PERFECT BREAKS

Dorothy Topfer

Perfect Breaks

First published in Australia by Dorothy Topfer 2022
www.dorothy.topfer.com

 A catalogue record for this
book is available from the
National Library of Australia

ISBN: 978-0-6451559-2-1 (pbk)
ISBN: 978-0-6451559-3-8 (ebk)

Book cover photography by Maria Orlova (Pexels Stock Images) ©

Typesetting and design by Publicious Book Publishing
Published in collaboration with Publicious Book Publishing
www.publicious.com.au

Dedicated to John, my ever patient life partner
and reluctant cattle farmer.

Other titles by this author:

Past Presence

Also available on Kindle:

The Lost Spirit

Unravelling

The Legacy

Remembrance

The Life and Death of Gypsy Carmichael

Chapter One

OK. I get it that you want to know my story. Are you sure? It really is rather tedious. So much of my life has been like everyone else's—family, pets and living in a small community. But there once was a time when I was known as *Australia's sweetheart*—that didn't last and like so much in my life, it came spectacularly undone.

Until I became the famous Francesa McAdam, my life was rather boring—living in a small seaside town on the NSW South Coast with my parents, surfing whenever I could. There were friends of course, but no one with whom I felt really close. At the age of seventeen, I had yet to meet anyone who interested me enough to become my significant other. Then, one summer in the school holidays, when I was wasting time down at the beach, this young man came into my life. Not as you might expect, not in any romantically exciting way.

It was one of those perfect summer days and the waves were just humming. We were two people out of many out there bodysurfing, when we both caught the same wave and collided. Heads crashing, bodies thumping into each other, before both being caught by the swirling after wash of the wave. Finally, I came up to the surface, gasping for air, water up my nose and sand entangling my hair. No surprise that I was indignant. I immediately confronted the culprit who paid me no heed, as he was too busy shaking water out of his ears.

'What do you think you are doing? Can't you watch where you are going? Why were you cutting across my wave? You idiot!'

You could tell I was a bit cross.

He said nothing. Just kept bashing the side of his head with his hand, presumably in an attempt to dislodge the water from his ears—all the while gazing at me contemplatively.

I ran out of words and steam and just stood there, still glaring at him of course, but unsure what I should do next.

Then he smiled with a smile that transformed his features, and spoke:

'Come on. Let's do that again, but this time no more crashing into me.'

I rolled my eyes and followed him back into the surf. After seeing that smile, how could I resist?

We spent the rest of that afternoon catching wave after wave and fortunately not colliding. While floating in the sea and waiting for the next wave to appear, we exchanged random snippets of conversation.

His name—Charlie Saddler.

I told him my name—Francesca McAdam—called 'Frankie' by my family, but sometimes known to my friends as 'Freckle'. You see, I hated my full name and did everything I could not to use it. I came undone each year at the school speech night when, as prizes were awarded, my name would be called out in full, to the accompanying sniggers from my classmates. There weren't many Francescas in our neck of the woods.

Did he still go to school? Yes, but he attended the nearby all-boys school. No wonder I hadn't seen him before. We students at the local co-ed school wouldn't be seen dead mixing with those losers!

Yet as the afternoon wore on, I decided that this loser was worth getting to know a bit better. He was gorgeous. Shaggy blond hair of the dedicated surfer. Body muscled and tanned. Grin as wide as a slice of cake and laughing eyes the colour of a summer sea. What was there not to like?

We laughed. We swam. By the end of that afternoon, I felt like I had known Charlie forever. When he was summonsed to leave by the prolonged shouting from a shadowy figure on the beach, I felt like I was bidding farewell to an old friend. Yet, he really wasn't, and I had no idea where he lived, except that he was a local. Being mindful of my image, I was careful not to sound too desperate. But how to see him again?

'I have to go now. That's my brother, Archie, come to collect me. We're supposed to help with the milking this afternoon, so I have to get a move on. Don't want to be too late. Luckily, the old girls will be waiting for us to let them in. See you down here again?'

The last part was said in a slightly hopeful tone, giving me some encouragement.

'Sure. I'm here most days after I help my mum with cleaning up after the guests. Or you can find me up at the *Ocean Breeze Guesthouse*. That's where we live.'

Yep, I'm desperate. My love life is a desert. This one is so not getting away.

With a smiley see ya, he turned and swam for shore, caught up with the waving figure and walked slowly away, a random wave in my direction as a sort of farewell. Suddenly, I became conscious of my water pickled skin and also headed for the shore.

***

That evening I casually mentioned meeting Charlie to my mum as she tended my back and shoulders, now being reinterpreted by sunburn.

Mum knows everyone. She was born here and has never left.

'Why would I?' she would say if asked if she would ever leave. 'Everything I could ever want is here. The beach, the mountains, the climate, and my most precious family. No, I take that back. On a bad day, I would happily trade in my precious family. Especially your father!'

That night though, I had no time for her usual patter.

'Mum! Pay attention. He said his name was Charlie Saddler. Do you know the Saddlers? Maybe they have a dairy farm? He said something about having to help with the milking.'

Mum paused in her anointing and responded. 'Ah yes, the Saddlers. Of course, I know them. I grew up with his parents, Charles and Elsie.

We were all at school together. Haven't seen them for a while, but I suppose the boys are about your age or possibly a bit older. They live out *Back Valley Way* on a farm that belonged to Charles' parents. Yep, that'd be them. Nice family. Maybe you'll see him again?'

Maybe.

Days passed. When I could get away from home, I hung around the beach, surreptitiously checking out each new arrival. No, not him. Sometimes my school friends turned up and we spent the afternoon idly chatting and surfing. Not totally wasted time, but still no Charlie.

Then one afternoon as I was walking down the track to the beach, I heard my name being called by someone jogging up behind me.

'Frankie … Freckle. Hey wait for me.'

I turned and there he was, hurrying to catch up and looking like he was pleased to see me. I permitted myself a small smile of welcome. It was enough.

That summer was amazing. I won't go on about it as I'm sure I would bore you to death. Every spare moment we spent together. Usually at the beach, but sometimes just mooching around our small town, hanging out in the local milk bar on the main street or sitting out in the garden at my place.

We talked. About everything. About ourselves, our families and life in a small town. What we wanted to do when we left school. Charlie knew for certain he would stay on the family farm. He saw no need to do anything else. Me? I had no idea. For starters, I knew I wasn't yet ready to leave our town, even though career opportunities were limited. Mum and Dad were encouraging me to move away and undertake further study once I finished school in a year's time. After all, that is what my brother and sister had done. My sister, now a qualified teacher of young children, had returned to the district once her training was complete. She had settled in a nearby town, happy with her career, and in a budding romance with a local builder. My brother? Well, he had stayed away, seduced by the big city career and the excitement of a corporate lifestyle, only returning to us at Christmas. With each year his attachment to his childhood home lessened. His visits became more infrequent and for a shorter duration. I knew Mum and Dad missed him. They tried to make the best of it and spoke to their friends with pride concerning his achievements, but I sensed that their words rung hollow. For that reason, I was reluctant to commit myself to another life far away up in the *big smoke* as I didn't want to inflict any further pain on my parents.

Each time Charlie and I discussed the future, I grappled with what future there was for me. Nothing as far as I could tell. The only certainty for me was that any future had to include Charlie. He was my everything.

How can I describe him to you? Not too tall—about five foot eleven to my five foot nine. Blond hair—but you already know that. Surfie hair, surfie tan and always, when I saw him, dressed in board shorts, T-shirt and thongs. Eyes the colour of the sea he swam in every day. Like the sea, they changed colour from a clear turquoise to a stormy grey blue whenever the mood took him.

It took me a while to appreciate that his nature wasn't always sunny. At times he could be solemn, silent and almost depressed in his negativity. The first time it happened I thought I had offended him and was at pains to find out what I had done wrong and to seek forgiveness. He brushed me off with few words and a dismissive gesture. I felt mortified and walked home alone from the beach.

He later apologised, wrapping me up in his arms, his firm muscles holding me close and secure, providing comfort and security.

'Sorry, Freckle. I don't know why I behaved as I did. I'm a bit of a shit sometimes. When I'm like that, its best you leave me alone to recover. A bit of time out so to speak.'

With a kiss on the top of my head, he stepped back and considered my tear-stained face.

'I love you. Don't you ever doubt it.'

My first declaration of love! Why then did I not feel

overwhelmed with excitement? The manner in which Charlie delivered those words of such great significance was more akin to a man heading to the execution block.

Did I love him? I think so. Yes, I'm certain I did. He made me laugh and we had so much in common. Surfing for instance, eating (I cooked, and he ate), animals, and of course, living in our small seaside town. He loved his family and I loved mine. It all seemed so simple.

We even had pet names for each other. How pathetic! My nickname, *Freckle,* was his name of choice. Rather accurate as I had a fair smattering of freckles across my nose and shoulders. Sun kisses he called them, as he proceeded to kiss each freckle, one by one. My diminutive for him? CJ. Not very creative, I know. It was his initials—Charlie John. No one else called him that, so it was something I could lay claim to as mine alone.

I started to fantasise about a life together—Charlie working on his parents' farm and me helping Mum. But all the while I ignored the small voice in my head which told me I was way too young to commit to such a boring life.

We kissed. We cuddled. Occasionally, we went very close to the full thing, but for some reason I hung back. Not that I'm sure why I did. Maybe it had something to do with mum being six months pregnant when she married Dad. I wasn't ready for that happening to me. Despite my reluctance, we managed to entertain each other on those summer evenings, lying on the grass under the Norfolk Pines down by the beach and quaffing way too much Green Ginger Wine. Even now, years afterwards, I still can't drink that stuff. It brings back too many sad memories.

So, what happened I hear you ask. Why aren't we still together?

Chapter Two

It was the last week of the summer holidays. The heat was diabolical and a group of us decided to head out of town to a favourite picnic spot on a nearby river. The riverbanks were sandy and sloped gently into the water. The water, deep and cold, was held back by a weir built a long time ago when the river water was needed for agricultural uses. On weekends, this part of the river would be swarmed by families and frolicking children. That day, being a weekday, no one else was expected to be there. Only us— three carloads of young people.

Much to my disgust, I wasn't allowed to go. At the very last moment, Mum had insisted I stay behind to help her. New guests were expected in all the holiday units that evening and she couldn't manage the preparation on her own. As you can imagine, I was not happy. Charlie, who had stopped by to collect me, tried his best to calm me down.

'It's okay. We can go some other time—just you and me. I've promised to take the others for a swim, but I won't stay long. I'll be back before you know it and we can go out or do something.'

The last words were delivered with a suggestive wiggle of his eyebrows and a leer at me behind Mum's turned back.

Charlie left, and never returned. Many times in the months afterwards, I wished I had given my man more than a token kiss on his cheek as he left my side.

By dusk, when I had not heard from him, I became anxious and rang some of my friends who had gone with Charlie. No answer.

I rang Charlie's home. No answer. It wasn't until much later that I discovered everyone was at the hospital.

I later learned that there had been a massive car accident as they returned home after the outing. Charlie, who had only recently got his driver's licence, was behind the wheel of his parent's car—a large family station wagon of venerable age. The others were crammed inside—more people than the five seat belts permitted. The coroner determined that the accident was a result of Charlie failing to negotiate a sharp bend, crashing into the guard rail and tipping over the embankment. The car rolled, over and over, until it came to rest by the side of a tree. People dead and dying everywhere. A car following sounded the alarm and the paramedics were soon on the scene. Although, they were not quick enough to save some. Three died at the scene of the crash. Charlie and two others were rushed to hospital in a critical condition and two others, who suffered minor breaks, were subsequently tended to.

Charlie died that night. I didn't know. In fact, it wasn't until the next morning that I heard about the accident from a neighbour, who had popped in to see us and share the news.

'Frankie. You probably know these people?' she asked, while taking a cautious sip of the scalding hot tea Mum had just made for her.

'What people?'

I had only just entered the room so had missed the start of the conversation.

'The people involved in yesterday's car crash. They are said to be about your age, and they were on their way back here from the weir. The young lad driving the car died overnight and I understand a few others have also died.'

I stared at Mum with dawning horror. She understood and reached for the phone. Too soon we learned the reality of what had occurred. I won't go into any further detail. You see, I had no life experience to prepare me for the horror of suddenly losing a loved one. If that is even possible. One minute he was there, the next he was gone. Perhaps the hardest part was that I never had a chance to say goodbye. Nor did I ever see Charlie again. The coffin at the funeral was closed, something Mum said was probably for the best, given the horrific nature of the crash.

His funeral was one of many held that week. I attended them all. Somehow, I felt guilty for still being alive. Like I had cheated death. I should have been in one of those coffins. If it wasn't for Mum insisting that she needed my assistance on that fateful day, I would have been.

Seeing Charlie's parents and his brother—so forlorn, yet resolute, crammed together in the front pew of our tiny church made my feelings of guilt even worse.

After the service ended, when we were all huddled in a massed grouping outside the church, I left the group and wandered over to Charlie's parents to offer my condolences. They smiled blankly when I said my words of sympathy. After all, they had never met me and didn't know of my important place in Charlie's life. Charlie's mum recognised my mum standing next to me, and with a sorrowful smile she accepted a hug and the softly spoken words delivered by my mum. I stood by her side, at a loss as to what to do, my hands hanging limply by my side. I sensed someone drawing near. A warmth and a feeling of comfort. A hand reached for my arm and a head bent down as if from a great height.

'He loved you. Never doubt that. This summer has been the happiest I have ever seen Charlie, and it was all up to meeting you.'

I turned and looked up at a towering man. A sort of version of Charlie on steroids. Of course, it was Charlie's brother, Archie. He was uncomfortably dressed in a suit that I could see was not his natural attire. His face was gaunt, and eyes were shadowed with grief. He was a different man to the one I had recently observed at the beach coming to fetch his brother.

He wasn't finished yet and with a pat on my arm he continued:

'It was an accident. A terrible one at that, but we cannot hold it against him. Sometimes bad things happen. Yet, we must carry on. I know he would want you to get on with life and live your dreams. If you can.'

I just stared at him. His brother had just died, and he was trying to console me? Surely it should be the other way around? I really couldn't deal with this. I just shook my head and moved away to stand by my father.

'Dad, can we go home now? I don't think I can do this anymore.'

My father, a man of few words but deep emotions, immediately understood. He signalled across the crowd to Mum, and we all departed.

There's not much more to say about that day and the twelve months that followed. Feeling numb with grief, I moved through each day like an automaton. I did the chores as directed around our guest house, attended school, studied, wrote essays, and sat exams, all the while feeling like the real Frankie was sealed away behind a glass wall. Sealed away where she could no longer feel pain nor any emotion and could no longer be hurt. All forms of emotion were to be avoided, and like a nun approaching her vows, I was determined to turn my back on all that life had to offer. Safe at home on a Friday or a Saturday night, I assured my parents that I was happy to be with them and to study. I resolutely refused all invitations to social events and focused on staying in my room. Safe and secure. Locked away with my memories of Charlie, refreshed by constant study of the few photos I had of us. I was regretful that I had not prolonged our intimacies when we had the chance under those Norfolk pines or hugged him harder on that fateful day.

I sat my final exams and passed. I was at a loose end as to what to do with the rest of my life now that I was no longer safe in the confines of school. For as long as I was still a student in Year 12, my routine was clearly mapped out for me. Term time I would go to school. In the holidays I would study and help Mum. No more outings to the beach for me. The beach meant Charlie, and that just meant unbearable pain. Maybe one day I would be able to return to surfing, but not now—not when every wave reminded me of my time with Charlie.

My parents and my sister, Amy, conferred in a huddle from which I was excluded. There were several phone calls during which anxious voices could be heard, dropping to a whisper whenever I walked into the room. Then a decision was made and agreed to with the person on the other side of the phone, and the result was made known to me by my parents and my sister. I knew I was in for it when I saw all three seated in a line at the dining table, waiting for me as I re-entered the room. My dad spoke first, smiling his usual gentle smile.

'Frankie, dear. Come and sit with us. We want to talk to you.'

I could see from their stern expressions that this was about to get serious. Was someone ill? Was I adopted? What was going on? I took a seat and stared at my sister. She shrugged and left it for Dad to explain.

'You've finished school. You've got your results. Fantastic results by the way. Congratulations. But as far as we know, you've made no plans. Is that correct?'

I nodded. To make plans for my future required more energy than I could presently muster. All my plans, such as they were, left this world with Charlie when he died. Now I was directionless, with no wish to do anything other than to repeat the daily chores over and over.

'Frankie, dear, we think a change of scene might do you the world of good.'

This time it was my mother speaking. She rushed on before I could object to her words. 'I've spoken to your brother, and he says there's room for you to live in his house. He assures me he can find you some work to do at his office. Not sure what this work will be, but it will pay and give you time to settle into city life and see what else is out there.'

I shook my head. 'No way, I'm not ready. Please don't force me to go somewhere that requires effort from me.' I shook my head even harder as I could feel tears welling. 'No Mum and Dad. I don't want to leave here. This is home.'

'Just give it a go, Frankie,' said Dad, his plea obvious by the tone of his voice. 'This will always be your home. You know that. But for now, there's nothing here for you. Just more grief. Please? For our sakes, go for a little while and see how you find it. We can't bear to see you suffer so. Something has to change and maybe just spending some time away in Sydney in a new location, but with your big brother to care for you, might be just what you need.'

Don't get me wrong. I love my parents and understand they always want the best for me. But this time Dad's comments gave me pause. Maybe I had been selfish in my grief. After all, what did I have to lose? My brother, Simon, was about six years older than me. We had always been close, so it was possible that some time spent with him would not be time wasted. What my parents said did make sense. I realised I couldn't continue to stagnate here even though it seemed like the easiest choice. With my family urging me on, I realised it would take more energy than I currently possessed to resist them.

Before I knew it, I was packed and deposited on the bus which regularly headed to Sydney. In those days, it was a long trip—nine hours more or less. That evening, by the time we reached Central Station in Sydney, I was so stiff and tired that I was beginning to regret I had even agreed to this visit. Yet, all was forgotten when the bus door opened with a hiss, and I stumbled out into my brother's arms and his enthusiastic welcome.

'Hooray! You're here at last. I've been waiting for ages. Let's get you home and you can settle. I can't believe you are here—finally. I've been nagging Mum and Dad for so long to send you up to stay with me.'

With an enthusiastic grin, he added: 'Wait till you see where I live. You're going to love it. Where are your bags?'

Beyond tired, I submitted and let Simon organise me. I pointed at my two bags as they were unloaded from the bus, then permitted myself to be led to his car.

I had never been to Sydney before and my initial impression that evening was of feeling overwhelmed by the noise and the densely packed buildings. To my exhausted eyes, the trip to Balmain was a mass of colour and confusion. The night, if you could really call it that, was lit by countless illuminations—neon signs, traffic lights and car lights. I seem to recall that it had been raining sometime during the evening. The rain had lifted by the time the bus reached Sydney, yet the streets still gleamed with remnant moisture. The signs and lit buildings shimmered and reflected on the wet roads, their wavering movement making me feel even more disorientated.

I had no sense of direction and did not understand where we were heading. As usual, Simon was full of chatter and kept up a constant monologue as he pointed out local points of interest. We crossed an architectural bridge, which I later learned was called ANZAC Bridge. I looked out of the car window at lights from nearby suburbs reflecting onto the harbour. Slightly behind me now, I could glimpse the towering lights of the city—the Central Business District Simon called it. Somewhere in that mass of buildings was his office and my soon to be workplace. It was all so spread out and overwhelming, and for a moment I yearned for our small township where life was less complex. Then we turned off the busy road and headed up a hill towards Balmain, Simon explained. My sense of disorientation increased as we negotiated a series of turns. By now I had completely lost all sense of where we were. The streets quietened, and around me were houses grouped in a haphazard manner, almost as if they were the result of some child's random creation or built as if they evolved without consultation with their neighbours and to no set plan. Some two-storey terraces in a row leaned in as if they were supporting each other. Other tiny weatherboard cottages, complete with a front porch and dormer windows, stood next to others built of stone as if they had been hewed out of the ground on which the cottages now rested.

I was enchanted. I had never seen anything like it in my life. Even in my dazed and bemused state, I knew this place was magic and that I had found myself in a wonderland. Maybe, with a bit of luck, I could remake myself and my life would get to start again.

Chapter Three

What can I say? Sydney was amazing. After all, I was only eighteen and this was the first time I had ever left home. Until now, I had only ever known a country environment and my eyes were familiar with the vistas of sea and the sheltering mountain range. This city was beyond anything I had ever envisaged. It throbbed with life and noise and smelled so different to the clean sea salt freshened breezes of home.

I wondered if I would ever become accustomed to the traffic noise—a constant murmured hum in the background. That first night, the smells that greeted me when I stepped out of the car onto the narrow street in front of my brother's home were so confusing that it took me a moment to separate and identify them. The food aromas from nearby restaurants reminded me that I had not eaten for some time and awakened the rumble in my stomach. The industrial smell of asphalt rising from the rain drenched streets assaulted my nostrils. As I stumbled to the front gate, I was greeted by the sweet scent from the frangipani tree that flourished nearby, dripping its waxen flowers on me when I brushed past. Although I knew the harbour was not far away, its presence was not made known in the myriad of smells that wafted around me.

That first night, there was not much more my overwhelmed senses could absorb. I stumbled into the house, paying little attention to its layout, and was asleep almost as soon as my head hit the pillow.

It wasn't until the following morning when I woke early that I had the opportunity to take in my new home. So different to my childhood residence, this house was old, weatherboard and quirky. The floorboards creaked as I stepped down from my bed and sounded off with each step when I progressed around the room exploring my new bedroom. Not much to see really. It was clearly a spare room and a repository for cast off stuff. A double bed, a wardrobe in one corner, and a desk covered with papers. The bookcase by my bed was crammed with assorted paperbacks. On the walls hung posters that had seen better days—faded and ripped. There was a window over which a length of batik cloth was secured by tacks. The daylight was obscured by the patterned cloth. I was reluctant to push it aside as I suspected those tacks would quickly fall away. There was a lot I could do to make this room mine. That is if I intended to stay—and that was something I had yet to decide.

Simon of course was still asleep, and unless he had changed dramatically, I expected he would be for quite some time. I had time to explore. First thing though was to locate the kitchen, which was easily found down the corridor towards the back of the house, and to make myself a morning cup of tea. While the kettle was coming to the boil, I peered around. The kitchen, small but workable, opened onto a paved courtyard. Several bicycles were stacked against an outdoor table surrounded by four chairs. A few plants in raised brick beds formed the back boundary of the courtyard with a backdrop of a dilapidated paling fence. No gardeners here, as the plants had that bedraggled thirsty appearance common with the neglected and those things suffering from lack of love. Cup of tea in hand, I leaned against the kitchen island and perused my surroundings. In front of me the view of the courtyard. To my left a small lounge area, two sofas and a TV. Cosy. To my right there was just room enough for a small pine dining table – big enough to seat four.

Sipping my cup of tea, I headed back past my bedroom. The corridor was wide with honey-coloured floorboards that creaked my progress. My bedroom was the first to be reached. It was on my left across the hall from a bathroom. I reached the two doors across from each other that led to the front two bedrooms: one was Simon's bedroom, and the other Ruth's room. I had yet to meet Ruth, but Simon assured me she would be my new best friend. I really hoped so, yet I also wondered how she would react to a total stranger lobbing into her home unannounced.

There was no sound of life from either room, so I took myself and my cup of tea out onto the front verandah, sat on the front step and contemplated the day.

That first day was very confusing. My overwhelming impression was how weird this city was. In many ways it could not have been any more confusing if I had woken up in a strange new land. Simon, probably with the best intentions, focused his energies in getting me up to speed with city living as quickly as possible. He spoke constantly of where to go to find food, to have my hair cut or to buy clothes. His directions on how to get to the city by bus or ferry were like some foreign language to me. All my life, up until now, I was a person who had only ever walked to school or the beach. I must have looked as overwhelmed as I felt, as he soon gave up.

'Never mind,' he said. 'Let's wander up the street. I'll point out a few shops to you, and we might stop somewhere and find something for lunch. Then, maybe in a day or so, once you are prepared to get up early, you can catch the ferry with me into town and have a look around the city. You don't need to start work until next week. That'll give you time to get your bearings and find some new clothes.'

At that, I looked down at my clothes with concern. What was wrong with my black leggings and checked shirt?

Simon, seeing my confusion, laughed. 'Trust me, kiddo. If you want a career in PR, you need to look more city mouse and ditch the country mouse attire. Ruth can give you a hand. She knows fashion.'

Ruth, who had been sitting in the corner scrolling through her phone messages, looked up and agreed.

'Happy to help. I have the day off work tomorrow. We can go

find you a few things. Just a couple of outfits should do you for now. Black, I suppose, Simon?'

He nodded.

'Of course!'

Did I mention Simon is a partner in some hot shot public relations firm? PR, as they call it, is a big thing. He never talked about it much when he came home for a visit other than to say he was always busy with product launches and parties. Whenever he visited, he always brought me samples of new products from some of his clients—fragrances, handbags and cosmetics. My friends were impressed and nagged me to get more stuff from him. But it really wasn't stuff I needed or used, so I couldn't see the point. But now that I was becoming a city girl, I wondered if I would change my mind.

Simon assured me there was plenty of work for me in the business. Nothing glamorous he told me. I would be a sort of dogsbody and help wherever I was needed. What he said I would be doing didn't sound very exciting—running errands, answering the phone, photocopying, and doing what I was told. but, as he explained, I would be paid a salary and it would give me a chance to get to know Sydney. It was not like I had any choice. The only alternative was heading back home, and I knew that life was behind me. For now.

It's hard to describe Simon to you. Not only because he is my big brother who I have always taken for granted and never really looked at, but also because Simon has always been so much more than his appearance which, when I considered him that morning, I was forced to admit really was rather ordinary. The same light brown hair as mine, cut short so the curl was much more pronounced. He was almost the same height as me—not too tall and not too short. The sort of height and colouring that would help him blend into a crowd—if he was a spy that is, and not some PR guru. He had even features and boring brown eyes, yet it was not Simon's looks that made him memorable. There was no doubt about that! It was his energy and enthusiasm for absolutely everyone and everything that made him so unforgettable. Simon had never been bored or boring. There was always something attracting his attention or provoking his interest. Need I say it? He was also rather exhausting. Even when he was younger, I found it hard to keep up with his many interests and joy for living. He was good in small doses you might say. As we made our plans that morning, I wondered how I could possibly manage to cope once more sharing the same house with my brother—and working with him.

***

The next few days were, as I expected, busy. True to her word on the Monday, Ruth took me to some nearby fashion outlet warehouse where we were able to pick up several heavily discounted outfits. Two pairs of trousers and a few floaty tops—all in black, of course. She did permit me to buy one black and white spotted top. I fell in love with a linen jacket of the most amazing burnt orange colour and spent my remaining funds on that. I had no money for a haircut. My long brown hair I would just tie back into a ponytail or put up in a bun. My old sandals would do for now—at least until payday.

Ruth was good company. A country girl herself, she told me she came to Sydney to do a degree in journalism and had never left. Like Simon, she worked in PR, but for a different firm and with different clients. She and Simon had met at a function and had immediately hit it off. When his housemate moved out, he somehow convinced her to rent the spare room. Ruth was at pains to assure me they were just friends and nothing more. Although I did wonder why she was going to such lengths to convince me of this. Did she really fancy him? Not that it worried me. She was fun to be with. Like an older sister, yet much more sophisticated than my big sister. With a ready smile and warm engaging manner, Ruth was easy to be around. We spent that Monday together as she showed me the parts of Balmain that she loved—her favourite café, a nearby bakery, and her preferred walks through winding streets that allowed you to take in glimpses of the harbour.

The following days, having scrounged some funds from my brother, I kept busy exploring—catching buses to nearby suburbs, or just walking around and getting my bearings. As a contribution to the household, each evening I prepared dinner for the workers. Nothing very fancy, for my cooking skills were pretty basic. I could manage a stir fry or a variety of pasta dishes. That was about it. But it was more than enough for my appreciative audience, who showered me with praise for my prowess. At some stage, I knew I would be expected to contribute to the rent, but for now my brother kept silent. For that I was glad, as I had absolutely no funds of my own.

That first weekend, Simon and Ruth took me to the beach. Tamarama, I think it was. We had fun—along with all the other hordes of people. Being by the sea again resonated with me, and I felt like it was finally time to return to my natural environment. I did my best to ignore the folk splashing around me and focused on the feel of the water as I slipped under the waves. I luxuriated in the taste of salt on my lips and the sting in my eyes as I came up for air after each wave had passed. In these crowds, it wasn't perfect. But it was enough.

With so many other people in the water, it was a battle to find sufficient space to catch a wave to the shore. But battle I did, and I managed to catch a few. The joy of being propelled by the energy of the water sent shivers of delight through me. For a moment, I reminisced about the endless beach at home, the luxury of waves to myself, and how it felt to surrender myself to the power of nature as the wave and I surged to the shore. Then those thoughts invoked memories of Charlie and our collision on the wave on the day we first met. With grief flooding back, it was fortunate I had the sea water washing over me, swamping my tears.

By now it was a bit more than twelve months since Charlie had died, yet the pain was as raw as if a part of me had recently been amputated. Would I ever heal?

Chapter Four

First day at work and I woke up terrified. How could I do this? I had no skills—or none that would be of any use. My life experience to this stage was comprised of studying at school, surfing and helping Mum clean the guest apartments. Sure, I might have acquired a few people skills from looking after those difficult guests that occasionally descended on us, but what did I know about how an office operated or how to survive office politics? Nothing! Apart from what I had seen on those sitcoms on TV, and surely they couldn't be realistic. For if they were, then I was definitely out of my depth and destined for total catastrophe!

That morning we left home early—all three of us—and headed to Balmain East Wharf to catch the ferry that took commuters to the city. By now I had already caught the ferry several times as part of my exploration and was familiar with the process. I knew I could also catch a bus into the city, but unless the weather was appalling, I wondered why anyone would choose that method of transportation when they could travel to work over this amazing harbour?

Waiting for the ferry to arrive, and watching the water sparkling in the morning sunlight, I knew commuting by ferry was a no-brainer. The sunlight and the beauty that surrounded us infected my fellow commuters with good cheer. So many obviously knew each other as indicated by the chat that surrounded me. Simon greeted a few arrivals and introduced me as his kid sister who had come to experience *the big smoke*. I was welcomed with genuine smiles and questions from those interested in my intentions. Seeing me struggle to respond—you see, I was still very shy in those days—Simon interjected:

'She's going to work with me in the office for a while until she finds her feet. Who knows, PR might be in Frankie's blood?'

Travelling across the harbour was a delight. First, we headed towards McMahons Point then we turned and travelled across the harbour in the direction of the city. I refused to join my brother and Ruth in the confines of the cabin. Instead, I found a seat on a wooden bench at the bow of the ferry and gloried at the vista that was unfurling before me. The Harbour Bridge towered over the scene, looming over us as we grew closer, The houses and apartments on the other side of the harbour so densely packed and the waterway busy with other craft: ferries, motor and sail boats. I felt like I could sit there all day and take in the sights, just like any other visitor to this city. Yet, too soon we had arrived at Circular Quay and were disembarking into a chaos of commuters, buskers and tourists.

Simon's office was located a short walk away in the direction of The Rocks and behind the Museum of Contemporary Art. I struggled to keep up with Simon, who clearly was now running late, rushing along while bellowing orders to someone on his mobile phone and paying me no mind. Desperate not to lose sight of his back as he pushed his way through the crowd, I tried not to be distracted by the displays in the shop windows and the delicious breakfast smells wafting out of some of the cafés. We turned a corner, ducked up a narrow alley way and passed through a doorway beside which a painted sign was displayed proclaiming in large bold letters: *Perfectly PR – Marketing and Communications*.

My first day was a blur. As soon as we arrived, Simon introduced me to Lena, his assistant. With a muttered direction to me to help Lena however she wanted and that he would see me later as he had *heaps to do*, he disappeared into his office and shut the door behind him.

Fortunately, Lena was welcoming. She already knew I would

be starting work that day and had arranged several tasks for me. In fact, Lena was more than welcoming. She made it very clear that she was so grateful to have someone to share the workload with. It helped to feel needed, even when I wasn't sure what exactly I was meant to be doing. Lena assured me that within a week or so, I would be on top of it all and maybe even getting bored. In my present state of feeling overwhelmed, that was hard to imagine.

The first thing she did was show me around the office and introduce me to the others as they arrived. It was a small office. Straight in off the street was a foyer with some comfortable armchairs and a reception desk. Lena told me she usually sat there but said I would help with the reception duties once I was up to speed. There was a door into a corridor which led to an open plan office and behind it two offices—one for Simon and one for his partner, Bryan Landry. I was told Bryan was off-site today, but I would meet him later in the week. I met Jasmine and Mark who greeted me with enthusiasm. They weren't much older than me— maybe 22 or 23, but they were streets ahead in style—clothes, hair and adornments such as jewellery and subtle tattoos proclaiming them to be city sophisticates. My own black attire, which only this morning I had considered suitable for a life in PR, now seemed sadly shabby in comparison. Still, they were enthusiastic in their welcome.

'Great to meet you at last, Frankie. Simon has said so much about you,' beamed Jasmine.

'We've been looking forward to showing you around. We work in the best location; so much to see here—and eat …'

'And drink!' interrupted Mark.

'Friday nights we usually go to a pub down near the Quay and meet up with others from the business. Don't go rushing off on Friday. You can come with us and meet a few of the others. With a name like Frankie, you are just meant to be in PR. Such a trendy name.'

'That's enough you guys.'

Lena, clearly the task mistress, fixed her steely gaze onto Jasmine and Mark.

'You know we have a team meeting at 10.00 am to discuss this week's work programme. Isn't there something you both need to do to prepare? I'll send Frankie out for coffee for us all once I have finished showing her around.'

With a good natured *'yeah whateve boss'* from Mark and a wave of the hand from Jasmine, they both turned away and headed for their adjoining cubicles. The rest of the tour didn't take long. I was shown a tiny kitchenette, a small stationery area complete with photocopier in an alcove off the main room, and a toilet area out the back which we shared with the other tenant on our floor—a theatrical agent.

'You'll meet him at some stage,' said Lena. 'He and Simon are great mates, so Tom is often in here. I think he just likes a chat. It gets a bit lonely working on your own I suppose.'

'Tom?'

'Tom Georgiades. You must have heard of him? He's one of the top theatrical agents. Looks after all sorts of stars—movie and TV. Sometimes they will come into our little office by mistake. If you are quick and they're in the right mood, you might even be ablet to grab an autograph or they'll let you take a photo with them. That or you get snubbed. It's amazing how the ones you think might be nice are just ... well ... they are just complete bitches!'

By the end of the day, I knew my tasks included getting coffee for everyone, morning and afternoon, from the café around the corner. Once I explained to the barista where I was from, there was no issue with my order. Clearly, we were regulars, the preferences of the others in the office already known. All I needed to do was include my coffee of choice in the order. Not an easy thing because I was not sure what it was, I preferred. I was puzzled as I considered the coffee menu. Some of them I had never heard of. Piccolo? Macchiato? Chai? Over the following days, I sampled all. Did I have a favourite? Not really. It was even more overloading of my senses.

Lena was amazing. So professional and organised, I think she would make a better job of running the country than our present lot. They'd be left behind eating her dust! That first day I sat quietly by Lena's side as I had a speed lesson in what she did most days. Gobsmacked I was! I only left her side for those coffee runs or to do the photocopying. It looked like both those tasks were something I would have to do every day. Sometimes I would be expected to do a run for sandwiches at lunchtime when all were working to some tight deadline. On the rare occasion we had letters to post, I would be tasked with taking them to the local post box. When I had those outings, I took my time, delighting in the bustle of tourists and locals around me.

It wasn't until Wednesday that I met Simon's partner, Bryan. So different to my chirpy, high energy brother, Bryan was older and more sombre. By my estimate, and at only 18 at the time, I was not a good judge of age, but Bryan looked to be in his forties. Immaculately groomed with not one hair of his slicked back style out of place, he was in stark contrast to my casually attired brother. In a designer charcoal suit set off by an open-necked grey and white striped shirt, and feet shod with black riding boots polished to a high shine, he looked like he would be more at home in a legal office or hanging out in the financial district. Yet, he too was welcoming, although not in an effusive way. I suspected my contact with him would be limited.

'Francesca, isn't it? I know your brother calls you 'Frankie', but it seems a bit casual. Welcome to our little office. I hope the others are looking after you.'

All this was said in a kindly avuncular manner, almost as if he was an elderly relative greeting a long-lost niece. Still, I had no doubt he was pleased to have me here. It was just that Bryan was so formal. I found out later that he and Simon made the perfect business partnership. Bryan, so old school and charming, appealed to the more established brands who trusted him as he *spoke their language* and was *one of them*. Such a contrast to Simon who was so on trend—young and progressive and who could tailor those enticing campaigns that caused controversy and resonated with a younger demographic.

After a month, I was in love. In love with Balmain—its funny, old-world charm and close-knit community. In love with my daily commute across the harbour—my daily fix of sea water, sun and waves. In love with The Rocks and the history that seeped out of the quirky buildings and the landscape at every turn. And I was in love with my new job. Every day was different and every day I learnt something new—about the PR industry, about the people who were our clients, and about the photocopier! I hated that photocopier and on a bad day I suspect it hated me. The printer wasn't much better, always jamming and in the most inaccessible places.

My workmates were all so fascinating. Their lives so different to mine. They were all Sydney siders who took the amazing landscape in which they lived for granted. I often felt like the country cousin when listening to their chatter about cultural events and the latest must visit restaurant or bar.

Yet, I was also changing. Every week and following each payday, my wardrobe was supplemented with new *must haves*. My attire was becoming edgier, but still black. I had no need to lose any weight, having lost heaps in that year of grief after Charlie's death. My hair I was reluctant to cut. When loose, it still hung down almost to my waist in a swishing waterfall of soft light brown curls. On workdays, when I was keen to conform with the appearance of those fellow travellers I saw on the ferry commute, I would tie my hair back into a high-topped ponytail or pile it on top of my head into a haphazard bun.

Every Sunday evening, I would ring or skype Mum and Dad to report in. I could tell they missed me, but being the people that they are, they did their best to hide it and share in my enthusiasm for Sydney life and my new career. When I could, I tried to remember to email them photos of the places and people I was seeing. I knew it was too hard for them to get away from their business, and photos were at least a way they could vicariously experience what was happening to me.

On weekends, I would try to get to the beach, dragging Ruth or Simon along with me. Sometimes, if it was overcast, we would forsake the beach and walk along the clifftops from Bondi to the Heads. On a stormy day, that walk would be spectacular, especially when the sea churned so far below us, sending waves crashing onto the rock platforms with such force and fury it made me feel like I too was part of those elements and not the urbanite I was fast turning into.

Just as I was starting to feel confident about my place in this, my new little family, and at my workplace, it all changed. Overnight.

Chapter Five

I t was all Tom's doing.

I've already mentioned him to you. Tom Georgiades, the theatrical agent who also rented some rooms next to *Perfectly PR*. Just like Lena had said, Tom was often in our offices. Usually, at the end of the day, he would pop in for a bit of a gossip with Simon and/ or Bryan. Some Fridays he would join us at the local pub. He was great company. Full of so much gossip—the latest tall tales from the theatrical world or details about an unfurling political scandal. I don't know who his sources were, but they were impeccable. The stories I could tell you! But I won't! It's not worth my while.

He was fun. About my height and much older. A bit on the chubby side, but cuddly chubby. Like a teddy bear. A twinkle in his eye and a smile that said, 'trust me'. And we all did. He was sort of like everybody's favourite uncle. He was someone with whom we had no hesitation about sharing all our concerns and secrets. He was always kind to me. Still, being shy, I often held back, staying on the edges of the conversation, and not joining in. Content to listen. Tom noticed this and made the effort to draw me in. He was so skilful at this that I didn't realise and found myself confiding in him, sharing with him stories about my love of the beach and surfing.

I suppose it came as no surprise that he immediately thought of me when he received a request to find a young woman who was a capable surfer and who could fill a role in the latest *must watch* soapie.

That afternoon was like all others. When Tom wandered in at about 5.30 pm, his arrival was greeted with a chorus of *about time* and *let's get to the pub now Tom's here.*

'Not so fast,' Tom said. 'I want to talk to Frankie here.'

'Me?'

I couldn't imagine what on Earth he would want to discuss with me.

'That's right. This could be your lucky day, my girl. I've just this very minute got off the phone. The director of *On the Rocks* rang me in a flap.'

Still a mystery. What did that have to do with me? I raised my eyebrows and looked around at the others. Jasmine shrugged her shoulders and Mark pulled a face. Obviously, a mystery to them as well.

'You see. They have a new part. A bit of a romantic interest for that surfing hero. Drew, is it?'

He looked around at all of us.

'No idea,' said Lena giving a grimace. 'Not in the demographic. It all sounds a bit young for me, but I'll believe you. So, what's that got to do with our Frankie?'

Our Frankie? I like that.

'The person they cast in this role has pulled out. Some unspecified serious illness I'm told. Filming of the planned episode starts the week after next, but they're having trouble finding a replacement at such short notice—especially someone who can surf convincingly. They don't want to rewrite the script as Drew the surfer needs a fresh bit of love interest to up his profile.'

He beamed at us all. 'Then I had a brainwave. Such a genius I am! The solution was staring me in the face.'

The solution stared back at him blankly.

'Frankie, this part is made just for you! You only need to be yourself and you'll shine. It's not a very demanding part, being a cameo role. I think they intend for you to break his heart and then move away. A no-brainer! Maybe two, possibly three episodes. But if you wow them, they might write you in and you could have a role in the show for much longer. What do you say? Interested?'

Lena, Jasmine and Mark were loud in their enthusiasm.

'You ripper!' said Mark with gusto.

'Frankie, how amazing. You just HAVE to do it,' gushed Jasmine.

'Tom, what a great opportunity and I agree, the part sounds just perfect for our Frankie,' Lena added. 'You must dear,' she continued, turning to me, and patting me on the shoulder.

Me? I just sat there staring at Tom. My brain refused to register what had just been said. Of course, I knew about *On the Rocks.* Who didn't? It had been running in the early evening time slot on TV for some years now, in competition with *Neighbours* and appealing to younger viewers. A lot of my school friends had watched it, so I was vaguely familiar with the story line although I had never bothered to tune in. I knew Drew was one of the lead characters. A troubled young man who worked for the local mechanic. His parents ran a beachside café, the scene of many of the episodes. Drew had two close friends and their misadventures occupied much of the show. The local policeman had a heart of gold—as always! And the community rallied behind whichever character was suffering grief that week. A sort of endearing, everyday soapie with characters everyone could relate to—just not me.

Simon, on hearing the commotion, appeared from his office and was updated by Tom.

'No way! That's amazing! You have to try out Frankie. There's no guarantee you will get the part. But you should at least give it a go. Try to think of it as an experience in promoting yourself. Good training and all that.'

Tom drew closer and peered at me. Lena and Jasmine were also training their eyes on me, so intently I wondered if I had a dirty mark on my face. Their focus intensified. I now felt like an insect under the microscope.

Feeling apprehensive I backed away. Not too far, as the wall was right behind me.

'What's wrong? Why are you all staring at me like that?'

'I'm not,' piped up Mark. 'But now you mention it, why are you all staring at our Frankie? Am I missing something?'

As if by some unseen communication, Lena nodded, and Tom spoke.

'Yes, you are right. The hair—good length for a beach babe. But the colour is wrong.'

'Blonde, it needs to be blonde. That sort of streaked look you get when you have spent all summer at the beach,' said Lena.

'How long before they want to see her?' asked Simon.

'I haven't got back to the director yet. I wanted to speak to Frankie before I did so. But if you are interested, young Frankie, I need to tell him straight away and he will want to test you—maybe even tomorrow.'

He looked across to Lena and Jasmine.

'Can you sort Frankie out before then? Do something with the hair? Find a strappy beachy number and thongs. Oh, and some swimmers—a bikini, I suppose. Yes, that'll do for tomorrow.'

'I'm on the case,' said Lena, reaching for her phone.

'Hang on a minute. I haven't said yes,' I said.

Five pairs of eyes turned and peered at me.

I felt the need to assert my authority. This was all way too terrifying. I had only just started to feel comfortable in my new home and vaguely confident about my work duties in this previously unfamiliar office environment. Now they were wanting to uproot me and dump me on some film set populated with complete strangers? Waves of terror washed over me. Simon, as if sensing my panic, drew near.

'Hey, sis. What've you got to lose by checking it out? If you want, I'll come with you tomorrow and be your spokesman if you are feeling too nervous. Think about it. This could be fun. Maybe a bit terrifying to start with. But look at how you've already put yourself out of your comfort zone by coming here and joining us. You took all those changes in your stride. I reckon you can do this as well. And as Tom says, it could only be for a few episodes. Think of the extra cash and the chance to surf. Whaddya reckon?'

It was the thought of the surf that did it. Being paid to surf. Without conscious thought, I found myself nodding.

'OK. I'll try out. But only if you are there with me Simon, and maybe you too, Tom?'

Tom rubbed his hands together, his gleeful smile illuminating his face.

'Of course. You won't keep me away from this. Now I'll go and make the call and hopefully sort out an audition time for tomorrow. You girls, transform our Frankie. I just knew I was right that this was the part for Frankie. How brilliant am I?'

I already had practical experience as to how Lena could make things happen, so I wasn't at all surprised that two hours later I found myself in some fancy hairdressing salon in her company. A charming hairdresser consulted with Lena regarding the desired look for me. As they spoke, he stood behind me lifting my long hair, pushing it to and fro, while peering earnestly in the mirror.

'I'm thinking, Lena, we need to keep this light brown base but give her streaks of different shades of blonde—golden highlights to show a life spent at the beach.'

Ignoring me completely, he continued, 'She has a pretty face. Almost heart shaped. I'm thinking a shaggy feathered fringe—not too blunt, mind you—might set off her features. Those brows need work. Do you want my beautician to sort that out once we get the foils in? Yes? Good.'

He now spoke to me.

Finally!

'Good thing you came to me, Frankie. By the time we are finished, you will look incredible. Just relax and let me get you transformed.'

He jiggled with excitement.

'What a story! It's all a bit like Cinderella. Unlike most of my clients, you have given me the most amazing material to work with. Lucky girl and lucky me!'

All the while the hairdresser and his beautician fussed over me, Lena stayed by my side. Being conscious of the time, I tried to encourage her to go home, but she brushed my objections away.

'It's no bother. I think Marty is right. This is a bit like a fairy tale. I so want to be here to see your transformation. Think of me as your fairy godmother. Lie back and relax while Marty does his magic. Now I'll just go and get some sushi for us to have for dinner and then I'll be back. You and I need to do a bit of online research about this show and learn something more about this character you are meant to be romancing—Drew, wasn't it? I'll be back shortly.'

Relax? As if! My stomach was churning, my mind whirling, and I had the dreaded feeling that I had just made the most tremendous mistake. What had I done? Yet, there was no possibility I could pull out of this commitment. I felt like I had been plonked onto a conveyer belt to be hurtled into a new world and a new me. Despite it all, and underneath all those feelings of queasiness, there was a vague tingling—an inkling that this might be a bit of fun after all. With the foils now in place, I succumbed to Marty's urgings and leaned back to let the beautician do her work on my eyebrows. It was hard to relax when pain was being inflicted. Hot wax, then the pinprick of the tweezers and the sting of the dye—for I had been assured my lashes and brows would be so much more dramatic after the application of some dye.

The reveal was—as they say—amazing! The woman staring back at me in the mirror was totally unrecognisable to the one that came into the salon not that long ago. Shimmering long hair reflecting strands of gold, silver and strawberry blonde that now trailed over my shoulders to just above my waist in an artful curled mass. My eyes, defined by strongly arched brows and darkened lashes, shone with amazement. I swivelled around in my chair and faced Marty.

'Marty. This is wonderful. You've worked miracles. I can't believe how different you have made me look. Thank you so much. Now I truly feel like Cinderella!'

'No worries. Just make me proud when you do your audition tomorrow. You really do look the part of a beach babe. The rest is up to you.'

Outside, Lena put me into a cab with stern directions to go home and get some sleep. Somehow, I knew that would be easier said than done!

Chapter Six

We were up early the next morning. Ruth, who had been updated by Simon about my audition, was also awake and took charge of my proposed attire.

'A strappy dress is what you need. Let me see what you've got. Is that all?' she exclaimed as she inspected my sparse selection of clothes that were taking up only a small amount of space in the wardrobe.

'Well, I suppose this one will have to do,' she said while pulling out a pretty floral number—a relic from the family Christmas gathering last summer.

Now dressed and wearing my old sandals, I headed to the kitchen to find Simon. Draped over my shoulder, a striped beach bag containing towel, swimmers and floppy hat completed the look.

Simon, sipping the first of his many coffees for the day, contemplated my approach, gazing at me thoughtfully over the rim of his mug.

'Not bad. I can see you have totally got into character and dressed for the role. But how is your preparation for this part?'

'Well, Lena and I did some research last night while we were at the hairdressers. This Drew bloke I am meant to fall for sounds like a bit of a drop kick. His past behaviour seems very inconsistent. He no sooner falls in love than he dumps them. He looks like he has no ambition—is content to work for the local mechanic, go surfing and hang out with his mates. He just seems like a magnet for attracting trouble. Car crashes, shark attacks, assaults, the list goes on and on.'

'Yeah, they have to keep the story churning to attract and keep the viewers.'

'He is kind of cute though, so I can see why the female viewers must like him. Surely that means they won't be too keen on any of his love interests. Is that why they don't last on the show too long?'

'Who knows? Just focus on being the gorgeous beach babe for three episodes or perhaps more if you are lucky and maybe you will win the male viewers over! Come on. Let's get going. We have to pick up Tom on the way. We're collecting him from his home, which is just over the Bridge and then we are meeting the producer and the director at Manly Beach. They want to be certain that you can swim and ride a surfboard. If you pass that test, don't be surprised if they get you to read a few lines. Got your swimmers?'

I opened my bag for his inspection. Simon nodded and then called out to Ruth.

'Wish us luck! Maybe we will be celebrating tonight.'

The drive to Manly seemed to take forever. It was my first visit to the North Shore and my first harbour crossing on the Sydney Harbour Bridge. Yet, I was way too nervous to enjoy the experience. We took the Lavender Bay exit and stopped to collect Tom from a small duplex with views across to the city. Simon had rung Tom just as we were leaving Balmain, so he was outside waiting for us when we drove up. His level of excitement outweighed mine, obvious by the way he bounced up and down as he waited for us to turn into his driveway. Jumping into the back seat, he was full of praise for the new me.

'How amazing you look. Yesterday you were plain Frankie, today you have transformed into this gorgeous Francesca. Not a country mouse anymore! Before you would have been asked for your ID at every pub. Now, you look like a woman any man could only dream about. Well done you!'

'Nothing to do with me. Well done, Lena—and Marty.'

'Marty?'

'The hairdresser.'

Ever the agent, Tom immediately stopped gushing and focussed on the upcoming audition. He explained what I should expect. He consulted his notes and told me to expect a grilling from the director, a bloke called Ivo Simpson.

'I've known him for years. A bit of a perfectionist and with an eye for detail. He will know what he wants, and you will either fit the bill or you won't. In a way, that should take the pressure off you. You are either it or you aren't. Just be yourself and answer his questions as best as you can. You don't have to be perfect. All he needs is to see your potential, to identify something in you that he can work with. OK?'

Tom peered at me intently.

I nodded, feeling strangely relieved. No need to perform. Just be polite and be myself. Too easy. I should be able to do that. Tom continued, 'Now the producer. She is Dana da Silva, and she is new to me. Don't know much about her. Dana also rang me yesterday—at Ivo's suggestion. Seemed perfectly pleasant on the phone. She's the one who keeps track of the money, sorts out the contracts, etc. If they decide you'll suit the part, then best to leave her to Simon and me, and we'll negotiate on your behalf.'

Simon reversed the car out of the driveway and retraced our direction back to the expressway. The traffic was heavy, but by and large going in the other direction, towards the city. After a little while, we turned off and headed into suburbs I had only ever heard of and never actually seen—Neutral Bay, Cremorne, Mosman, and then down the hill to cross a bridge. *Spit Bridge* I read from the sign. To my right and left a vision of blue drenched harbour was overlooked by massive houses clinging onto treed cliffs. We climbed up a hill and then headed for the coast. Already I could smell the salt on the breeze wafting through the open car window. My excitement mounted. No longer any stomach churn. No need to worry when I had these two wonderful people as my support team. All I had to do was to trust them and enjoy the swim. If nothing else, at least I would get to swim at this Manly place I had heard so much about.

It was just after 9.00 am when we finally arrived at the beach and located a car park. I could see that the beach was already busy. A workday yet so many people were already here—jogging or pushing prams along the esplanade—either in groups or escorted by their dogs, sitting on the beach soaking up the early morning's sun or already in the surf.

It was a perfect morning. Clear sky, warm but not too warm, and the waves not too high. A moderate swell—just right for a not too challenging swim and maybe sufficient in size to enable me to catch a wave or two.

Tom waved at three people hovering by the steps to the beach. They waved back. Three people? Of course, the third person would have to be the actor who plays Drew—my new person of interest. Thoughtfully, I gazed at them all as they approached. The man whom I assumed was Ivo Simpson greeted Tom with enthusiasm and clapped him on the shoulder. Ivo, about Tom's age, was tall and rangy, and was dressed in what appeared to be cast offs—a faded misshapen T-shirt and bedraggled shorts. His battered straw hat had clearly seen better days. Yet, his smile was broad and friendly. He enthusiastically shook Simon's hand then drew Dana across to introduce her. Dana, a perfectly styled woman, in complete contrast to Ivo, said her hellos and then introduced the 'Drew actor person' to everyone. He was everything his publicity said he would be. Utterly gorgeous.

With the introductions completed, they looked around for the person of interest. Me. I moved forward and put out my hand. Producer first, then director, then Drew. Saying 'Hello, I'm Francesca,' I shook each person's hand in turn and smiled in what I hoped was a friendly manner. There. That's my part done. Now the rest is up to them.

Dana smiled back at me coolly, yet not with hostility. More a neutral welcome. Ivo's expression was initially questioning, then it became warm and welcoming. Presumably, he liked what he saw. As did the actor who I soon discovered was called Luke. He greeted me like a long-lost friend.

'Francesca. Great you could make it. So pleased to meet you.'
Luke turned to Ivo. 'Good one Ivo. I feel that this is going to work.
What do you want us to do?'

'First thing I need to do is to check out Francesca's surfing skills.
Later, I will get the two of you to read through a bit of the script, so
I can see how the chemistry between you two is. Francesca, I take it
you can surf—body and board?'

I nodded. I could do both.

'Excellent. Looks like you need to go and get changed. The
change shed is over there,' he said while waving his hand in the
direction up the beach. 'Then we can get started.'

As I walked away towards the change sheds, I heard Ivo say to Tom:

'Tom, she's gorgeous. Just what I wanted. Where did you find her?'

'Oh, I have my contacts,' came the not-so-humble reply.

If only Ivo knew how inexperienced I was. But I guessed he
would soon find out.

Diving into the water, closely followed by Luke, who I had to
remind myself to keep thinking of as Drew, I immediately forgot
about the need to impress Ivo and Dana and instead focussed on
the delight of once more being in my element. The water, cool but
not too cool, foamed around us as we pushed through the breaking
waves. Further out past the other swimmers, and now treading
water, I turned to Luke.

'What are we supposed to do now?'

'Catch a wave.'

'OK, you're on. How about this one?' I gestured at a wave
forming and heading our way. Luke grinned back at me. We turned
back to face the beach and commenced swimming in preparation.

He was not too bad this Luke/Drew. Shoulder to shoulder, we
body surfed the wave to the shore. Then we stood up, laughing at
each other and turned, preparing to go again.

'Not so quick you two. No more body surfing. I want to see
Francesca on a surfboard. Take that one,' Ivo said, pointing to a
board lying on the sand.

I busied myself squeezing water from my bedraggled hair, which now fell in limp hanks around my face. I hadn't ridden a board for quite a long time—since my time with Charlie—but surely it was a skill so long ingrained that I would never forget what to do? Anyway, with a surf this size, I thought I should be able to manage it. Doing my best to look like a seasoned professional, I grabbed the board and attached the leg rope. I breathed a quick sigh of relief when I realised this was not too tricky a style of board. Stability should be OK, just so long as I concentrated and focussed on getting to my feet as quickly as possible.

Pushing the board into the waves, I positioned myself, lying tummy down on top of the surfboard and started paddling out—over and through the breaking waves back to where I was only a few minutes before. A few other board riders were already there, some sitting casually on their boards, legs dangling into the water. Others, like myself, were lying on their boards. The waves came and went—rocking under us. Some we let pass. Others were considered suitable, and a few riders took the opportunity to paddle furiously with the hope of matching their momentum to the wave before being propelled by it into the shore. Sometimes, this works and sometimes it doesn't. But that is part of the trick of successfully catching a wave. The other trick is being able to stand up quickly in time to progress with the momentum. That's what makes it fun.

Me? I took my time. It was important not to rush. I steadied myself and focussed on all I knew about catching the perfect wave. I didn't need too demanding a wave. After all, I suspected I might only have one chance to get it right. Soon, I spotted the swell of what looked like a promising wave developing and turned my board to the shore. This could be it. Not too big and not too small. The wave came closer, taking shape with each second as it approached. I started to paddle, timing my speed to that of the wave. It surged under me. Lifted me with its motion and the energy impelled me forward. Now for the tricky bit. No time to hesitate, and with one movement, I thrust myself onto my feet. Toes splayed and gripping,

I balanced and commenced to steer the board to the shore. Arms out wide to keep me steady, I focussed on staying upright. No fancy moves this time. Just a simple demonstration that I could stand upright on a board, catch a wave and ride it to the shore. It might be a simple wave, but the smile on my face spoke of the delight I felt in this experience.

Once I reached the shallow water, I step glided off the board and in one seasoned movement, I hoisted the board under my arm and moved forwards through the ankle-deep wash. Reaching the sand, I bent down and removed the ankle strap, and stood and gazed at my judges. Simon gave me a furtive thumbs up. Everyone else's broad smiles confirmed that I had nailed it.

'OK. What next?' I asked, while squeezing the water out of my hair with my free hand.

'Let's get out of here,' said Ivo. 'Back to my place and we can just run through a bit of the script. Nothing too strenuous, Francesca. Tom, you know the way?'

Tom nodded and we all set off up the beach. Luke took the board and with a muttered thanks, he returned it to a bystander—presumably the owner of the board. Me? I took my dripping self and followed Tom and Simon. I had hoped for a longer swim. But that's show business for you!

Ivo lived in a penthouse apartment with panoramic views of the beach. However, we didn't stay long enough to enjoy it. Once I had changed back into my dress and scraped my hair into a ponytail, I was handed a few pages of a script and told to read it with Luke.

As I perused the script, butterflies fluttered in my midriff, but then came to settle once I realised I would not have to act at all. I could just be myself. For bizarrely, what I was about to read was so like real life. No need to pretend. The script was outlining my first meeting with the character Drew, and you guessed it, our meeting involved my character crashing into him while catching a wave. No wonder they wanted someone who could surf. The words I had to say, well, they were not quite what I had said to Charlie that time, but they were awfully similar. It was no stretch to remember the range of emotions I felt on that occasion and just play myself. So, I did.

'Yes,' said Ivo after I had finished speaking. He looked thoughtfully across at Dana.

'She's fine for this role. Tom, Dana will send you the paperwork this afternoon. We won't be filming this episode for a week or so, but Francesca has to get started straight away. Rehearsals, voice coach, costumes, and just getting involved in the publicity stuff. Steep learning curve for you, Francesca, but I think you'll enjoy it. Luke here will look after you.'

'Yeah, sure boss,' said Luke.

Turning to look at me, Luke grinned and continued, 'Don't you worry. We are one big happy family—by and large. And I will take care of you. After all, you are my new romantic interest. We're going to wow the ratings; I just know it!'

As we drove back to Simon's office in The Rocks, I sat quietly on the back seat, processing all that had just taken place, while Simon and Tom conferred in the front. They spoke softly but I could tell it was all about me—stuff like contracts, options, fees, and working hours filtered across to the back of the car. I had no experience with any of these concepts and the novice that I was, I trusted those two to get it right. Maybe I was lucky but having Tom and Simon on my side ensured I secured the best possible contract from the production company. When my character became a hit, and I was offered a longer-term contract, it was Tom and Simon who negotiated a phenomenal deal. And I was to need that when things turned sour.

Chapter Seven

When we finally got back to the office—Sydney traffic, you know, is just the pits—we were greeted by four anxious people.

'You could have texted us,' grumbled Lena. 'We've been beside ourselves wondering what had happened. How did it go?'

'Like clockwork,' gloated Tom. 'I felt just like Henry Higgins. I knew she could do it. I could burst into song, but I will be considerate and spare your eardrums. What a champ!'

Suddenly, I was overwhelmed by a group hug from Lena, Jasmine, Mark, and Bryan—all of them speaking at once.

'Steady on. Slow down. Let me get my breath.'

Once seated, I gave the anxious audience a blow-by-blow description of the audition—for audition I suppose it was, although it had been much more casual than I had expected.

'You should have seen her catch the wave. Leapt up on the board like she was a true surfing professional and then cruised into shore right to our feet. Amazing. And looking like a princess, thanks to you Lena,' said Simon, smiling his gratitude at Lena.

'You wouldn't know it now though Lena,' I said, flicking my bedraggled ponytail over my shoulder.

'No worries. You made the perfect first impression and that is what always counts.'

Simon, looking at his watch, resumed his boss role.

'Come on, you lot. Unless Bryan has you all sorted, don't we need a team meeting to at least let Frankie and I know what is happening for the rest of this week?'

'I'm pretty sure Frankie knows. She's about to start a new career and leave us all behind!' laughed Jasmine. I hoped that glint in her eye was empathetic excitement and not jealousy.

It didn't happen that quickly, but in time I did leave them all behind. Yet, I couldn't completely let them go. For the team at *Perfectly PR* remained my number one fans and my dose of reality when I started to believe my own publicity. I could rely on any of them to tell me like it was. To not bullshit, and to always be there for me when I just wanted to chill and leave the fantasy world behind.

Mum and Dad were so proud. You would think I had discovered a cure for cancer or achieved world peace by the way they carried on. But I didn't mind. It's rather lovely to be adored by your folks. Mum made sure that everyone in my hometown knew about the screening of my very first appearance on TV. It even earned a mention in the local newspaper. I knew this because Mum made sure to send me a clipping. *Local Girl Makes Good*—complete with some daggy photo Mum had dragged out from who knows where. Still, it made her and Dad happy.

Once my character became part of the regular cast and I was earning good money, I could easily have moved out on my own, but I remained with Simon and Ruth. Although now I insisted on paying my share of the rent and I upgraded the furnishings in my bedroom. There are only so many cast offs a girl can bear.

However, I'm getting ahead of myself.

I was initially signed up for three episodes, as the powers that be deemed that sufficient for me to be the side story of Drew's latest romance. The chance visit by the daughter of an ex-local who was just passing through, my character, Trudi Hamilton, was said to be a bit of a restless spirit only visiting the seaside town in order to trace her family history. She was meant to be a fleeting romance for Drew, who would then wake up to the attractions of Maia, his longstanding and long-suffering love interest. But no one counted on the way Luke and I sparked off each other, and the surge in the clamouring from the devoted fan base, who just couldn't get enough of our story.

The fans were hooked from the moment we crashed into each other in the surf then the ensuing spat—both of us standing knee deep in the surf, glowering face to face, me trying to keep hold of my sagging bikini top and Luke just looking ferocious. Initially, I was cast as a bit part in three episodes but with my increasing popularity, I quickly found myself being written into a bigger and more substantial role. My screen mother then appeared in the community and was written into the script with her misadventures also forming part of the story line. Our escapades were intricately woven into the mesh of every episode. My love story with Drew was a roller coaster, as he prevaricated between the two women in his life. Like I said earlier, his character really was a bit of a tosser!

My initial contract was extended for twelve episodes and then extended further. I was delighted because being on the set was fun. I got to surf every day, or at least paddle in the water. Although, sometimes in mid-winter, when we were filming me surfing or running in and out of the waves or striding thoughtfully along the shore with my faithful dog, I was just plain freezing!

The story line seemed to require me to be attired either in a bikini or in skimpy cut off shorts and a bikini top. But I didn't mind. Until I moved to Sydney, that was my everyday attire when I wasn't in my school uniform. There was a lot of fussing over my hair and my makeup, which took some getting used to. I hadn't realised how much makeup you need to achieve the natural look.

Apart from the beach, the two best things about this new life were Luke and Skeeter—maybe not necessarily in that order.

Skeeter—well, he was the most gorgeous terrier I have ever met. Let me get this right. Skeeter was a wire-haired fox terrier of ferocious intelligence and personality. He had a trainer whom he adored, which was just as well as he pretty much ignored everyone else. In the story, he was meant to be my dog. Ivo, the director, was particularly keen on getting shots of me walking pensively along the beach with Skeeter at my side. His intent, I think, was to get the audience all emotional at those times when it looked like Drew and my character Trudi were estranged and possibly splitting up. Usually filmed at dusk or at some other atmospheric moment, such as when a storm was brewing, I was required to walk slowly, stopping from time to time to stare pensively out to sea and occasionally wipe away a stray tear that might be seeping down my cheek. All the while Skeeter, my loyal companion, was meant to be by my side. Getting the perfect shot often took many takes and we finally achieved it courtesy of the doggy treats secretly hidden in my shorts pocket or in my hand. With these enticements in place, Skeeter by and large stayed with me and sometimes even trotted beside me. Trouble was, he often looked a bit too excited for such pensive shots and every time I stopped to gaze thoughtfully out to sea, he would jump up to get to the treats. Before Ivo had a freak out, I quickly learned to bend down, pick up Skeeter and hold him in my arms. Cuddling him, and sneakily giving him a treat out of my hand, and with my head resting on his, we would both stare sadly out to sea. The effect was only spoilt on close examination by any diligent viewer, who might be able to detect the smacking of lips by said pooch.

From day one, Luke became my dear friend. Despite the speculation in the press that we were dating, the truth was that we were not an item, although it suited our publicity team to hint that we might be. Luke was my partner of choice at any awards night or media event. Many times, you would find us glammed up to the nines at an opening night for a movie or at the launch of a new celebrity product. Although occasionally I would give into Simon's whingeing and go with him. I suppose you could say Luke and I had joined the big time and become part of the A-List crowd. All that adoration and media attention is kind of addictive. I revelled in the glamour and started to forget about the small-town girl I once had been.

We made a fine couple, Luke and me. Much the same height. Maybe he was an inch or so taller than me. We photographed well. His dark complexion a foil to my blonde hair. Courtesy of fake tan and professional make up, we both epitomised the outdoorsy goodness of our TV characters.

The speculation about our relationship was just that—

speculation. We were friends—dear friends and nothing more. I nailed it almost immediately, but no one else seemed to work it out, and Luke swore me to secrecy. You guessed it. He was gay and as a heart throb for all those young female viewers, it would have been career suicide to have come out at this stage of his career.

I can't remember when we had our first heart to heart about his career dilemma, but it was the first of many. Luke would regularly agonise about how he felt conflicted playing the role of Drew and not being open about his true self. Me, I had no such concerns. This was just pretend and not of any importance as far as I could see. Froth and bubble. Why get worked up about that? I tried to set Luke's mind at ease.

'Hey, it's just acting. It's all pretend and not really you. You're on the TV like some cardboard cut-out. No one really believes that it is the real you. Like no one really believes I'm as stupid as this Trudi. Surely, they don't? And the publicity? It's just to sell the show and hook the viewers. None of it's real. It doesn't show who we really are. If our fans knew how boring I was, they would turn off in droves.'

'Don't you believe it. Have you read the fan mail? How many marriage proposals have you had this week?'

'Like I take those seriously! Anyway, I let the PR team look after those.'

Then one day I met the love of Luke's life—Harry. Somehow, they had kept it a deep dark secret, but I thought it was only a matter of time before the whole world worked it out. Occasionally, I would take Harry as my date to an event or to a dinner. At least that way the three of us could be seen having a good time without raising any suspicions. And we did have a good time. It was like Luke and Harry were my best friends. When people thought they saw Luke and I sparking off each other in the various contrived situations our writers dreamed up, it was really two close friends taking the mickey out of each other. He could always make me laugh with his asides and I must say, he was a pleasure to kiss!

The rest of the cast weren't too bad and over the 18 months that

I was on the show they were, as Luke said on that first day I met him, by and large welcoming. My screen mother was a hoot and I think ... no, I know ... she had a fondness for a certain white powder. The actors, who played the proprietors of the local café, were stalwarts of the Australian acting scene and were no trouble so long as they were given the respect they felt was their due.

In the story, Luke's character, Drew, regularly had adventures with two young men who were his old mates from school. All troubled characters, of course there were various scenarios involving danger, potentially fatal illnesses, and run ins with the law—almost on a weekly basis. For a while it looked highly likely that my character might dump Drew and take it up with one of these young men—a slightly shady but highly muscled man called Lex. I quite enjoyed those scenes. Gino, the actor who played Lex, was a bit like his character—dangerous, but oh so tempting, yet rather dumb. His public persona was scripted like a movie. Married to a model, and now the father of an adorable toddler, photos of the young family out and about were regularly featured in the women's magazines. We all knew though, that this image of domestic bliss was a façade. With monotonous predictability, he worked his way through any of the fresh faces on the set, trying out both cast and crew. Luke had prewarned me about him, so I was able to give him a regretful flick off. Like I said, he wasn't too smart. He took my refusal in good grace, interpreting it as a deferral rather than a rebuff.

Occasionally, new characters would appear in the show for three or four episodes—often to be in the role of love interest for some poor unfortunate with the aim of spicing things up when the ratings started to slide. These actors, being new to the set, always caused a frisson of excitement for the crew and cast. Consistent with their role as love interest, they were, by and large amazingly good looking. We young females in the cast would vie for their attention—nothing like a bit of variety to break up the long days on the set! I wasn't immune from this excitement and, well, if I am to be honest, confess that there were one or two of these blow-in actors that I fancied. No names mind you as I went to great lengths to keep these trysts secret. I didn't want to sully the speculation about the romance between me and Luke after all. You see, by then I knew how to play the game. But that didn't stop me completely, and I found time to enjoy … how would you describe it? Some added benefits! Yet, something held me back from committing to anything further than a casual relationship. Sex—yes please! A long-term relationship—no way! I think deep down I still believed that I belonged to Charlie.

Eighteen months all up I was part of that show. During that time, I certainly learned a lot. You might say that I grew up. From being the naive country girl who had no understanding of herself, let alone the devious ways of the TV industry, I transformed into a young woman who knew it all and had pretty much tried it all. I guess it was inevitable that I came to model myself on my screen persona and began to believe my publicity. I really thought I was important. In time, I started to believe the airbrushed over made-up image that regularly appeared on the magazine covers was all my own work and portrayed the real me. I forgot that what the public saw really was the creation of the publicity machine and not me at all. In hindsight, I came to see it was only a matter of time before it all came undone and the real me, that naïve country girl, was left to pick up the pieces.

Chapter Eight

We had just wrapped up filming of the last episode for the year before a four-week summer break. And what an episode it was. It was a cliff hanger for so many of the characters—mine included. Drew and Trudi had been reconciled in the previous episode. In the season finale, Drew brought me to tears (real tears – can you believe it?) with his heartfelt proposal—on bent knees down at the beach by the gently washing waves. In accordance with the script, he knelt down just out of reach of the incoming tide and spoke with utter sincerity the schmaltzy lines our writers had dreamed up. In response, I had to stand there saying nothing and looking overcome with emotion. It's a measure of my development as an actor that I managed to dredge up some tears and didn't dissolve into laughter. For the scene had all the elements of high farce. The tide creeping closer and closer with each take. Skeeter circling us barking with excitement and every so often leaping up and licking Luke on the face. As far as Skeeter was concerned, this new game was the best one yet. Every so often he would jump up at me looking for the treats he knew were in my pocket.

Ivo was having a meltdown.

'Can't anyone control that blasted dog?' he shouted to the assembled crowd.

'I don't know. It's kinda cute,' said Luke. 'But I think the problem is that I'm crouched down at his height, and he is expecting me to fuss over him and join in his game. Perhaps we could try the scene with me standing by Trudi and holding her somehow. Even if Skeeter jumps up it will then look like he is wanting to participate in the proposal.'

We tried that approach and it worked. My character then had to burst into tears and say something like, *'Drew I can't … not now'* and then run off up the beach with Skeeter in hot pursuit. This Skeeter and I did perfectly. After all, I still had treats in my pocket, and he was fanatical about chasing anyone. Then music swelled and faded and that was it for the season. The love story of Drew and Trudi still unresolved because as the viewers had discovered at the start of that episode, there was an added complexity to the story. You see, the viewers were in on the secret and knew Trudi's first love had turned up unexpectedly and she was now in turmoil. Turmoil being the default setting for my character. That or tears!

Anyway, with filming now finished, the end of year party could commence. A party for cast and crew this year being held on some swish motor cruiser which would cruise up and down Sydney harbour all evening. It was a bit like an end of school party. Everyone was in high spirits—some naturally high and some artificially enhanced. All of us were relieved another year of production had passed. We were still in work and had next year to look forward to once we had rested and recharged. Well, maybe not for the script writers. I had no idea if they ever had a break. They didn't really mix with us.

I had taken great care with my appearance and was rather pleased with how I looked that evening. A designer dress in this most amazing shimmering sea green/blue, changing from leaf green to aquamarine blue with every movement I made. Strappy and flared to the calf, the fabric was so fine that it floated in the gentle breeze. My hair I had left loose with two small plaits pulling my hair away from my face. Some dangly earrings and glittery sandals completed the look. No high heels tonight.

Our PR team had tipped off the media. A few of the paparazzi were hanging about when we arrived and took photos as we boarded the cruiser. I linked arms with Luke and smiled for the camera. No harm in continuing the speculation. Luke whispered something in my ear and I laughed. It was an appalling joke. I heard the click of cameras and knew that this image would be sold for a goodly sum.

The summer's evening was perfect for a party. Balmy weather, clear sky and the harbour so smooth that the boat barely rocked. We cruised up and down the harbour, all the while dodging the other watercraft and the occasional ferry. Every so often the boat would pause to give us the opportunity to admire the beauty of our surroundings and the nearby ever-changing shoreline. The glowing sunset promised further good weather for the next day. All the well-known Sydney icons were on display every which way we looked—the Opera House, the Harbour Bridge towering over us, the billowing sails of so many pleasure craft lapping up every last moment of daylight and those ever-present Sydney Harbour Ferries carting countless sad commuters to their homes. Watching one such ferry cross our path, I felt a brief flicker of contentment. How lucky was I to have this life away from boring 9 to 5 drudgery? So what if occasionally I had to brave freezing cold water and make it look like it was fun. The alternative could be so much worse.

Dinner was finger food, and I ate selectively taking care not to spill anything on my dress. Designer the dress certainly was. It belonged to a designer and was on loan for the evening. That meant no spills or rips, or I would have to pay for it.

I ate. I drank—Champagne of course—and I danced. A DJ played a mix of music that just begged to be danced to. Impossible to resist. Unless you were deaf, that is. I danced with Luke, with the other girls in a swirling group and with my screen mother, who was totally off her tree. Now that I looked around, I saw quite a few others in that condition. Me? I just stuck with Champagne.

At some stage, and I'm not sure exactly when it was as I had lost track of time, I decided I needed some fresh air. For some time, I had been back on the dance floor dancing in a group with some of the younger members of the cast. It was easy to slide away out of the gyrating mass and head out to the stern of the cruiser, onto the deck that was open to the sky. I remember the feeling of relief as I registered the cool evening air on my sweaty skin, and the shock when I realised it was now completely dark. The harbour foreshore twinkled with light—a bit like a Sydney fairy land. The Harbour Bridge receding behind us as we headed for the Heads, was a curve of light with its reflection waving back at it from the waters below, now being churned by watercraft.

I found myself a secluded space in a corner and rested while watching the others chat and mingle. I really was feeling knackered and found myself wondering how much longer this party would continue. If I could find myself a spot in which to curl up and hide, at that moment I would have done so. I had just closed my eyes and was relaxing into the rock of the boat and the smell of the salt water when I sensed someone approaching. I opened my eyes and there he was—Gino, who played the character, Lex, was drawing near with two glasses of Champagne in his hands.

'Here, beautiful one. Take this,' he said proffering one glass to me. 'I knew you would be out here, and you were so easy to spot. That dress just shimmers in the dark.'

I accepted the glass. Another glass of Champagne was the last thing I needed after the amount I had already drunk that evening. But what's a girl to do? To refuse would be bad manners. Or so I thought.

We stood side by side thoughtfully sipping our drinks and gazing out into the darkness and the lights beyond. Gino/Lex spoke first.

'I've really enjoyed working with you this year, Francesca. You are such a happy person. You make everything fun. Even when Ivo makes outrageous demands, you never get in a flap. Unlike some of the cast who can be right prima donnas. You know, I think you and I had something special in our scenes together. I just hope we get to do more next year—get a bit closer maybe?'

His smile became a smirk.

It was clear what he had in mind.

'Yeah, something special,' I said dryly. 'Like you have with all your other interests?'

I'll say this for Gino. He never takes anything too seriously and certainly was never too full of himself. He just grinned and chuckled at my response. That grin—it's amazing. Like that of a naughty little boy charming himself out of trouble.

Then, still smiling, he took my glass out of my hand, put it along with his own glass on a ledge, and gently took my face between his hands. What did I do? Well, I smiled back at him and instinctively leaned in closer—all the better to kiss him. And kiss we did. From previous professional experience, I already knew how to kiss Gino and was fully aware of how amazing it could be. After all, we had plenty of practice being filmed in this manner during the season.

We kissed and kissed some more. Deepening kisses, lips opening to reveal and share questing tongues. Pressing closer and closer together. My hands ran along his back, gliding over muscles honed from hours of work in the gym. His hands slid up under my dress and under my 'barely there' knickers, curving over my buttocks and rubbing between my legs.

We were in a corner of the deck in darkness and hopefully unnoticed by the others. But even if we had been, I'm not sure we would have paid them any mind. I was rather drunk you see, and I am certain Gino had been hitting his favourite white powder. There was so much of it there that night I'm sure he would have had the opportunity. And with intoxication comes recklessness. We neither knew nor cared if anyone was watching. At that moment, they could have joined in for all I cared. I hadn't ever slept with or had sex with Gino and now I wondered why I had not ever done so. What I was feeling was so incredible and I wanted more—NOW!

He pushed me against the rails and with one movement he unzipped his pants and with practised ease, he connected with me. Clearly lots of experience with a quickie. Not that I objected. I clenched myself around him and we started the timeless ritual of sex—in and out with increasing speed and force. I groaned. He groaned. It felt so good. And then suddenly it didn't.

You see, the rails Gino had pushed me against were not wooden but made of metal wires supported by metal posts. Although the bit below was solid, it was of no help when the wires, with a sudden pop, snapped and we tumbled over the side, still joined in some bizarre cuddle, only unlocking as we hit the water. Down and down I tumbled, taking in water as I sank.

I don't really have much recollection as to how I managed to survive, but I now understand that eventually I was located and dragged onto a rescue boat. Maybe it was the iridescence of my dress that somehow saved me, for I was later told that hope had almost been completely lost for both of us before one of my rescuers spotted me, barely conscious and trying to float.

I was lucky. Gino was not so. His body was not found until the next day.

Drowned.

Then the scandal hit. Photos taken by someone else on the boat of Gino thrusting into me were circulated. Rather dark and blurry photos at that, but with a bit of explanation, people could work out what was happening. Gino's widow, grieving and devastated, issued a media release asking for privacy *at this difficult time*. Then other people spoke *confidentially* of course of Gino's open marriage and his addiction to sex. The storm grew in its fury and worsened as some women came forward and spoke of how he forced himself on them, and the media now speculated that this was what was happening on the night of the party.

All this was going on while I was in hospital recovering. So much of what was swirling around on the social network and in the press, was being kept from me. Security kindly provided by Dana kept most of my visitors away. It wasn't until two days after the party that a sombre Simon and Tom came to see me.

'How are you feeling?' asked a concerned Simon after giving me a hug.

'Okay, I guess. They say I might be able to go home tomorrow if I keep improving. The doctor was a bit concerned about water in my lungs and the bang they say I took to my head, but I think I'm doing alright.'

Tom, after handing me a fragrant bunch of multicoloured flowers, peered at me intently.

'What do you remember?'

'Not much. I was there with Gino and then the railing must have snapped, as the next thing I remember is hitting the water. It stung and then was so cold and I kept sinking. I must have lost consciousness 'cause I don't remember anything until someone was wrapping me up and telling me I was safe. I'm just looking forward to getting home and back to normal.'

Tom's face looked grim.

'Frankie. There is no *back to normal* for you. Life has changed irrevocably. Gino is dead—drowned—and the scandal that is erupting is also threatening to drown your career.'

I didn't understand. In fact, at that stage the memory of what Gino and I had been up to was rather hazy. I was drunk, remember? Sure, there was kissing. But was there anything else? I just couldn't recall. My puzzled expression was a clear indicator that I had no idea what they were talking about.

'You don't remember, do you?' Simon said.

I shook my head.

'How do I put this? You and Gino were in an intimate position when you crashed through into the water. Not unusual at a party, especially an end of year celebration. It happens all the time at PR parties. Trouble is, someone took a photo. Maybe you thought you were being discreet, but no matter. That photo has now been shared with half the world—or those people that might be interested, which probably is more than half the world. The media is beside itself with excitement and is writing up a storm. The so-called grieving widow is distancing herself from this scandal and Gino's past activities are providing fodder for so much speculation. It's only a matter of time until they turn their attention to you. So far you are being seen as the innocent victim and have everyone's sympathy, but it is almost certain that the story line will change. The media likes variety, you see.'

My look of horror said all I need to say, which was fortunate as I found myself unable to find any words. I frantically trawled through my memory of that night but was unable to recollect anything about those vital few minutes. It can't have been long. Gino was always quick in his couplings. I knew as much from the shared gossip on the set. I could remember us sharing the Champagne, the kissing, and then the water. That was it. I shook my head.

'No. Surely not. We were in the shadows. I certainly remember where we were, outside on the deck, but not much more.'

'That might explain the quality of the photo—being in the shadows and all that. Look. See. Here,' Simon said, as he passed his phone across to me.

I took his phone and stared at the image on the screen in dismay. The background of the image was dark being the shadowy harbour, but it was clearly Gino in the foreground. No one else was so well built. He was wearing a white shirt, which stood out against the background and his pants were loose around his hips. They were not falling any lower as they were being held in place by two shapely legs wrapped around him. Long legs, together with slender arms, clasped him close. The face of his partner was not visible. It could have been anyone, except for the glistening mane of blonde hair falling down his side and across his shoulders as we kissed. That hair, my trademark, belonged to no one else.

'Oh shit,' I said and handed the phone back to Simon. 'What do we do now?'

'Don't panic and don't say anything to anyone, especially the media,' said Tom, patting me reassuringly on the cotton bedspread that covered my ankles.

'All comments from you should come through me. Maybe in time a remorseful interview on *60 Minutes* or the like, but we should see what else is flushed out about Gino's behaviour. Leave it to me. First thing we need to do is to arrange for you to be discharged from here and get you home undetected. I also need to talk to Dana about how we protect you. Simon, you should be in on that conversation. Your PR skills might be needed.'

They kept talking, planning a strategy while I lay back, my mind awhirl. How could so much go so wrong from one simple bonk? I'm not a strait-laced person, but believe me, if I had been sober, I would not have let any coupling with Gino happen. Maybe after a kiss or two, and with a laugh, I would have pushed him away encouraging him to prowl elsewhere. But my defences were down and let's admit it, Gino is, no make that *was,* gorgeous and fun. Who could resist a quick romp with him? Not many judging by his track record!

The night of the party Gino was just doing what he always did—getting high and finding a lay. Now he was dead. I couldn't help thinking that all that had happened was somehow my fault. If I hadn't succumbed to his overtures, then the railing would not have snapped, and the chances are he might still be here, up to his usual tricks and trying it on with someone else. I lay there, feeling stunned that life could catastrophically change in just one instant and without any deliberate thought. I thought of his wife—unlikely she would mourn him if what Gino had regularly said about their relationship was accurate. But the toddler? Now that was a tragedy. Gino adored his daughter and she adored him.

With that thought, a wave of grief deluged me. Gino, for all his faults, was real and I had always thought of him with a kind of weary affection. He made me laugh with his constant attempts to try it on with me. Not in a sleazy way but in a *this is what best buddies do* sort of way. Who would have known that the one time I finally succumbed to his advances would be the very last bonk of his life? I just hoped he didn't suffer.

I rolled over and stared at the wall, ignored by Tom and Simon who continued with their conferring. Alone in my misery, I pondered the disaster that had now become my life.

How had things gone so wrong?

Chapter Nine

I didn't leave the hospital until the next evening. Simon was in charge of Operation Get Frankie Home and took to it with all the enthusiasm he was capable of mustering. Should his PR business end in tears, I can see a new career awaiting him in international espionage, given his skill in avoiding detection.

We waited until close to midnight before leaving the ward. Simon had already located a rear exit from the hospital—generally used by staff—but somehow, he convinced the authorities we could use it. Or maybe he hadn't, and we used it anyway. Disguised in the most appalling long flowing outfit resembling a nightie, which Simon said belonged to Ruth, and with hair tied back and hidden under a scarf, I followed him down the stairs and along what seemed to be a rabbit warren of shadowy corridors built many decades ago. Finally, once outside in some sort of courtyard, he took my hand and led me towards the back gate, all the while keeping us both in the shadows. There the night porter opened a metal gate—*Locked for security purposes after 10pm* according to the sign—and we scuttled across the road to the waiting car. With Tom at the wheel with the engine running, we eased away from the kerb. All this took less than five minutes. I was impressed.

'Just put your head down in case anyone is hiding behind the bushes. I think we are in the clear, but you never know,' said Tom, as he eased the car onto Elizabeth Street and turned down Market Street heading in the direction of inner west Sydney.

Undetected, we finally reached our Balmain home. By now it was well after midnight. All the other houses in the street were dark, their inhabitants sound asleep. The only light still burning was the one out on the front porch of our house. It all felt so surreal—opening the squeaking gate, walking up the front path towards the house, the concrete path still warm with the accumulation of that day's heat. It could be just like any other day, returning home late from an evening shoot on the set. As I approached the door, it opened, and I was greeted by a cuddle and an emotional hello from Ruth.

'Come in, Frankie dear. You must be all in. It's so late. You need to get to bed.'

I shook my head. 'I'm not sure I can. I feel all wired. Must be an adrenaline rush from being *007's* buddy.'

I elbowed Simon and grinned at him. He grinned back. For a moment we were children again, partners in our latest escapade and fleeing from the inevitable parental punishment. Then reality hit. I was no longer a child, but an adult who had stuffed up big time. Simon took my arm.

'Come on, baby sister. Out the back with you. A cup of tea? Or maybe a hot chocolate? We have a bit to talk about.'

A short while later, all of us were seated around the dining table sipping our beverage of choice—tea being Ruth's and my preference, and a beer each for Simon and Tom. The discussion then commenced. Tom went first by updating us about the current situation.

Unofficially, he had been informed of the toxicology results. Tapping his finger to the side of his nose, Tom indicated that we were not to ask how he knew. Gino, it appeared, had a massive amount of cocaine in his blood—no surprise there—and hardly any alcohol in his system. Me on the other hand—no drugs in my system, but lots of alcohol. If I'd been driving a car, I would have lost my licence. I was that drunk. But no drugs. And Tom assured me that made me look less of a criminal than Gino, and just plain stupid.

'Which you were,' said Simon.

'Don't beat her up,' admonished Tom. 'There's more to come.'

He then explained how he had been informed that day that the production company was cancelling my contract. They would pay me out of course. He assured me that he had negotiated a very respectable payout which should keep me comfortable for some time. But my career with them was over. I was damaged goods, and it was unlikely I would be able to get a gig with anyone else for some time. He assured me that in time I would be redeemed. After all, my only sin was being stupid. For many, my youth was a sufficient excuse for my behaviour. You know, too much fame too soon and not being equipped to handle the lifestyle and so on. That excuse is trotted out all the time. Tom said if I played my cards right, and because I was pretty and generally well liked, he thought that eventually I could expect to be forgiven. Although it may take some time.

In an ideal world, that would be right. But Tom, sweetie that he is, had not allowed for some of the bitches I had worked with on set—two of them in particular who had had it in for me from day one. One of them played the role of Luke's long-suffering love interest, Maia. The other, cast as Maia's best buddy, had hoped to be rebirthed as Trudi. Then I came on the scene, and they had to get used to being second fiddle. Well, not anymore. The very next day they were interviewed on a morning TV program and spoke of my appalling behaviour on set. How I was a prima donna and a pain to work with. How Luke went out of his way to placate me and how Luke's and my romance was a farce. They were right about the last bit, but the rest was all lies, the product of their jealous imaginations and a desire to get even.

The next morning Luke rang me to warn me to stay inside.

'The paparazzi are after you. It's only a matter of time until they find out where you live. You can't risk going outside the house at all and definitely not up the street. Don't worry about those bitches. Dana and Ivo have read them the riot act and they've gone into hiding. Not that Dana and Ivo care about you. They're just worried about their precious soapie and its sponsors. They have to stay squeaky clean, you know. I suspect the days are numbered for your screen mother with her drug problem. But seriously, you need to lay low.'

Tom rang me soon after and confirmed all that Luke had said.

I was a prisoner. It was mid-December—hot and steamy—and I was stuck in this charming, but unventilated cottage. I couldn't even sit out on the front porch for fear of discovery. I wanted to go home. To my mother—and father, of course.

I texted Simon.

I want to go home. Can I take your car?

The texted reply was almost instantaneous.

No way. I don't trust you with my precious car. I'll take you this weekend. Hang in there and stay calm. First thing though, you need to lose your hair, then no one will know who you are. I'm bringing home clippers tonight.

I had no emotional attachment to my hair. It had just brought me trouble. Maybe Simon was right. Without that blonde curtain, I could be anyone—especially if I wore slightly different clothes and ditched the makeup. Rummaging in the junk drawer I located some old, sharp scissors—dressmaking scissors by the look. I moved to the bathroom and studied myself in the mirror. It had been so long since I had worn my hair short—ten years at least. I paused and contemplated my image in the mirror as I tried to imagine myself without what had been an integral part of my personality. The tanned beach babe with flowing blonde hair. Who would I be without it? Did it really matter? Decision made I reached for the scissors. But something made me pause. I looked at myself in the mirror with this golden curtain hanging thick and glossy, framing my face, tumbling over my shoulders, and falling to my waist. Then it came to me. I knew what I must do.

Dividing my hair into four, I set to and created four plaits topped and tailed with rubber bands. Before I had a chance to chicken out, I cut all four braids off. With the four braids placed carefully onto a clean towel, I once more glanced at myself in the mirror. Short tufty hair spiked out from my head. Now I looked like some street urchin of less than half my age, straight out of a novel by Charles Dickens. Still, it would do for now until Simon came home with the clippers. The braiding had been for a purpose and my severed braids now had a use—a much more worthwhile use than their previous life. Instead of being an adornment for a useless star in a soapie, I would now send them off to the charity that created wigs for those in need.

'At least you've done one worthwhile thing,' I told myself. *'Not sure it makes up for the mess you've made of your life. But it's a start.'*

That night both Simon and Ruth greeted my changed appearance with horror.

'I know the hair has to go, but does it have to look this bad?' Simon said as he handed over the clippers.

'It's going to look much worse in a few minutes. Thanks,' I said after taking the clippers from him. 'You both stay there, and I'll be right back.'

As I predicted, it only took a minute or so to clip my hair using a number one blade. The spiky, straggly hair peeled off into the bathroom sink. I ran my hand over my now almost smooth scalp, while gazing thoughtfully at the new me.

Not too bad, I thought. Fortunately, for this look my skull was a rather dainty shape with a gently curving dome. There is no way a pointy head could be hidden with this reveal.

My housemates' reaction though … was different.

'OMG,' cried Ruth in alarm when I returned to the room. 'You look like a starving waif.'

'Or a cancer sufferer,' said Simon. 'Put a scarf around your head, or one of those turban thingos, and no one will even glance your way. You know how funny folks are around people with cancer? Can't even look them in the eye. You'll be totally unnoticed.'

'Mind you …' Ruth continued her analysis of the new me, walking around me and staring at my face intently. '… This style really makes your eyes look enormous. I hadn't noticed before those specks of green in your brown eyes. Rather unusual. A bit like emerald chips. Maybe it is the contrast with your brown fuzz that is bringing out the green.'

I patted my head and smiled. It really was a relief to finally get rid of that hair. Like shedding a skin. I could finally let go of the soapie star, Francesca McAdam, and move on. Literally, it was also a physical feeling of release as if I had shed a heavy weight. I hadn't realised how heavy all that hair was, as it was so long since I had worn it short. All that hair had weighed a ton and was almost like another person, the amount of attention it demanded. No longer the blonde beach babe, I was now transformed into an ordinary person, just like any other sickly-looking brunette you'd pass by on the street without a second glance.

Now, all I wanted to do was forget the disaster that had been my life. And maybe, with time, the rest of the world would too.

Chapter Ten

But I couldn't forget. It was agony. I felt trapped. Like I was some tortured soul in Limbo. Unable to return to my old life—even if I wanted to—and, even if I knew what I wanted to do next, I was also constrained from moving on. The events of that fateful night played over and over in my mind. Asleep or awake, I just couldn't get away.

Floating. I felt like a piece of unwanted rubbish cast overboard, drifting in the ocean—directionless and without any idea where I was heading. No, not exactly. With my luck I would be sucked down some black hole or lost in the Bermuda Triangle.

My life was a misery. Each evening when Simon returned home from work, I would pounce on him, pleading with him to take me home.

'Please Simon. I can't cope with this much longer,' I would say, grabbing him as soon as he came through the front door.

'Hey Frankie. And good evening to you too! It's okay. You just need to hang in there for the time being. A bit of patience is what you need. Anyway, you are best staying here in Balmain until the weekend, and then I'll take you home and you can hide there. I can't go any earlier than that—Christmas rush and all that. But once we are both home, I can stay for a while over Christmas and maybe your life will get back to normal. Whatever *normal* is,' he said, while prying my clinging hands off his arms and doing his best to give me a comforting pat at the same time—quite a feat in contortion.

Not that his attempted comforting soothed me in the slightest. I had become so used to getting my way and was well and truly on my way to a full-scale tantrum when Ruth intervened.

'Frankie. Listen to me. You need to grow up. This is not all about you. Someone died the other night. A little girl lost her father and all you seem to be doing is worrying about yourself. You survived. Okay, it *is* a bit embarrassing what you were up to. But we are all so relieved you are still with us and not with Gino in the morgue. Have you thought about how we are all feeling—and your folks too? Have you spoken to them? I know Simon has and your mum is going out of her mind with worry about you.'

I just stared at Ruth. Her words were harsh but true. What sort of person had I become?

Now I was awash with shame and self-blame. Images of those final few moments before we plunged overboard played and replayed in my mind. It was all my fault. Why had I not, like so many other times, neatly turned Gino away with a laughing response, allowing him to move onto someone else? If I had, maybe he would have survived. Why did I weaken then and why did the railing snap? Perhaps it wasn't completely my fault after all, but I couldn't help but blame myself.

Ruth suggested it might bring me some comfort if I wrote a sympathy card to the grieving widow. I spent some hours trying, but I eventually gave up as I couldn't find the words. How do you comfort someone who you are fairly certain is not so grief stricken and who most likely will re-partner at least once within the next twelve months?

I tried to be patient and not nag Simon who, with each passing day, looked more and more exhausted. Work deadlines and Christmas parties were taking their toll. I spent my days reorganising and tidying the little cottage. By the time I was finished, it had never looked so good—trim and sparkling with everything tidied away. So unnatural and so unlived in. Its cosy, jumbled mess was a thing of the past.

With my new shaven look, I soon discovered that I was able to wander the streets unnoticed. As I had suspected, people took great care not to look at me at all or for too long. A quick glance in my direction determined my bald-headed existence, and their eyes would slide away so as to avoid a second look. It was almost as if I had become a ghost—able to drift around undetected. Each day I walked the back streets until I ended up in Darling Street at my favourite coffee shop. A short stop to enjoy a coffee and a quick read of the papers and then I resumed my perambulations.

One afternoon, as I was wandering back to our house, I glanced up and noticed a man with a camera hovering near our front gate. I had been located! Fortunately, I was far enough away that he had not seen me. I ducked into a nearby driveway and studied him from behind the safety of a flowering shrub. Scruffy, unshaven and clutching a camera, he was furtively examining our house for signs of life. I lurked there for some fifteen minutes until he appeared to be satisfied no one was at home and, after taking one snap of the exterior, he wandered over to a parked car, hopped in and drove away—fortunately not in my direction. Breathing a sigh of relief, I left the security of my hiding place and walked back home on slightly trembling legs. I had no idea what I would have done if he had spotted me. Run away, I suppose.

When I told Simon that evening, he reacted exactly as I expected.

'That does it. The mongrels. Can't they leave you alone? They don't care about you. All they want to do is sell their photos for the best possible price and have no compassion for the people they're persecuting and the pain they might be inflicting.'

'That's a bit steep coming from someone who works in PR,' I laughed. 'Seriously though. It's okay and I'm fine,' I continued. 'Although seeing him there snooping did give me a bit of a shock. But I managed to remain undetected. You should have seen me there hiding behind the bush in the front yard of that terrace over there. You would have been proud of me.'

'Hah! You were brave. It's a wonder the dragon that lives there didn't hose you off her property or call the police. A close call all around!'

Still, joking aside we agreed to head for our parents' home the following evening as soon as Simon had finished work. It was less than a week to go before Christmas and he thought he could delegate the few outstanding tasks to the rest of the office team to complete. He was meant to be taking leave after all. I knew that wouldn't happen as most days he would still be on his laptop and phone.

I was so relieved that, after giving him an enormous hug—which he reciprocated—I immediately rang Mum.

'Mum, we will be home tomorrow night. Late probably so don't wait up for us. Just leave the back porch light on.'

Mum, who is the world's biggest softy, wouldn't have a bar of that.

'No, dear. We will be here waiting. Just call when you are close, and I will put the kettle on.

The drive home seemed to take forever. But that may have been because I was so desperate to leave Sydney—and the life I had once so loved—far behind me. Of course, Simon had to be delayed at work that evening. By the time he arrived home, I was completely packed and ready to go: my bags were stacked in the hallway and me, well I was wearing a path in the floor with all my pacing.

Ruth waved us off with motherly admonitions and told us to drive carefully. She was going to spend Christmas Day in Sydney but would brave the Boxing Day traffic to join us. As we drove away, I leaned out the car window calling last minute instructions concerning the purchase of gourmet supplies to bring with her. Simon laughed.

'We're not going out to the sticks you know, baby sister. They do have food down there and even some decent cafés these days now that the tourists have discovered us.'

I half wound up the window—it was still warm even this late in the evening—and I turned to Simon.

'I'm so pleased to be going home. Now I can forget this life in Sydney ever happened. First thing tomorrow I'm going surfing.'

Simon, a serious note in his voice, questioned, 'It wasn't all bad, was it? You made new friends, like Luke and Tom, and my team. And I got the impression you had fun. Well, you never complained, and you looked rather happy.'

'Yeah okay. There were some good bits. And Luke and Harry are both pretty special—and your gang too. I hope they don't all dump me. But I can't help feeling like all the good times have been overshadowed by what happened that night on the harbour. Tainted somehow. I just can't see myself ever returning to Sydney.'

'I hate to spoil this little fantasy of you galloping off into the sunset never to return little sister, but I'm afraid I have to give you a reality check, Frankie. It's not certain yet, but there is every chance there will be a coronial inquiry as to the circumstances of Gino's death. You see, there could be a safety or manufacturing issue that explains why the railing collapsed. If there is a hearing, you may be called to give evidence.'

Sensing my shudder, he continued, 'Don't panic yet. Nothing has been decided and it may take a few months before the powers that be come to a decision. But as a betting man, I reckon there is a fair chance they will convene a hearing and you will need to be there.'

Our conversation faltered after that. Simon tuned the car radio to a music station—Triple J, I think it was—and focused on his driving. Me? I slumped in my seat and gazed mindlessly out the car window into the darkness. In my misery, I decided that the darkness outside was a fitting analogy for my inner state. Even the twinkling lights of the passing towns and hamlets did nothing to elevate my mood.

After some time, Simon spoke again, his gentle voice intruding on my thoughts.

'It's not the end of the world, Frankie. Maybe the end of the world you were coming to enjoy, but maybe not. Only time will tell. Promise me you won't be a misery guts for Mum and Dad. They've been so worried about you. If they see you like this, it'll just make it worse for them. You know how hard they work with their business. That is a heavy enough load. They don't need to carry you as well.'

He was right of course. I owed it to Mum and Dad to not be a burden. It might take a bit of acting on my part. But hey, aren't I an actress?

'Yeah okay. Fair comment. I'll do my best to not be a wet blanket and maybe do a bit around the guesthouse. Maybe that way Mum and Dad could have a day or two off while you are staying. You could do front of house—reception and serving breakfast, and I could do the hidden stuff—cleaning, cooking the bacon and eggs. I just don't want to be seen by the public until this all dies down.'

'Deal. That can be our Christmas present to them. I'm assuming in all your misery you forgot about presents?'

No surprise there! My brother had me pegged.

Once more, silence descended, and I found myself slipping into a semi-doze, still vaguely aware of Simon's tuneless humming to the songs being played on the radio but sounding as if it was coming from a long way away. I slumped down into the seat and relaxed into a semi-conscious state until sometime later when Simon's voice again intruded into my thoughts. I jerked awake, shaking my head as if to dislodge the jumbled thoughts that had been crowding my foggy brain.

'Nearly there. And about time too. It's almost midnight. Frankie, time to wake up!'

'Where are we now?'

'We're approaching the town. See? The lights are ahead.'

I wound down the car window and sniffed the salty air that gushed in. Yes, definitely home. I would know that smell anywhere. My nostrils were assailed by that unique aroma of surf and dairy country that could only exist in this part of the world. I inhaled deeply and relaxed into the car seat. Now I knew I was really almost home.

We drove along the deserted main street (it was very late after all) that snaked up and down a steep hill. Then, turning left, we headed towards the sea.

We made a sharp turn into a driveway beside which a sign proclaimed, *Ocean Breeze Guesthouse – Boutique Bed and Breakfast Accommodation*. We followed a narrow driveway flanked by tall flowering shrubs, past a shadowy house and around to the rear where we stopped.

It had been a long time since I had last been home. So much had happened, and I hesitated to move.

'Come on, sis. You can't sleep in the car, you know. Time to get moving.' Simon urged me on.

Shrugging, I made my move. With the seatbelt unbuckled, I opened the car door, stepped into the night and stretched, my body aching with tiredness and with what could also have been a slight feeling of relief.

The evening so still and warm enveloped me. The sound of cicadas with their ear-piercing shriek deafened me and drowned out all else. Their call reverberated through my very being, so much so that I could feel my innards vibrating in tune.

Moths circled and battered themselves against the lone lightbulb shining outside the back door. Then, with a shudder and a squeak the door opened and slammed shut, scattering the circling moths as my mother burst through.

'At last. I was starting to worry.'

With the warmth of arms and a softness of kisses, I was safely cocooned in my mother's loving arms. Not a bad feeling, but after a moment or two, rather suffocating. Taking action, I squirmed and came up for air.

'Hi Mum. You shouldn't have waited up for us. It's way too late. But it's lovely to see you and to be home at last,' I said. 'Never again,' I added, trying but failing to repress a shudder that travelled through me from head to toe.

Mum once again reached for me as if to protect me from any further harm. 'It's alright, my dear. That's all behind you. You're safe here. No one can hurt you.'

'Don't you bet on it,' muttered Simon, moving to Mum's side and kissing her on the cheek.

'Trouble just follows our Frankie.'

Mum batted at him and with a murmured 'Oh do behave,' she continued to cluck over me as if nothing had been said.

I should explain that Mum is one of the most unfussed people I have ever met. Nothing and no one ever upsets her, which is just as well given the erratic and undisciplined behaviour of her husband and children. I recall how, during our childhood, when all was chaos around her with rampaging children and a husband obsessing with his latest hobby, she would just smile serenely and ignore us all. Maybe she was deaf, but I doubt it. I think Mum is just a supreme optimist who has always expected life to work itself out in time. And it generally did.

People say I look like her with my curly light brown hair and muddy-dam-water-coloured eyes. Our fine bones bely our strength—something Mum needs every day as she lugs the vacuum cleaner or armfuls of bed linen to the various guest rooms.

She and Dad had got involved with the B&B business by accident. Dad had been raised in this house—once his parents' home. Set on a secluded headland a short walk away from the main beach, it had been a perfect location for my childhood adventures whenever we visited our grandparents. Following his parents' deaths, Mum and Dad and the three of us relocated to this house—a move of which we three children all thoroughly approved. Living so close to the beach, we were the envy of our schoolfriends. We were still only young when we moved in: Amy was 15, Simon 13, and I was only 7—all legs and wonky teeth.

It didn't take long for my parents to identify the tourist potential of our place. With some help from the local bank, they built tourist accommodation—six separate bedrooms with individual sitting areas and ensuites in two blocks of three. Built a short way from the main house, and scattered under remnant coastal gums, they were discreetly hidden from view. Each with their own private timber deck, these apartments had proven to be a winner. Our bookings were steady with many repeat visitors. The cabin apartments were connected to the main house by various gravel paths that meandered through the bush. Breakfast was always provided in a dining room or, if the day was fine, on the deck out the front of the house. Nothing fancy, but perfectly comfortable in a scenic location and, judging from the glowing reviews from our guests, always appreciated.

Yet, that night when we arrived home, we didn't enter via the front door but did as we had always done—went in via the back door into a broad enclosed verandah which functioned as our sitting room.

I plonked my various bags onto the floor just inside the door, then wandered into the large internal kitchen to put the kettle on. Although it had received a thorough refurbishment some years ago to make it suitable for commercial operations, the kitchen still had the feel of a homely family meeting place. Photos randomly stuck on the fridge, and notices, cards and invitations pinned to a corkboard all spoke of a busy connected life.

A short time later, Mum and I were both settled on the couch and sipping our cups of tea while Simon contented himself with a cup of coffee.

Between sips I asked, 'Where's Dad?'

'Asleep. It's way too late you know,' said Mum.

'No, I'm not,' came a voice from the doorway.

A sleepy figure resplendent in vivid Christmas pyjamas appeared.

'You lot would wake the dead you would. Lucky for us that we have no guests tonight. They'd be full of complaints otherwise.'

There were more cuddles and laughter when Simon and I, as always, battled for prime position with our father. You see, Dad has not just been our own much-loved dad, but has always been everyone's favourite person. Years ago, when he was the sports master at the local high school, he was the trusted confidant of students and teachers alike.

Tall and gangly, yet blessed with a winning smile, Dad has always oozed charm and genuine interest in all others. With a distinctive shaved head—premature baldness, you know—he stood out and was easy to find in a crowd. Sometimes, especially in my early teens, I begrudged the way everyone else in this town seemed to act as if they had a special claim to my father or to his time. Yet, on other occasions, I was happy to bask in the admiration of my friends who envied me for having such a *cool* father.

About four years ago, Dad retired from the teaching business to help Mum. He said Mum needed his help as the B&B was getting so popular. I suspect he really was ready for a change and helping Mum was just an excuse that suited him at the time. Since then, he has never looked back. Dad has never been one for tidying the rooms or making the beds, but he has always been happy to perform as host and make the breakfasts each morning, while charming the guests with his repartee and suggestions as to what to see and do. He has also always been a general Mr Fixit and when he isn't repairing taps or changing lightbulbs, he can be found out the back in the garage working on his latest project. This could be anything from rebuilding a motor bike, repairing a car, or generally just playing around with gadgets. Sadly, none of us have inherited his mechanical skills, but he seems to love us anyway, despite this lack.

We sat quietly and talked about this and that until the single chime of the hall clock signalled the hour.

'Well, that's it for me then,' said Dad rising from his chair. 'Lots to do in the morning—well, you could say it's already morning. So, I suppose that means lots to do very soon once it is daybreak and before the next lot arrive to stay. Maybe you two can help your mum set up in the morning?' he asked, looking at us hopefully.

As if we had a choice!

'Of course,' we both chorused. Then, with good night kisses and hugs, we made our way to our various bedrooms.

My room is up a steep flight of stairs to an attic bedroom— unchanged since my childhood—a vision of surfing posters and the odd sporting trophy. At least the bed had been upgraded to a double since I was last here, but the rest of my mess was untouched. A small ensuite for my sole use completed the look. Again, I was the envy of my girlfriends when I was a teen. Not only did I have the best dad in town, but I also had a bathroom that I didn't have to share with a sibling.

Simon's bedroom is outside over the garage. Not really his childhood bedroom, as it has been years since he moved away and what was once his room at the front of the house has been repurposed as a guest lounge/reading/TV room.

It was late—way too late—but I still didn't feel tired. I sat on my new bed. I gave it a few test bounces and decided it would be fine. Firm but not too firm. Plenty of pillows. A feather doona and a cotton quilt draped decoratively at the foot of the bed. Mum had been busy.

I contemplated the posters and the inspirational texts stuck to the walls. Time for them to go. The girl that drew inspiration from them was long gone. I told myself that it was well past the time when I should grow up and act like the adult I really was. I needed to move on and surround myself with more age-appropriate decoration.

My eye was caught by a framed photo on top of the bookcase. I stood up, gathered it in, and sat back on the bed in pensive contemplation of the image.

It was a photo of me and Charlie from that summer so long ago. With arms entwined, we were both laughing at the photographer. Whatever the joke was, it must have been hilarious judging by the expressions of delight on our faces. Or maybe it was our delight with each other and our lives that was on display. If I took myself back to that day when the photograph was taken, and if I had known that in a matter of weeks after that day our lives would all come undone, the joy so obvious in this image would have vanished forever.

But for a moment, holding that photo and gazing at the glowing faces of me and Charlie, I remembered how it felt to be young and so completely in love. Would that ever happen to me again?

With each toss and turn through what remained of that night, this thought kept on returning. Was Charlie my only chance at love?

Chapter Eleven

It probably helped my readjustment to life back in this small coastal town that the next few days were frantic, leaving me with no time to think. It had been a long time since I had visited home for more than a rushed weekend visit. I had been dreading returning, especially as I felt like I was coming home under a cloud, tainted by the recent scandal and by my eviction from the show. Both Mum and Simon assured me this wasn't the case. Apparently, I was still seen by the media as the innocent victim of *Gino the Groper*, as he was now being called. And the producer of *On the Rocks* had yet to publicly divulge that I had been *let go*.

Mum assured me that people would be pleased to see me. 'That is …' she added after a doubtful look at my shorn appearance, '… if they would even recognise you.'

The B&B was booked out over Christmas, so I spent the next two days helping Mum make beds, clean bathrooms and tidy the garden. Doesn't sound very exciting, I know, but after my time recently spent under *house arrest* in Balmain, I was so pleased to have the freedom to come and go that even scrubbing the guest bathrooms was a welcome relief.

We didn't have much planned for Christmas. A bit of a family celebration on Christmas Eve and maybe an outing to the beach or a visit to the relatives once the guests had been fed on Christmas morning.

Mum said she was expecting my sister to show up sometime on Christmas Eve. Yet, she sounded a bit hesitant when she said this. I needed to find out more. I so hate surprises.

'Okay, what's happened to Amy?'

'Frankie, I just don't know. She never tells me much at the best of times. But lately she's been even more secretive. I'm not sure if she is still seeing that boyfriend of hers. Not that he's any loss, but he was useful around here. Fixing things, you know. Still, I suppose that's no reason to keep him on ...' Mum's voice trailed off as she looked thoughtfully at the mop clutched in her hands, poised in mid swipe.

'You can rely on Simon to find out more. He's such a busy body. You don't need to do anything, Mum. Just let him loose on Amy and stand back!'

Amy, my big sister, has always been a mystery to me. Born eight years before me and two years before Simon, all through our childhood she was the one in charge. When I was little, Amy seemed to me to be as much an adult as my parents, and like my parents, she was adept at telling me what to do. In fact, I was secretly rather scared of her, as I suspect were many others. Typical firstborn sibling, Amy was the responsible one—the person who would always take control of a situation and direct others. You know, the sort of person who was a shoo-in to be captain of the netball team, captain of the debating team and, basically, captain of everything.

Never hanging around in the shadows like me, Amy had always been a leader—at home and at school. Of course, all that bossiness had to be channelled into a career as a schoolteacher—a teacher of primary school age students. And, like everything else she did in life, Amy excelled at being a teacher. Any child in her care blossomed and acquired skills that were beyond anyone's expectations.

For many years now, Amy and Shane had been an item. Shane Jervis, a local builder, had been hovering around our family since late high school. At some stage, the hovering became more intense. As far as I could tell and with no overt declaration, it gradually became clear to the rest of us that they had become a couple. As the years went by, we all assumed that Shane and Amy were together for life. Yet, still nothing specific in that regard had ever been said.

I suspect Mum and Dad had hoped Amy would move on, that she could do better and find someone who would look after her and not vice versa. It wasn't that Shane was unlikeable. It was just that he was, how do I describe him? He was just … average. Having our enthusiastic, high-energy parents as role models, it struck me as strange that my sister would settle for someone who was content to live a life that didn't change—same job, same house and the same girlfriend. Boring! It did my head in just to think about it.

So, by the time my sister appeared on Christmas Eve, I was bursting to know her news. Would it be the same as always or, as Mum suspected, had something changed?

Hearing her car pull up out the back near the garage, I rushed out to greet her, arriving just as Amy was opening the car door and forgetting that my sister had yet to see the new me. Her shocked face said it all.

'Oh my God, Frankie. Your hair! What happened? Is this a new look or is it … head lice? If it's head lice, I'm used to that. The kids get them at school—so much so that you wouldn't believe! But I know the best stuff to use. The stuff that really works. I can help you if you like.'

Yep, that's my sister. Not only can she talk for Australia, but she can jump to conclusions quicker than you can blink. Luckily, I am used to it and don't take offence. Mind you, there are many that do.

'Hey, big sis. Great to see you too. Don't panic. There are no head lice. Well, I don't think so.'

I ran a tentative hand across my now spiky hair. Was the itch I was now feeling from the salt water after my recent swim in the ocean or could she be right? Surely not!

Amy, her eyes wide with concern, drew closer as if to comfort a dying sister. I felt the need to reassure her.

'This is just my new look. That long hair just had to go, and I must say that after the initial shock, I'm starting to like it. So much less to look after and maybe in a week or so I might be able to style it with a bit of hair gel.'

I tried my best to sound more confident about my latest hairstyle than I was actually feeling. Amy stood back and considered me.

'But you look so different. Almost unrecognisable.' Her eyes narrowed and she continued, 'Or was that what you intended?'

I grimaced and shrugged. Not much more I could say about that. She had nailed it—as always.

Amy busied herself getting copious bags of presents out of the car and passing them to me with instructions to take care. Then, the two of us loaded with presents and suitcases, made our procession to the house—walking in a measured manner as if we were part of some Christmas pageant. You know, a sort of procession of *The Two Wise Women* – or maybe, given the bombshell Amy was about to drop, and given my recent behaviour, *The Two Not-So-Wise Women.*

Inside, all was cheer and lightness of spirit as if the rest of my family had already been infected by Christmas jollity. Amy's presents joined the pile under the overly decorated Christmas tree, and Amy and suitcases were directed to the downstairs spare room.

It wasn't until we were seated outside on the front porch with its filtered view of the sea down below, that conversation shifted to Shane, or more accurately the absence of Shane.

'Amy, dear …' Mum launched forth after having taken a fortifying slurp of her lethal gin and tonic prepared by Dad. 'Amy, dear,' she repeated. 'Just wondering if Shane is joining us later tonight or has he commitments with his family?'

Amy's expression darkened. In full glower, she replied, 'Don't you mention that man's name to me ever again. He's history!'

Mum was no longer looking concerned. Now she was openly curious. As were we all. With a caring hand placed gently on her daughter's arm, Mum continued, 'Has something happened, Amy dear? Is he okay?'

'Hah! How would I know? He could be dead for all I care!'

Amy's indignation was made clear by the way she spat out the words. Her reluctance to mention Shane's name was clearly forgotten as the growing anger overwhelmed her.

'The bastard! You wouldn't believe it, but he two timed me. And with my best friend. The bitch! After all these years and just as we were about to become engaged. Or I thought we were—if only he would have done as I wanted and ask the question! I'd given him lots of hints it was time and then he did this ...'

Flooding tears drowned out her anger and with noisy sobs, Amy collapsed into her mother's arms. Mum tried to pat Amy's back with one hand, while murmuring consoling words. All the while, Mum was endeavouring not to spill the drink still clutched in her other hand, as she signalled to Dad for help with raised eyebrows and a comical expression. Dad, who generally is not at ease with emotional excess, stared back at his wife, mouthed, *'What?'* then contented himself with another mouthful of beer.

It was Simon, as always, who saved the day.

'What is this about my two sisters and men? You should both be like me and swear off romance. Simpler that way. Get a dog or something. Or take up knitting! Now there's a thought. World peace through knitting. Maybe I should patent that or something.' He smiled complacently, satisfied with his own genius even if no one else was.

Amy snorted, dried her eyes with a rather grotty handkerchief, and reached for her soft drink. Now calmer, she continued, 'I told him that we were over and maybe it will be better that way. To end it before we got too committed. Trouble is ...,' she paused and looked around at her family who were hanging on her every word.

'Trouble is ... I'm pregnant.'

Amy took in the transfixed expressions on the faces of her mother, father and two siblings, and once again snorted.

'It happens, you know. Don't look so surprised. I'm not a virgin,' she said, pausing as if uncertain as to how to continue, before adding, 'The real trouble is ... well, how do I put it? You see ... Shane's not the father.'

The last few words were delivered in a rush. Then with mouth clamped shut, Amy turned her head away, as if signalling that no further words on the matter would be said by her.

Not surprisingly, given the unexpected nature of this news, Dad was still processing Amy's disclosure and ignored her discouraging signals.

'Come again? Run that past me one more time Amy love.'

'Dad! Don't you get it? I'm having a baby. You'll be a grandfather, but it isn't Shane who is the father. In fact, the father of my baby isn't in the picture and never will be.'

'Wow!' said Simon. 'No need to be bored in this family. Still, I like the idea of being an uncle. Count me in. I'll be there for you, sis.' He smiled encouragingly at Amy, who reflected the emotion back at him, albeit in a rather diluted and waterlogged way.

Mum, focusing on the baby news, Shane now forgotten, moved into mother hen mode and started clucking. Under Mum's warm regard and solicitous cross-examining, Amy eventually, and in a stumbling manner, told the full story.

It appeared that some weeks ago, Amy left school for home early, the planned after school activity having been cancelled. On her way home she dropped into Shane's house. His car was parked in the driveway, alongside a small red hatchback. Amy let herself in by the back door but couldn't find anyone around. She headed down the corridor towards the master bedroom when the unmistakeable sounds of lovemaking became all too audible.

'It was disgusting what she was saying. Calling him *Big Boy*. As if! And then I opened the door and caught them at it. I screamed. They screamed. You know, if only it hadn't been happening to me, I might have found it a bit funny. You should've seen their faces! Shane caught in mid-thrust. The panic and then the immediate droop! Hah!'

'Dear. Too much information,' said Mum, fanning herself.

'Yeah, right. So, the long and short of it is, I left, after scratching both their cars with my keys. I went to the wine bar. I was so angry I got absolutely smashed, picked someone up and well, one thing led to another and here I am—no man in my life and now preggers. The doctor tells me I'm six weeks gone, which exactly coincides with that fateful night.'

Amy paused for a breath and took a mouthful of her drink—a non-alcoholic drink I noticed, the reason for which was now obvious. At the time Dad poured it for her I had just thought she was pacing herself for the evening of celebrations ahead.

Silence descended. We all sat still in a frozen tableau, looking like we were struck dumb, staring blankly at my sister as if she was some total stranger, unrecognisable to us. For a moment, I wondered if some alien life form had moved in to colonise my sister's body. The sister I thought I knew—a calm, organised and responsible adult who would never have behaved in the manner described. Getting drunk, picking up someone at a bar and having unsafe sex. No, not the perfect firstborn. If anyone in this family was to behave in this manner, it would be me, the irresponsible baby of the family.

My face must have mirrored some of my thoughts as Amy, with a wry smile, continued, 'Yes, just so Frankie. Who would have thought this would happen to me? You and I are more alike than I thought. Both capable of stuffing up our lives without any conscious thought!'

'Steady on,' Dad interjected. 'You're both human. That's all. Amy dear, it sounds like you've had quite a bit of provocation to behave like you did. I know it's early days, but whatever you decide to do, we, your mum and I, are here for you,'

'Too right,' chimed in Simon. 'We're family, together through thick and thin, remember? But hang on. What do you mean, Dad? *Whatever you decide to do?*'

'Dumb arse!' explained Amy, once again in superior older sister mode. 'He's trying to find out if I'm going to have an abortion!'

Amy, taking her time, looked at us all in turn, her eyes solemn, yet still watery, with tears ready to fall at the slightest provocation.

'I think the answer to that is obvious. If I had decided to have an abortion, I wouldn't have told you about any of this. It would have been my secret. Something I would have to live with for the rest of my life. But, for whatever reason, and I don't think there is any logic associated with it, I have decided to keep this baby. After all, I am almost 29. Who knows if I'll ever get the chance to get pregnant again. The way my love life has gone down the toilet and living down here with a dearth of fellas, eligible or not, who am I going to meet? Once the baby is born, I'll get maternity leave and hopefully, Mum and Dad, you'll help me out?'

Amy looked across at her parents with a hopeful, yet slightly vulnerable expression on her face. Almost as if she was expecting them to reject her. This was an Amy I had never seen before.

Mum and Dad didn't disappoint. With loving promises of assistance, they overwhelmed their firstborn with hugs and kisses.

Meanwhile, Simon and I sat back and observed the entertainment. Whoever said Christmas at home with this family would be dull?

Simon whispered in my ear, 'You're off the hook, kiddo. I think Amy has outperformed you in the misbehaving kids stakes. You are positively dull and boring by comparison. Mind you, though ...,' he twinkled at me, '... if you were also to be pregnant, that might elevate your status somewhat!'

His mischievous smirk was sufficient justification for me to dig Simon in the ribs.

With a stifled laugh, Simon whispered, 'This family. We're certainly going to give the old biddies in our small town something to talk about!'

Chapter Twelve

After all the excitement associated with Amy's disclosure, the rest of Christmas Eve was something of an anti-climax. That's not to say it wasn't fun, but there was nothing else said that could top Amy's announcement.

Mum had pulled out all the stops and somehow had found time to create an amazing Christmas feast. Poached salmon for the fish eaters—Mum, Amy and me. Rare roast beef with hollandaise sauce for the red meat eaters—Dad and Simon. All served with masses of salad and crispy roast potatoes, followed by a boozy fruity ice-cream and fresh fruit salad (the latter deemed to be appropriate desert for the pregnant one). The ice-cream made a perfect Christmas pudding substitute.

Conversation flowed about everything and about nothing in particular, and a fair bit of silliness ensued. It was a bit surreal really, almost as if everyone was feeling relieved after the earlier drama associated with Amy's revelations.

While Mum was dishing out dessert, I leaned back in my chair and looked around the table at this—my family—with a feeling of utter contentment. Dad smiling lovingly at his wife as she gesticulated with the serving spoon, splattering small icy droplets in all directions. His brown eyes twinkling at his vivacious wife, who was in full flow mistelling some anecdote of local interest. Mum, as usual in pocket dynamo mode, now with both arms flying as she reached the dramatic conclusion of her tale. Simon leaning back in his chair, possibly to avoid the ice-cream splatters, arms crossed and chuckling with delight at Mum's performance, every now and then interjecting with a smart retort, which just prompted Mum to up the ante and make the story even more outrageous.

My sister, sitting calmly looking almost serene, like a survivor who had endured the storm and come out the other side, slightly battered but safe. She glanced across at me and we both smiled.

After dinner was done, Mum pushed all three of her children out the door saying Dad would be happy to help her clear up and that we should all go for a walk. Dad hmphed but not surprisingly backed her up and lent his support by flicking the tea towel at us to speed up our departure.

'Okay, Okay,' grumbled Simon. 'I get the message. I suppose you oldies need time to wrap up our Christmas presents. Come on siblings. We are all clearly unwanted by our parents. Let's go console ourselves elsewhere.'

The moon, just off full, lit our way along the gravel path that wound through the gum trees and scattered clumps of native grasses leading us to the beach. There the moonlight shone a path across the rolling waves.

'The path to fairyland. Remember? That's what granny used to say when we were little,' I said overcome with memories of that loving lady who encouraged us to believe in those magical creatures that inhabited the bush.

'Yeah, I remember,' said Simon. 'You were such a baby, believing everything our granny said, but it was us who were kept busy keeping you from finding that road. Always pulling you out of the water. I suppose you want to try now?'

'Why not?'

The sea was calm. The waves murmured softly as, being close to low tide, they lapped gently on the shore. The beach was deserted, yet brightly lit by the moon, almost as if it was daylight.

No time for hesitation, I pulled off my shift dress and in bra and knickers, I raced for the sea. The water splashed my ankles, then my knees and then my thighs—cool, yet not too cool.

'Wait for us,' I heard from behind me, but I was too focused on returning to my element—the water, the salty taste of the sea, the magical sensation of bathing in the moonlight. This was where I belonged. This was where I was meant to be. I swam into the deeper water and sprawled out onto my back, trusting the saltwater to support me. And it did. Lying back, with only my head out of the water and with arms outstretched, I contemplated the heavens above. A passing wave wobbled me, so I had to briefly flap my arms to rebalance. The waves moved under me and onwards to the shore in time with the eternal watery motion. There was no other sound in my ears but the swooshing of the sea water to its own rhythmic beat in time with the beating of my heart. Then ,the spell was broken as with splashes and hoots, Simon and Amy arrived by my side and proceeded to splash water in my face.

'How excellent is this?' chortled Simon. 'Just the thing to wash away dinner. Perfect. So long as we don't become dinner for anyone else.'

Amy looked around in alarm.

'You mean?'

'Yes, I do. But let's live it up and take a few risks. How good is this?'

Although we all agreed with Simon that being together in the water was perfect, somehow the enchantment had been broken and we surreptitiously, as if by unspoken agreement, found ourselves edging towards the shore. Not openly wanting to concede we suffered from a fear of sharks, but also being reluctant to challenge the others.

With clothes dragged over wet undies, we headed home, exchanged chorused good nights, and made our way to our separate bedrooms.

That night sleep came easily. As I lay in bed relaxing into the comfort of home, I was sung to sleep by the rush and sigh of the waves—my childhood lullaby.

Chapter Thirteen

The next morning—Christmas Day—Mum woke me with a cup of tea and Christmas kisses.

'Merry Christmas, my dear. Don't get up straight away. Your dad just had to pop out, so you probably have about half an hour before he will be back hassling us all.'

I rolled over and regarded my mother. Dad going out on Christmas Day. Now that's strange. Yet Mum, mistress of secrets, just smiled at me mysteriously, placed the cup of tea on my bedside table and left the room. As I listened to her shoes tap tapping a rhythm down the wooden stairs, I speculated.

There was nothing to it. I needed to get up and find out what was going on. I had never been one for secrets. I needed to know.

Ten minutes later, now freshly washed and dressed only in my bra and knickers, I stood considering my clothes, trying to determine what was the appropriate outfit for Christmas Day. With no long hair to fuss over, washing takes no time at all. And as for getting dressed, I didn't have much to choose from. All my trendy Sydney clothes had been left behind in Balmain. A limited choice made for a quick choice, and it didn't take me long to select some leggings and a floaty, embroidered muslin top.

Finishing my tea, I took my mug and headed for the stairs. Already I could hear voices out in the kitchen, so I headed in that direction. Dad's rumbling bass was punctuated by Mum's higher tone as their conversation proceeded in as smooth a rhythm as a duet—now and then punctuated by a giggle from Amy.

A giggle?

I entered the kitchen, and all heads turned my way to regard me—faces lit with anticipation. Even Simon was present—awake in a sleep rumpled way with hair standing out in all directions. But nevertheless, Simon appeared to be sufficiently alert for his expression to register expectation.

Finally, Dad said, 'Here she is ... at last. Merry Christmas, Frankie dear. I've got something for you. Well actually this is from all of us. Close your eyes and hold out your hands.'

'Mind you, no peeping!' warned Simon as he took me by the arm and led me out into the family room. With faltering steps, I allowed myself to be moved forward. Obeying my father's direction, I kept my eyes firmly shut. Not because I'm essentially obedient, but more because of my brother's hissed warnings ringing in my ears. I sensed that I was now standing in a shaft of early morning sunlight. The golden hue filtered through my not so firmly shut eyes as I was told to halt. I did not resist when Simon moved both my arms forward and positioned my hands together in a slightly open yet cupped manner. I felt something warm and somewhat damp being placed into my hands. Feeling its slight wriggle, I moved my hands to hold this 'thing' more firmly and bring it towards my chest.

'You can open your eyes now,' said Dad.

With open eyes I gazed in wonder at the wriggling mite barely contained in my cupped hands. A tiny pup regarded me with those milky grey eyes peculiar to the very young. I clutched him ... or was it *her* more tightly and pulled the pup closer to my chest. The puppy nuzzled me, then reached up and licked my chin with its raspy tongue. I squealed with delight.

'This is amazing. Is this puppy for me?'

'Yes. Merry Christmas from all of us,' said Dad, a grin as wide as the moon splitting his face. 'We thought it was time you had a dog of your own. Remember all those years you hassled us? So, when I heard from the Saddlers that they had some pups looking for a home, I thought it was time we got you one.'

'Mind you ...,' he added while considering the mite. '... Her mum might be a blue heeler—a cattle dog you know, but none of the Saddlers are too sure who the dad is. A bit of a lucky dip you might say. I suppose we will know more as she matures. She's only just weaned, and it was thought best that she come immediately to you, so she can really bond with you.'

By now I had settled onto the floor rug in front of the lounge and had nested the pup into my lap. Mum had passed me a soft towel and I used this to make a sort of bed for the pup in my lap.

'She's only just left her mum and her litter mates. You'll have to be everything to her now, especially for the next few days, if not weeks, as she could be a bit unsettled.'

I nodded, while taking in the wonder that was this new life. Tiny—obviously —and with that peculiar puppy smell. An aroma that was slightly milky, yet with an undertone of eau de puppy pee—distinctive but not too objectionable.

Already her coat had that distinctive blue/black flecking often seen on blue heeler dogs. A black patch over one eye and four black paws that made her look like she was wearing galoshes completed the look. No sign of any white hair except for a white tip at the end of her tail. Any evidence as to the identity of the father had yet to be revealed. With luck, the blue heeler might triumph and overwhelm all other genetic contributions.

I was overcome by the unexpected generosity of this gift. Dad was right. For years I had pleaded with my parents for a dog of my own. Our elderly family dog, no matter how loveable, did not cut it as far as I was concerned.

As the puppy squirmed in my lap and chewed on my finger, I struggled to put into words the emotions that were swirling around inside me. Despite my disjointed words, somehow my family understood.

'Just take good care of her, Frankie,' Dad said. 'I promised the Saddlers that she was coming to an excellent home. She needs to be with you day and night so she can bond with you and you alone.'

'Worse than a baby,' muttered Amy.

'Well just like a baby,' smiled Mum. 'For that is exactly what she is.'

Turning to me, Mum continued: 'We thought that after your recent experiences you could do with a bit of cheering up and some fun. Someone to love we thought might be just what you need.'

'Yeah, that and tidying up all its mess. Lucky you,' laughed Simon. 'Now where's breakfast? I' m starving. Didn't you promise ham and eggs Mum? Enough of this clucking over a baby when there are hungry people around. Although I suppose it is just the start. By this time next year our home will be a veritable crèche, eh Amy?' He said digging Amy in the ribs.

Fortunately, Amy was in a good mood and responded to his teasing with a smile and a laughing, 'Just you wait. I know you'll be the world's most devoted uncle.'

Christmas day had started with the family in good humour, and I hoped it would continue that way. As with many families, our Christmas celebrations could be a bit unpredictable. Sometimes the stresses invoked by demanding guests staying in the B&B or the need to spend time with distant relatives could tip emotions over the edge. But this year the day went better than I could have expected.

Because Mum and Dad were both born in this district, we had countless uncles, aunts and cousins who we were assured were looking forward to seeing us. And for some reason, most Christmases we were expected to go to them. To be honest though, this was sometimes a relief as it meant we could call time on our interaction and run home declaring commitments to our resident guests' demands.

This year it was clear both Amy and I were apprehensive about facing any scrutiny by relatives. The aunts were the worst. I convinced Mum that we should take two cars so I could leave early and bring the puppy home for a rest. Being mindful of Dad's directive not to leave the puppy alone, I was taking the puppy with me. She was now fed and soundly asleep, snuggled into the towel I had placed in a cardboard box.

'Excellent idea,' said Simon, also not keen on too much

interaction with the aunts who, each time he visited seemed desperate to know about his love life. They would grill him mercilessly about this and any Sydney gossip they expected him to know. When the mood took him, Simon would play up to them and delight/scandalise the aunts and cousins in turn with salacious tit bits about Sydney celebrities.

***

We set off in a two-car convoy—Simon, Amy and I bringing up the rear in the second car. We followed Dad's battered utility out of town and down the highway to the outskirts of the village of Berry. Dad's brother and family have lived there for years on a small rural acreage. Numerous cars of various ages and states of disrepair parked at random in the paddock adjoining the house indicated that the party was already in full swing. I grabbed the puppy and cloth, then clutching her to me, apprehensively headed in. Flanked by Amy and Simon, we trooped through the gate, up the path and around the back to our doom.

Thank heavens for that puppy! All that afternoon she was the focus of everyone's attention, the topic of conversation and the subject of many a question.

'A Saddler puppy, you say?' asked one of my uncles—Uncle Mike, I think it was. Sometimes it is hard to tell who is who when they are grouped together at family get togethers. They all look so much the same—tall, weathered, thin of hair, and smelling of cigarette smoke.

'Well, she'll grow up to be a good sort. The Saddler dogs have always been decent workers. Excellent choice, Vince,' he continued, nodding at my dad, who calmly accepted this praise as his due.

The puppy, as if knowing she was the star, behaved perfectly in a sleepy, licky sort of way and permitted herself to be passed around, cuddled and generally fussed over. With her existence attracting all the attention, questions to me concerning my time in Sydney or about my plans for the future were largely kept to a minimum. They were also generally satisfied with minimal response. In fact, I felt vaguely miffed that my life was of so little interest to my extended family. The one comment that was made over and over again was how glad I must be to have left that frenetic Sydney life behind and to be back with my family. No response seemed to be considered necessary, as it was beyond contemplation by my relatives that I could disagree with any opinion expressed by them. A smile and a nod in agreement from me seemed to be all that was expected.

Some of my younger cousins were keen to know all the background gossip from my time on set of the soapie. What they were really after was the dirt on the cast and particularly the intimate details about Luke. No, not that intimate! Their questions were largely about what he was like to work with. Was he really as nice as he seemed on TV? Of course he was! There was also more grilling about my character. Was I planning to return next season? A good question that! Most unlikely, I could have said given the termination of my contract, but as that news was still not public, it was impossible to say. So, I contented myself with saying nothing. I just looked mysterious and smiled sweetly.

Soon enough, a squirming puppy indicated it was time to get her home. I signalled to Amy and Simon that we needed to depart. Making our excuses and kissing every relative over and over, we made our escape and, waving out of the car window, we headed for home.

'Thank goodness that's now over,' said Amy. 'I felt like I was in court and being grilled by some expert barrister! Our aunts are dynamite. They seem to have an instinct and can sniff out a secret at a hundred paces. I kept being asked where Shane was and had to make up some sort of vague answer. Thank goodness they're yet to find out about the baby.'

She laughed dramatically and continued, 'Oh My God! Once the secret's out, it will be a major scandal. I'll have to go into hiding until it blows over.'

'Yeah, for a week or so,' Simon said and then added: 'You're not the first one here to have a baby or to be a single mum. In fact, a fair few of our cousins already are —must be a small town thing. Watch out, Frankie, it'll be your turn next!'

'Never.' I gave a shudder. 'I've given up on men!'

'Well, so did I,' sighed Amy. 'And look where that got me!'

At that we all laughed. I told Amy I intended to be the best aunt in the world and pup here would have to make do as her sprog's cousin.

'You can't keep calling her *pup*,' said Simon as he casually drove the car along the highway, one hand resting on the steering wheel, the other making quotation marks in the air as he spoke.

'I don't know,' I replied, glancing down at the puppy in my arms who, relaxed by the rhythm of the car, had once more settled into a restful doze, small head resting on outstretched front paws.

'Calling her Patch because of her black eyepatch seems a bit obvious. Likewise, with Bandit. That's rather cute—but no—it doesn't appeal. I'm not very good with names. Who knows, she might end up being called pup until she's an old lady.'

'Well, as the PR expert and for a fee, I could come up with a list of suggestions.'

'No. I have a better idea,' piped up Amy. 'Let's get the wine out when we reach home—well, wine for you two and I suppose mineral water for me, and we'll brainstorm a suitable name.'

'Sweet! You're on!'

It had been a long time since we three siblings had spent such quality time together. In fact, not since we had been little. Once Amy had met Shane all those years ago, her focus had been away from her own family. On the rare occasions that I saw her at our home, she was usually accompanied by Shane, who had a habit of monopolising the conversation—talking about himself of course! Amy's life had been largely focussed on her career and activities with Shane—neither of which were of any interest to me!

But this afternoon, once we returned home, fed the pup, and settled ourselves on the lawn under a shady tree, we bonded like it had only been weeks since we were young. A time when we had been a team allied against the perceived injustices inflicted on us by our parents. Old anecdotes were resurrected, discussed and dismissed with much laughter. Being a fair bit younger than my brother and sister, some of these recollections were new to me. While I had been busy being the cute and adored youngest child, I now heard about how Amy and Simon had got up to all sorts of mischief: putting coolant in the mower instead of petrol, clipping Mum's Persian cat with nail scissors—not a good look. They said the poor cat was so traumatised that he hid for weeks. When they were teens and I was still too young to join in, there was a period where they worked their way through the parents' cocktail cabinet, attempting to hide their tracks by topping up the bottles with water. Discovery was inevitable.

'Wow! I never knew you did that. You two were dynamite!'

'Yeah, what a team,' grinned Simon. 'Remember Dad's face when he found us out, Amy? I think we had visitors at the time. It all came undone when he poured himself and a guest a shot of whisky. The guest was being awfully polite when he made some comment about the whisky having a distinctive taste. Dad took a sip, spat it out and knew immediately what we had done. We'd filled up the bottle with black tea. It'd seemed like a good idea at the time. Maybe Dad had also done the same thing when he was young. Now there's a thought! Oh, how he roared at us! We knew we had been found out and scarpered. Didn't come home for hours. By then he had calmed down and could see the funny side. But we weren't trusted again. The grog was locked away. You know, it's funny. I didn't even like the taste of whisky then. Just thought we were being cool, I guess.'

'I still don't like the taste—especially whisky. Even when I can drink alcohol, I don't really want to,' said Amy.

Silence descended as all three of us contemplated the puppy who was now stirring and squirming in my lap. The puppy nuzzled my fingers and then commenced thoughtfully chewing my fingers with her needle-sharp teeth.

'Ow! That hurt. Stop that, you little nipper!'

'Nippa. Now that's a good name for a dog,' suggested Amy. 'And it looks like it could be an accurate description of this mite.'

I looked down at the little squirt who was still trying to chew on my fast-retreating fingers.

'Yeah. Maybe. It sounds kinda tough too. No one would mess with a dog called Nippa.'

I paused and gave the suggested name some thought. In the absence of any enticing alternative, I decided it would do.

'Done! Nippa it is.'

'Nippa is a bit cutesy,' objected Simon. 'Not scary at all. You need a name like Fang, Ripper or Jaws. Now they're really tough names. Sure to keep the intruders away if you have a dog called that!'

'Maybe if I had a different sort of lifestyle that might be necessary. You know, a stash that needed guarding. But no. No need for a scary name. I like Nippa and so that is what she will be called. Here Nippa!'

I tried out the name for size and effect. The puppy, who had by now squirmed off my lap, was busy inspecting a twig lying on the lawn. At the sound of my voice, she looked up and considered me, head cocked to one side. Whatever her limited brain had been contemplating in response to my call, it was not to return to the summons from her human. Clearly, she had decided that the siren call of the backyard was more important. With a shake that almost toppled her and on wobbling legs, Nippa moved away to pounce on a leaf blowing across the lawn.

'Clearly she knows who's boss—and it's not you!' laughed Simon. 'A bit of work to do there, hey sis?'

I laughed and lay back on the grass. Before I knew it, a small body had clambered onto my chest and had commenced an exploratory chew of my chin.

'Yep. Nippa it is. Definitely the best name for you, young lady!'

Chapter Fourteen

A fleeting visit from Ruth on Boxing Day meant that the Christmas celebrations were extended for a little while longer. This was Ruth's first visit to our home. Initially, she was rather polite and almost apprehensive. She kept calling Mum and Dad *Mr* and *Mrs McAdam* until, on the second day of her stay, Mum sat Ruth down and with a few stern words set her straight.

'Lovely though it is having you stay with us Ruth, dear. If you keep insisting on being so polite then I will have to start charging you like one of the guests. It's first names or nothing. Understand?'

It's not often I see Mum looking so scary but somehow it seemed to work. That or it was our muffled giggles that convinced Ruth to behave.

Our New Year celebrations were constrained by the need to be up early and not hung over the next day. One of the joys of being part of a B&B enterprise means that sleeping in is a mere fantasy. There is always a breakfast to be cooked, dishes to be washed or rooms to be cleaned. True to our agreement, Simon and I actually convinced Mum and Dad to have a sleep in one morning and we managed to produce a reasonable breakfast for the guests. Simon was the affable host and I stayed resolutely out of sight in the kitchen. Even with my shaved head, there was no way I was going to risk discovery.

As it was, there were a couple of close calls when one guest from Sydney surprised me when I was cleaning her room. She displayed an unusual interest in me and my background. After an initial moment of panic, I drew on my acting skills and channelled my artless country girl dialogue—and I think it worked. In any event, she quickly left me alone. Either I convinced her, or I scared her off. She left not long after that.

Simon stayed another week with us until after New Year had come and gone. On 2 January, he packed his car and headed off to Sydney—without me. I knew I couldn't return to Sydney for now, but I was reluctant to let him go. You see, through all the recent upheaval, Simon had been my main support and confidant. I didn't know how I could maintain sufficient equilibrium without his reassuring presence.

That day, as he packed the car to leave, I followed in his footsteps, just like the puppy who was following me and nipping at my heels. We made a strange sight, our funny mismatched procession.

At first Simon tolerated my behaviour, perhaps hoping I would lose interest and desist. But I didn't and finally he could take no more.

'Enough, Frankie!' he said, grasping me by the arms. 'It's not that I don't love you, but really this is too much. Trust me, it isn't the end of the world. You know I have to go back to work, and you'll be fine here. Can't you see that Mum and Dad need your help? And it'll give you time to work out whatever it is you really want to do with your life.'

He moved to pull me into a close cuddle and his voice gentled.

'I'll always be there for you, baby sister. You know that. But it's time for you and your buddy here to stand on your own six feet,' he said while looking down and pushing a jumping Nippa back onto all four paws.

'You need to work out what's best for you. Give it time, but I'm sure you'll sort that out. I have complete faith in you.'

He was right, of course. I wasn't a child anymore. Now over twenty, I should be capable of setting my own direction in life and without needing my brother to ride shotgun. Yet, when I contemplated my future, all I could see ahead was uncertainty, doubt and no clear path to follow. In the past I had let others make all the decisions for me. First, my parents with their loving guidance when I was a child. Then Charlie, full of plans for our future together. In Sydney, there was Simon creating a new and exciting life for me—with a little help from Tom, of course. All the while I had submitted to the directions of others, drifting along like one of those bluebottles at the mercy of the sea currents. I could tell myself that what I was doing was taking advantage of those opportunities that presented themselves to me. But that would not be the truth. The reality was that I was too apathetic. Making an independent decision seemed to be beyond me. To be honest, the thought of taking the initiative and choosing what I wanted to do with my life was frankly quite terrifying. But if other people could do it, why couldn't I?

Unable to articulate these thoughts, I mutely stared back at Simon, the terror I felt inside clearly reflected on my face.

Simon's voice softened and with affection clear in his voice, he continued: 'It will be fine—in time. You'll surprise yourself. Just look what you've achieved in the last two years. Believe in yourself, kid sister. I do.'

And with another hug and a cheery goodbye to our parents, who were standing anxiously behind me, Simon scrambled into his car, started the engine, and headed away, out of my life—for now.

I took Simon's guidance to heart and settled into a daily routine of helping Mum and Dad with the business—doing whatever they needed me to do.

Awake at first light, Nippa and I would start the day with a quick run along the deserted beach. Once we reached the other end of the beach, I would charge into the waves and dive under while Nippa pranced at the water's edge, barking furiously. Even at this young age, she knew better than I that the sea was a dangerous monster and in her own way she urged me to return to solid land. When I finally emerged from the churning water, Nippa greeted me as if she had personally secured my rescue from extreme danger. No matter how I tried to encourage her to experience the surf, nothing would convince Nippa that it was safe. However, she found endless entertainment in running along the beach snapping at the smaller waves as they lapped the shore, but there was no way she would venture into the water above paw depth.

With our swim over and feeling refreshed, we would both make our leisurely return along the beach. Each of us in our own individual way would examine the debris that had been washed ashore overnight. I would pick at the fragments of shell, driftwood and seaweed in the hope of locating a hitherto undiscovered item of treasure, and Nippa would roll in certain questionable discoveries— usually the rotting remains of dead birds or the odd fish carcass.

Back home, washed (both of us) and ready for the day, I would report to Mum for my day's work orders. This usually involved cleaning out the guest rooms once the guests had checked out and preparing them for the next arrivals. January and February were our peak times for holiday bookings. Even for those guests staying for longer periods, I was still expected to make the beds each day, replace the towels, and refresh the contents of the fridges, etc. I knew the routine. After all, I had been helping Mum with these tasks since I had been in my early teens. I did my best to be as unobtrusive as possible for I didn't want to be seen or recognised by anyone. As a result, Nippa and I became adept at keeping to the shadows, spotting when the guests had left or gone out for the day, then rushing to their rooms like a small ambush squad. I pushed the trolley loaded with cleaning gear and the clean linen, while a small, determined puppy followed me, keeping busy by nipping at the trolley wheels.

A small puppy, but not as small as she once was—growing a little each day —in size and energy. Maybe there had been some benefit in Nippa coming to live with us when she was such a baby because from that very first day, Nippa had decided I was her mother/pack leader and family rolled into one. Whoever I was in her eyes, she didn't let me out of her sight and was constantly at my heels or sitting by the trolley where I left it outside the door of whichever guest apartment I was cleaning. She didn't like the vacuum cleaner and made her dislike known by a spate of vigorous howling, which started as soon as I turned on the infernal machine and only ended when I switched it off.

At Dad's suggestion, I had enrolled Nippa at the local puppy school which, depending upon her mood, could be an astounding success or a total failure. On a good day we raced through the tasks set by our instructor and Nippa accepted the treats from my hand as her due. On a bad day, well it was an embarrassing disaster. On those days it was soon clear that Nippa had no intention of co-operating. She would either feign deafness or would just sit on her behind stubbornly refusing to listen to any command—except for the command to leave.

'Too smart for her own good, that one,' said the instructor. 'She needs to learn that you are boss and somehow you must convince her that she really needs your approval. Good luck!'

She laughed at me, and I could see that the instructor was already convinced that Nippa had the upper hand.

But I am stubborn, so I persevered. Each afternoon as soon as our chores were completed, we practised. Like Skeeter, my doggy friend and constant companion on the soapie, Nippa was receptive to bribery with doggy treats. After a few weeks, I started to believe we were making progress. She would now walk, sort of quietly, by my side, sit when asked and stay for a short time, so long as there were no tempting distractions enticing her away.

Mum and Dad were besotted with Nippa, something I totally understood.

'Our first fur grandbaby,' they would coo and vied with each other to mind Nippa when the surf was up and calling me and my board.

Although I was settled—sort of—and busy—kind of—in this new life, I knew deep down that it wasn't enough. In quiet moments, my thoughts would wander, and I would find myself speculating as to what might be happening in Sydney.

Fortunately, I didn't have to wonder for too long. Simon checked in with me regularly and kept me updated with the goings on at his office—the hiring of a new staff member and assurances me that he and Ruth missed me in their little cottage. They missed someone to tidy the house most likely, as I was the only neat person that had lived there. From time to time, I would receive a short email from Tom with encouragement to keep on living a quiet life out of the spotlight and hinting that he was still looking out for opportunities for me. That bit I didn't believe, as I was convinced my acting days were long behind me.

Every now and then Amy would stop by, full of the latest gossip and her baby news. Not that I needed to hear blow by blow descriptions of her nausea and aches and pains, but I was interested in seeing the photo from the recent ultrasound—a blurry image of a shape that was said to be my niece. Now that was exciting! Whatever they measure while doing the ultrasound had confirmed that Amy was on track for a late August delivery. Being tall and gangly like Dad, there was still very little indication that she was pregnant for those not in the know—apart from some expansion in her chest area, of which Amy was rather proud.

I hadn't expected to hear from Luke so when he rang one evening, I was surprised to find myself feeling rather emotional. His friendship had meant so much to me. I was relieved to find he still wanted to keep in contact, unlike the rest of the cast, who had dropped me quicker than you could say *scandal.*

Luke brought me up to date with the latest on the set—who was being the diva this week, who was on the up and up in the director's esteem, and who was doing the most drugs.

Luke confided in me that he thought he would see out his contract and then move on. He told me that he had already spoken to Tom about this. For the moment he had agreed with Tom's recommendation that he keep quiet about his future plans as he didn't want to give the director or producer the opportunity to prematurely end his role. But he thought another twelve months would see him gone—unless I returned that is. Luke said he really missed his partner in crime. He said his role had become positively boring—he had been reunited with his long suffering first love. My role was not quite written out at this stage. I was said to be travelling overseas *finding myself*, leaving the opportunity open for my return should the powers that be deem it appropriate for the ratings.

Yes, on occasion I still missed all that excitement—even the 4.00 am starts. But with each passing day, that part of my life seemed more and more unreal. Like it had happened to someone else and not to me.

Chapter Fifteen

L ife continued in this manner for the next few weeks—not too exciting and not too awful. Each day was enjoyable in its own way but edging towards tedium. I mean, who can say they really enjoy constant cleaning and bed making? These chores were only alleviated by my daily surf (or two) and the joy brought about by sharing my life with an enthusiastic, affectionate and destructive puppy. I never knew what she would trash next with those needle-sharp teeth. Or as my sister would often say in a gleeful voice—it was excellent training for when my niece arrived on the scene.

For the most part, I was successful in keeping thoughts of my final weeks in Sydney at bay. During the day when I was busy being a house maid or running after an exuberant puppy, my thoughts were on the here and now—had we run out of clean towels or where had Nippa hidden my sandals this time? It was only in the wee small hours that I remembered that night, when I woke from my sleep in a sweaty, thrashing, choking terror from dreams in which I was once more sinking into the harbour depths. Those dreams were haunted by images of Gino being propelled into the icy water, his eyes bulging with terror, my arms reaching out to save him but failing as I sunk deeper and deeper.

Nippa, sensing my distress, would also become agitated and attempt to scrabble up to me from her bedside basket. With her funny stumpy legs, she would keep falling back and become more frantic. Finally, I would give in and reach for her. Then, snuggled together, I would take comfort in the reality of her warm, solid body sprawled on my chest and allow her rasping tongue to lick my chin and chase the demons away.

In the glare of the daylight, it was so easy to rationally convince myself that nothing of what had happened that fatal night on the harbour was my fault. Yet, in those bleak early morning hours, the guilt and the overwhelming horror of my experiences that night always came flooding back. Once again, in my nightmares I felt like I was sinking and drowning in my terror. I did not know how to make the feeling go away.

It was this dilemma I was pondering one afternoon while Nippa and I were walking along the beach. Although it was a late, warm summer afternoon, we by and large had the beach to ourselves. The groups of family holiday makers had mostly departed, lured away by the prospect of refreshing showers or hot and salty fish and chips. A few stragglers remained, still in the throes of packing up. Nippa, on her lead, was trotting happily beside me. Every now and then she would look up at me expectantly as if she thought it was high time she should be released from her constraint. But I knew how, once freed, she would immediately race to every nearby small child to share her joy, but more likely invoke terror. So, I resolutely ignored those beseeching looks. Anyway, I was still preoccupied with considering last night's dream in all its technicolour glory and wondering whether I was becoming seriously deranged and needed help, when I heard a voice call out from behind me.

'Freckle? Is that you?'

Freckle? On hearing those words my heart raced. Now that's a nickname of mine that I hadn't heard for years. In fact, it was once my special nickname that was mainly used by Charlie. After he died, the use of this nickname fell into disuse. It was all too painful to me, and I had reverted to encouraging use of my childhood nickname Frankie as my nickname of choice. No painful memories associated with that name.

But there was no longer any living Charlie to call me by that name. Who could it be?

I turned around and considered the person striding towards me. Tall, muscled, face shaded by a broad brimmed hat, he looked familiar, but somehow not.

This person came close and then stopped, while peering intently into my face. Nippa, sensing a new friend, began cavorting in circles, then added a few jumps by way of variety.

'I wasn't sure if it was you. You look ... so ... so different. But then I saw this pup and recognised her immediately. Of course, she has to be one of ours. Looks like her mum. Well almost—except for those legs. Kind of stumpy, aren't they? As you probably heard, the father is rather a mystery, but I have my suspicions. The legs are a bit of a giveaway.'

All the while this stranger was speaking, I just continued to stand and stare at him. He seemed to assume I would know who he was. His words gave me a clue but if only my addled brain could sort it out. And then, it dawned on me. He must be a Saddler—one of the family that gave us this pup. That's it! He must be Charlie's brother. If only I knew his name.

Comprehension washed over his face.

'It's been ages, I know. But now that I can see you close up, there's no mistaking it IS you, Freckle. Although, for a moment, the hair, or lack of it, threw me for a moment. I like it by the way. But then I saw this fella. Hey, down little one,' he said as Nippa enthusiastically leapt up to greet him, more than making up for my appalling manners.

He crouched down and gave my dog his full attention. For a few minutes, they engaged in a mutual admiration exercise while I wracked my brain for the name of this rather gorgeous man.

'My, you've grown little dog. What a clever puppy and on a lead too!'

He looked up at me, blue-green eyes so like those of his brother, twinkling at me. No fool this one. He knew.

'Remember me yet? No offence. I quite understand. After all, I was rather a shadowy figure all those years ago. Forever being tasked by the parents to chase after Charlie.'

He stood up to his full height—well over six foot I would guess, brushed the sand off his hands and held one hand out to me. I took it, aware of the calloused strength in his grip. Still, I said nothing.

'Archie. Archie Saddler. Charlie's brother. I never thought I'd see you here again.'

I continued to hold his hand, strangely reluctant to let it go, and feeling hesitant, not sure what to say to this barely known brother of my first love. My past contact with him had been limited to less than a handful of occasions, usually when Archie was collecting his brother from the beach after we had spent all day together. On these occasions, our contact would be minimal, no exchange of polite conversation, merely a casual wave and from him a muttered *hurry* up to Charlie.

We spoke at the funeral. That I remember. The memory of his kind words murmured to me in passing after the service now came rushing back. How he sought to comfort me with assurances of Charlie's love and affection. Not something he needed to say to me in the midst of all the sorrow and grief overwhelming his own family. Yet, he chose to take time to speak to someone he barely knew. It spoke to me of a person with compassion for others—who cared. Just like now as he continued to gaze intently at me with questioning eyes, while still grasping my hand.

'How are you? It's great to see you back here again. When your dad said he wanted a pup as a present for you, I kinda hoped that meant you might be hanging around. What are you planning on doing?'

In response I said how I was back living with my parents and helping Mum with the guesthouse. My spare time, when I got any, was occupied in trying to train my overactive puppy. Even as I outlined the boring details of my current daily activities, I realised how dull my life now sounded but for some reason Archie considered my response with enthusiasm.

'Good on you. I'm sure your mum appreciates your help now its peak holiday time. And if this pup is anything like her mum, she will be way too smart for her own good.'

Was he always so enthusiastic?

'Hey, if at any time you are bored, bring the pup up to the farm so she can play with her siblings. Any time is fine. We kept two out of her litter. That way she might be able to burn off some of that energy. And we still have her mum, not that she'll remember her pup. Remarkable how they forget. You'll find me up at the dairy every afternoon after 2.00. Milking usually starts about 3.30. Just pop up anytime.'

He contemplated the puppy, who by now was mouthing at his hand. Archie once again crouched down to puppy height.

'What's her name?'

'Nippa.'

A delighted grin indicated an appreciation of my choice of name as he then pulled his hand away from the marauding beast.

'I see why you picked that name. Excellent choice. Shall we let her off?'

I looked up and down the beach. By now all the others had left for the day, probably encouraged to rush away because of the gathering darkening clouds and the distant grumble of thunder.

'Why not!'

Released from her restraint, Nippa scampered off in the direction of home, now and then diverting to chase a squawking seagull. As if of one accord, Archie and I set off in full chase. Nippa turned, saw us, and then raced back towards us, barking with pleasure that the two humans had finally seen sense and joined in her game. By the time she returned to us, I was breathless and collapsed on the sand to be monstered by a sandy yet still boisterous hairy bundle. No, I don't mean Archie! He, also breathless, collapsed on the sand next to me.

'Not as fit as I thought. Not much exercise involved in herding my cows. Hey, give over fella,' he said to a still jumping Nippa.

He pushed the pup away and then turned to face me. 'Freckle. I mean it. Do come up to the farm some time. I know Charlie never brought you up there. And maybe he had his reasons for not doing so, whatever they were. But I'm sure Mum and Dad would appreciate finally meeting you and getting to know you—and seeing the pup again, of course.' His last few words were directed at the pup who kept trying to squirm onto Archie's lap.

Ewww. Not quite sure whether I really want to do that but, feeling reluctant to offend this friendly giant of a man, I dredged up a smile and promised to let him know.

After the usual ritual of exchanging contact details by updating our phones, we once again got to our feet. I clipped Nippa onto her lead and we all headed further along the beach towards the rocky headland at the far end. From there I was able to access the path through the trees to home and where a carpark is located.

The thunder, now much closer, continued to growl. Raindrops fell and splattered on us with increasing intensity. When we reached the path to the carpark, I paused, said my goodbyes, then puppy and I sprinted for home through the deluge.

A short while later a towelled dry Nippa and I relaxed on the enclosed verandah and listened to the rain hammering on the roof. I just hoped Archie got to his car in time. I consoled myself with the thought that as a farmer he should be used to all sorts of inclement weather. While Mum made us both a cup of tea, I shared with her the details of that afternoon's adventure and my chance meeting with Archie.

'Not so chance, Frankie dear. He came here looking for you. Had heard you were back in town and said he wanted to say hello. I sent him down to the beach as I assumed you would be there. It's your happy place after all! Everyone knows that!'

'Can't see why he would want to see me. I barely knew him. He's a fair bit older than me I think and when I was out and about with Charlie, I only ever saw him in passing. Mind you, he is so like Charlie to look at. Well, taller I guess, but with the same colour eyes. And the way he looked at me, it took me right back. Although, I couldn't remember his name for a while. But I really don't remember much about him.'

'He's more like Amy's age—maybe a year behind her at school. A good lad though, but he has had a hard time of it. Always the responsible one, you know—helping with the farm and then keeping it all together when Charlie died, and his parents fell to pieces. Without Archie running the show, I'm sure the farm business would have gone under. Sometimes when I see him in town, he looks like he is carrying the cares of the world on his shoulders. I feel like I want to give him a hug and tell him it will all be fine. Not sure it will be though. His father is a piece of work. Issues and all. But that's not for me to say.'

'He asked me to visit. Said I should bring Nippa to play with her siblings and see her mother again. Said his folks would like to see me.'

'Maybe they would. They still hold Charlie's memory sacred. And that must be hard for Archie. Yet he never complains. Yes, I think you should go. For Archie's sake. Just don't get too fussed if the parents aren't very welcoming.'

I stared thoughtfully back at my mother. Her suggestion did make sense. It would be the considerate thing to do. But could I be bothered?

Chapter Sixteen

Apart from two reminders in the following days, Mum said nothing further about my visiting the Saddler farm. However, I knew Mum much better than to assume she had let the matter slip. I knew she was just biding her time and giving me the opportunity to respond appropriately—or in a manner she deemed appropriate.

Archie's invitation lingered in the atmosphere between us like an unwelcome smell. It wasn't that I was reluctant or that my diary was overbooked. In fact, I couldn't explain why I did nothing. Most of my afternoons were free for activities other than helping Mum.

From time to time, I would notice Mum looking thoughtfully at me. I knew what she was thinking. After all, I was thinking the same thoughts myself. Was now the time to head up to the Saddler farm? Yet, for no reason I could identify, I continued to hang back. Maybe one day I told myself, but not now. As if a party to my unspoken dialogue, one day my mother asked out of the blue:

'If not now. When?'

Dad, who had been seated nearby reading the newspaper, looked up when he heard Mum speak.

'Yes, dear? You said something.'

'No, not you! I was talking to Frankie. She knows exactly what I mean.'

'Yeah, Mum. I know. Soon. Promise.'

'Good then. Nippa would enjoy the outing.'

'What?'

Dad, still confused, sought clarification.

'Nothing!' Both Mum and I chorused.

Two days later, I found myself in Mum's small car heading out of town. The puppy, secured in the back seat, sniffed appreciatively out of the half open window at the farm aromas wafting by. Once out of the town, we turned off the highway onto a road appropriately named by our early settlers, *Back Valley Way*. We then headed inland along a much narrower road that tracked alongside a meandering rivulet. After about three kilometres, we turned right onto a narrow lane signposted *Saddler's Lane*. Although I had never been out this way that I could recall in all my years growing up here, I had always had a vague understanding of where the Saddler farm was located. Local knowledge, I guess. The lane didn't run for very far before it petered out in front of a gate flanked by two enormous monkey puzzle trees of venerable age and immense girth. This must be it.

The gate, shut but not locked, had the wonky look of something that had been in use for many years and was still fit for purpose—but only just. I got out, opened the gate, and drove through. Then, like the country girl I had been raised to be, I got out again and shut the gate. I momentarily wished for a passenger other than this puppy that could actually help with the gates, rather than drool out the window.

The dirt track curved through a paddock and then up a gentle rise. At the top stood a weatherboard farmhouse looking like it had always been there. It was painted white, was topped by a rusty red roof, and had a tall paling fence and sheltering greenery on the western side. But I wasn't heading for the house. It was 3.30 in the afternoon, and I knew where I would find Archie. So, driving with care to avoid the numerous potholes, I followed the track that veered off past the house to the sheds behind. There I could see the black and white cattle grouped patiently in the dairy yard waiting for their turn to be milked.

The dairy, like so many in the district, was not a thing of beauty. A functional shed built of corrugated iron and open to one side. By that opening I could see the cows standing at ease, almost as if they knew whose turn it would be next. Not wanting to disturb them, I stopped the car some way away and, leaving a disgruntled Nippa in the car, I headed for the shed. The chugging sound of machinery operating indicated that milking was in full swing. From inside, a radio played a background hum of music, and I could hear voices as they ordered the animals along. I stopped by a side gate and watched with wonder.

The vision before me was a revelation. In all my years in this little coastal town, I had never before been up close to a dairy shed at milking time. Sure, I had driven past such activities but, isolated in the sealed unit that is a motor vehicle, I had not appreciated the noise and the smell that was associated with running a dairy.

The noise ... well that was not too bad. Not as bad as I would expect at a city building site for instance. But the smell! The odour of cow manure was all pervasive! So many cows crowded together and all busy creating their own grassy brown discharges. I suppose a farmer gets used to it, but for a moment I fought against the gag reflex.

In the shed I could see two figures dressed in grubby khaki overalls. Presumably, the five cows that were in the shed had just finished and were being released by one person. Another washed the milking bay floors with a hose, before pulling a lever to fill up the feed bins and herd in the next lot. There appeared to be no need to encourage the cows to come inside as they seemed to know the routine and understood that dinner would be waiting for them. In they went to their allotted places and focussed on whatever was before them. Soon, busily snuffling at whatever delicious treat was in each bin, the cows then totally ignored the activity taking place at udder level. After being washed with some sort of squirter contraption, their udders were given a test squeeze. Then, the teat cups that form part of the milking machine suctioned on and, as if by magic, I could see the white stuff that was milk swirling through the tubing and heading who knows where. I leaned forward over the gate and watched with wonder. It all looked so easy.

One of the men glanced up and spotted me. He smiled and waved. It was Archie.

'Be with you soon,' he mouthed.

It didn't seem long, probably another ten minutes, before Archie came over. Wiping his hands on a cloth that was dangling out of his overall pocket, he smiled a greeting.

'Great to see you. We've just about finished for the day then I can show you around. Did you bring your friend?'

I knew he meant Nippa. My only friend really.

'Yes. She's in the car.'

'Get her out then but keep her on the lead until we can be sure she will behave around the cattle. You can lead her around and show her the sights while I finish up here. Then you can help me with the final chore before I give you the guided tour.'

By the time I returned with a very excited puppy, Archie was once more heading back to the gate. He smiled a greeting at Nippa, who responded with her own joyous reply.

'She recognises you,' I said, feeling rather miffed.

After only one meeting with this man, my disloyal puppy was showing signs of hero worship—for Archie and not for me.

'She probably remembers the farmyard smells. Come on, this way. Prepare to be impressed,' he said with a smirk.

Archie led Nippa and me around the corner to a back door of the dairy. He hopped onto the quad bike behind which was hitched a plastic rounded container on wheels.

'Follow me,' he said. 'We just have to take this milk to the calves in that shed over there.'

He pointed to a large shed past the dairy. The shed, open on one side, appeared to contain a massed herd of young calves, all of whom were clamouring for their supper. Nippa and I followed Archie as he slowly headed off on the bike. Once he arrived at the shed, we both watched with amazement as he proceeded to attach the container via tubing to a contraption that was beyond weird and looked rather indecent. Made of green plastic, it was attached to the railings and faced inside. The back part, the part that faced the calves, appeared to be some form of moulded plastic receptacle out of which protruded a line of pink udder-like teats—over twenty, I think. The calves were milling around in eager anticipation. Clearly, they knew what was about to happen, even if I didn't.

'Isn't she a beauty? Best thing I have ever purchased.' The proud owner stood back in awed contemplation of this monstrosity. I had the impression that he expected me to agree with him if only I knew what it was.

Archie must have sensed my puzzlement as he turned to me with a smile.

'I call it the milk bar. Each calf has access to a teat, and see how the plastic is moulded so each teat is attached to its own reservoir? That way they all get their fair share.

Just like the milk now flowing into those babies' stomachs, Archie was also in full flow and launched into a lengthy discourse about the art of calf raising. Separated from their mothers at three days of age, the time their mothers ceased producing colostrum and moved onto full milk production, the calves were fed twice a day with some of the milk produced by their mothers. They were also given some sort of supplementary calf feed in pellet form, which I could see in tubs in the middle of the shed. And as they grew older, the back gate on the shed would be left open in the day, so they could roam in the adjoining paddock. Once they were older and ready to be fully weaned, they would be turned out into a sheltered paddock where they could be left to grow up.

I tried not to feel too sorry for these babies separated from their mothers. The realities of farming aren't always pleasant.

'We have about twenty young calves in this batch at the moment,' Archie continued with his lecture. 'Some heifers and some steers— you know, bull calves that are no longer bulls. I know some people like to get rid of the bull calves at birth, but I prefer to grow them up and sell them on for meat when they are the right size. It just doesn't seem right to get rid of them at birth like they are garbage. This way they can have a good life here until it's time to go. The truth of it is that if we want to eat meat, then sooner or later the animals have to be sent to slaughter. The best I can do is to make sure I give them a good life for as long as possible while they are on the farm. The heifers of course get to stay here on the farm once they're grown. They are already marked for a future as part of the milking herd.'

I stood lost in wonder at the activity before me. I had never been up so close to a calf before and was amazed at how pretty these young animals were. Of course, all babies are beautiful. That's just Mother Nature at work, I suppose. Yet, as I considered these calves so focussed on their evening meal, I admired their fine textured coats, their large, dark eyes, and those eyelashes so indecently long.

One calf, obviously a greedy one, finished the milk before the others and came across to say hello. Or maybe it was to find more milk as it commenced to furiously suck on my fingers.

'That's enough now, young lady,' admonished Archie, pushing her away.

By now I had noticed this calf was a she.

He turned to me. 'You have to be careful. They can bite, you know, and even if they don't, their suck is mighty powerful. It can hurt and bruise. Come on, let me show you around. I'll yell out to Jo who is finishing in the dairy. He can come and clean up here once all of the calves have finished.'

We wandered back out of the calf shed and I hung about glancing idly around the yard as Archie went to find Jo, who I understood was a neighbour that helped from time to time. Then once Archie returned, we headed across the dusty farmyard in the direction of the house. As we walked, with puppy scampering at our heels, I listened to Archie speak at length about the farm. I could see from his enthusiasm that the farm was a passion of his, and looking around at the beauty of its surroundings, I could understand why he felt the way he did.

Although the Saddler farm was in a river valley, it was situated on a slight rise to one side of the rivulet. Paddocks down by the rivulet were lush with summery growth, an indicator of the fertile soil that bordered the flowing water. Even I was aware of the many times this plain had been flooded over the years; depositing nature's own fertiliser, just like in ancient Egypt. The early settlers, no doubt being mindful of the propensity for flooding, had built their homes and sheds on the rise. This gave an added benefit of an enhanced outlook across the valley to the wild bush beyond. But today, there was no time to admire the scenery as Archie urged me on.

'Nippa's mum, Bella, must be down at the house with Dad. I'm not sure if you have met my mum and dad.'

I shook my head in reply as I found myself reluctant to speak. The only time I had met Archie's parents was on that dreadful day—the day of the funeral. And I suspected that didn't count and I certainly didn't want to mention that meeting if I was to speak to them now. I'm sure on that terrible day I was just one of many nameless faces they had to contend with. Now that I think about it, I'm not sure if I even spoke to them on that day. I was so numb. All I can remember was the deluge of grief overwhelming me and the slight comfort brought to me by Archie's kind words. In fact, the last thing I wanted to do now was to meet Charlie's parents, but mindful of Archie's kindness to me, it seemed impolite to refuse to do so. With that in mind, I allowed myself to be led across the farmyard and towards a back gate that opened into the rear garden, along a cement path and up a step to an enclosed verandah. I looked at Archie with a question in my eyes. What should I do with Nippa?

'It's okay. Let me go get Bella and bring her out to say hello. With a bit of luck, that will also bring Mum and Dad out.'

Again, I waited. There seemed to be a lot of that happening today. I gazed at the farmhouse. It was cute with its steeply pitched roof and tidy garden but on closer inspection, it was a bit shabby. Paint flaking off weatherboards and a window propped open with a pile of books, spoke of general neglect or disregard for maintenance.

I glanced at my watch, wondering how long I needed to linger and why on Earth I had thought to visit. My puppy, entangling me with the lead, reminded me that it was for her benefit that I came.

The arrival of a taller, more mature version of Nippa, provided complete distraction for both puppy and me. The screen door opened with a creak and this dog bounded out, only to halt with hackles risen when she saw the puppy. She clearly had no memory of her baby. She moved forward with purpose, while said puppy hid behind me. The timeless ritual of bottom sniffing and a general once over of the now cowering puppy followed. Once satisfied that this pup was no threat, I was then subjected to the same treatment—minus the bottom sniffing, thank goodness. It was a relief to find that we had passed some sort of inspection because with some tail wagging, the dog proceeded to invite Nippa to play.

Archie, accompanied by two people—his parents I assumed— came across the lawn.

'Good one. Looks like they will be friends. You never know with Bella. She can be a bit territorial, even with her own babies.'

Turning to his parents, Archie proceeded to introduce me to them. His father was called Charles, so I suppose Charlie must have been named after him. Maybe a family name? Archie's mother, Elsie, was warm and welcoming, and immediately made me feel like I had known her for ages. She bustled forward and wrapped me in a warm, floury hug. I could smell the aroma of baking wafting around her as she moved forward.

'You must be Maggie's youngest. So lovely to meet you, Frankie. You have the look of your mother when she was younger. I would have known you anywhere.'

Elsie bent down and patted Nippa, who was still uncertain about the bigger dog and was playing it safe by leaning close to me.

'And you, little one. You have grown. Look like your mother too. But I'm not sure about those legs. Do you think the father could be the neighbour's Corgi?' Elsie looked across to Archie as she asked this question.

'Could be,' Archie smiled. 'Time will tell but I'm not sure it is going to help Nippa's career as a cattle dog with stumpy legs like that!'

Taking me by the arm, Elsie escorted me around the front of the house, talking all the time. No need for me to say anything. Not that I thought I had anything to say. It was clear to me that Elsie did not associate me with Charlie, and for some reason, that made me feel a bit miffed. After all, I thought I had been a big part of Charlie's life, even if only for a short period. Surely, they should have known about me. Hadn't Charlie mentioned me to his parents? If not, why not?

It wasn't until we had walked around the side and reached the front of the house, with its view down the valley, that Archie's father spoke. He was a gaunt, weathered giant of a man who took my hand briefly in a firm handshake, grunted a hello, then fell silent. I felt the need to say something. I gushed about how beautiful the farm was and how much I appreciated the gift of Nippa. I then fell silent as I had nothing else to say. By now, we had settled on some battered cane chairs on the front verandah, facing outwards and staring down the valley. Bella, who had followed us, sat by her master. I absentmindedly rubbed Nippa's ears and wondered how long it was considered polite to stay, and when I could make my exit. The only sounds were the scattered birdsong and the distant moo from the cows as they made their way back into the paddocks. It was Archie who spoke next.

'Let Nippa off the lead, Frankie. She will be fine.'

So, I did, and we all watched a determined young Nippa as she explored the verandah, wobbled down the step, and inspected the garden. Bella, immediately concerned about this pup in her garden, left her post by her master and shepherded the pup around.

'Do you think Bella knows that Nippa is her baby?' I asked.

'Hard to tell,' said Archie. 'But it's good for Nippa to spend time with her. You know, a bit of socialising and all that. There's only Bella here now as we ended up giving away the last two pups, but it looks like she will still play with Nippa when the mood takes her. Bring her up anytime. And if you come up before the afternoon milking, she can help get the cattle in. Not that she has to do much. The old girls know the routine. It wouldn't hurt Nippa to learn to walk behind them and become familiar with cattle. Even a half cattle dog should have an instinct for the job. Now that I think about it, if she is half Corgi, young Nippa could also have inherited a herding instinct from her pa. I seem to recall they were also bred as cattle dogs. Just a pity about the legs!'

Nippa, on her stumpy legs, ignored us all and proceeded with her exploration.

'Yes, Frankie, do come up any time.' Elsie reinforced her message with a broad smile.

Charles said nothing, although a thoughtful nod made me feel that perhaps he was in agreement with his wife, just not in exuberant agreement.

We chatted about this and that. I found that the conversation flowed much easier if I restricted the subject matter to the farm, the cattle, where the rest of Bella's litter ended up, and the weather. When in doubt, always talk about the weather. It works every time in this small community. Charles, it appears, has made a study of the rainfall since settlement, and talked at length about droughts, floods and the like. Fascinating—not!

When Charles finally paused for breath, I stood up, made my excuses, and left, dragging with me a very reluctant Nippa, who had finally decided Bella was her new best friend.

'Here, let me.'

Archie bent down and swooped Nippa into the air.

'Come here, rascal. Time to go. Settle down. No licking. Home with you. Next time you can do some real work and not just socialise. Both of you actually. That is if you want to, Frankie?'

He looked anxiously at me with those blue-green eyes, so like those of his brother. That did it—how could I refuse?

'Of course. Happy to help. Any time. Just call me.'

'You have no idea how much I would appreciate a hand. Jo

helps me out when he can, but I'm pretty much managing on my own. Dad's ... well, it's hard to explain.' Archie paused and drew breath and looked like he was having trouble finding the right words. Then he continued, 'Dad's not as strong as he used to be and can't do much on his own anymore. It's a long story. I'll tell you sometime, but let's just say it's so much better for him and me if he stays back here at the house.'

Archie's face clouded over, and I could sense from the way his body tensed that there was something causing him distress. I didn't want to prolong his pain as I was starting to like his gentleness. Reaching the car, I relieved Archie of the squirming bundle and shoved Nippa inside the car. Patting Archie on the arm, I said my farewells, got in the car and left. I waved casually out the window in the vague direction of this person, who was still standing, contemplating my departure. He remained that way as I headed down the rutted driveway—not moving, his hand, lifted in farewell, now slowly falling to rest by his side. I couldn't help but watch this solitary figure in the rear-view mirror staring until I drove out of sight.

On my drive home, I considered the situation at Saddler's farm. It was pretty obvious that something was a bit odd there. Maybe Mum's instincts were correct when she said that she thought Archie was carrying the workload of the dairy farm. His father, well, I couldn't put my finger on it, but it seemed to me there was something not quite right with him. And the way Archie just stood there and watched me leave. He looked so sad and desolate, like he didn't want me to leave. Maybe I did need to make a return visit. After all, it wouldn't do Nippa any harm. Looking in my rear-view mirror, I considered the pup, who had collapsed in an exhausted heap on the back seat and was gently snoring in time to the music playing on the car radio. Yes, the visit had definitely been a success as far as she was concerned!

Back home, I updated Mum on my visit. I spoke of the beauty of the calves and described the ritual of milking. Mum smiled.

'You've lived in this district all your life and you've only now noticed the dairy industry? What a beach girl you are,' she said, giving me a quick hug.

I remembered what else I had to ask.

'But Mum. It was weird. Archie's mum was so friendly and welcoming, but his father was rather reserved. He said hardly anything. It was like he didn't know how to interact. And Archie seemed kind of sad and forlorn. Is something wrong?'

'I'm not sure, Frankie. Charles Saddler has always been a difficult person. Even at school he was one of those people to be avoided—a bit of a bully, you know. Meeting Elsie seemed to soften him, but not as much as I'd expect. He was very strict with those boys. Living away from the town and up in that valley, they were fairly isolated from the rest of us. But I heard things. Nothing specific, of course, although I did wonder what sort of childhood those boys had. Yet, they seemed to turn out alright. When you were seeing Charlie, he always seemed to be happy and charming. And Archie, after he completed his degree, he came back to help on the farm. I suppose if things were really bad, he mightn't have done that, but left for good?'

'Maybe. He seems fond of his mum and certainly loves the farm. He has invited Nippa and me back. Maybe I should go. He seems nice. Different to Charlie, gentler somehow, and Nippa absolutely adores him.'

'Well, you know what they say about animals having the right instincts concerning people. Maybe that dog is correct and there is more to investigate about Archie. After all ...,' mum twinkled at me. '... it's not like there is a lot of talent down here on the coast. He may well be the only single man worth checking out. Even if he does smell of cow manure!'

'Mum!'

Chapter Seventeen

I slept well that night. No nightmares that I could recall. My sleep was restful and populated by dreams of Charlie and fantastic surf breaks. We were catching a perfect wave together when the ping of my phone, which I had left on the bedside table last night, brought me back to reality. I rolled over and reached for my phone. Through bleary eyes I could see that a text had just arrived from Simon.

'Check out today's paper. You're in it.'

That's it. No more detail. What paper? And why would I be in the news? Typical Simon. Rather than search the Internet, I rang him. He answered on the first ring with his usual breezy greeting.

'Good morning, little sister. Now aren't you the popular one! My, you get around.'

'What on Earth are you talking about?'

'Our local Sydney daily has you on the cover page. At least you have their sympathy. *Sad eyed Frankie on the rocks* it says. Not a bad use of words. Couldn't have done a better headline myself. And the photo isn't too bad either. So forlorn you look. Even I, your uncaring big brother, feel sorry for you.'

'What are you talking about?'

I know I was repeating myself, but I have absolutely no idea what he was on about.

'Just search the internet for the *Sydney Telegraph*. You'll see the cover story. Or you could always be a Luddite and go buy the paper. That is, if it isn't already sold out. I'm sure the locals will find this story oh so fascinating!'

I reached for my laptop, turned it on and started to search. The article quickly appeared. Yes, it did have the heading as described by Simon, accompanied by a photo of Nippa and I pensively walking along the beach. Both of us were looking down. It could be interpreted that I was feeling sad, but it was more likely that both Nippa and I were exhausted from another day of frantic activity associated with bed making and bathroom cleaning and were examining the beach debris for treasures.

'When was this taken?' I ask.

'How would I know? Sometime recently I would guess as your mate is with you. But more importantly it looks like the press has tracked you down. That means you now have no privacy while you and Gino continue to be newsworthy. Someone will think it worth their while to take photos of you. These people sell their photos for a goodly sum and the public will still want to see you, especially as you take a good photo—even with your current waif-like look. And there is a lot for the journos to speculate about. You know, has Frankie run away to this secluded spot to hide away and grieve in private? Or why has Frankie cut her hair so short? Is this a symptom of deep grief or mental instability or, shock horror, is Frankie seriously ill? Or, has Frankie been forced to run away and hide because she has been axed from *On the Rocks?* That's just a few ideas, off the top of my head. I could make up so many more once I warm up. But you get the drift?'

'Yeah, I do. Thanks,' I said dryly, not feeling thankful at all. 'So, what do I do now?'

'Lie low for the time being. Look, when I get to work this morning, I'll have a chat with Tom, who is probably fielding calls from the media as we speak. Basically, you need to keep out of sight. That means away from the beach. At least it is good that the photo is of you looking sad. You still have the sympathy of the public. If they were to see you skinny dipping or out clubbing, you would be on toast!'

'Like I care!'

After we hung up, I contemplated the story so artfully displayed on the laptop. At least the photo was flattering. Taken on the beach out the front of the guest house. It must have been taken some time in the last week on one of our afternoon walks. I had obviously been for a swim and was dressed in my old bikini. One hand was smoothing the drips out of my hair, and it may be my head was down and to one side in order to expel sea water that had lodged in my ear during the swim. I suppose a casual observer might speculate that I was being sadly pensive, but anyone who knew me would soon put them straight. That was so not my style.

But what to do? As always, I called for help from the number one fixer-upperer in the family.

'Mum!' I yelled at the top of my voice, giving Nippa such a scare she immediately started barking.

There was a clatter of footsteps from someone running up the stairs to my bedroom, then Mum soon appeared, wiping her hands on her apron.

'What is it, Frankie? Are you okay? Or is it Nippa? No, I can see she's alright. Be quiet young dog. No need to bark at me.'

The dog quietened at the arrival of her friend, while I mutely pointed to the story displayed on the laptop. Mum sat on the edge of my bed, drew the laptop close and started to read. After a moment, she paused and looked up.

'Well, I never. How did they find out you were here?'

'No idea, Mum. Any of the locals could've blabbed, I suppose. It's not like it was a state secret.'

We both considered the photo of me displayed in all my glory. I now noticed there was another photo of me further down the page. It really must be a slow news day if they had devoted so much space to me. That photo looked like it was taken the night of that party on the harbour. The contrast between my appearance then and now couldn't have been even more stark. In the *before* photo, I was every inch the starlet—glammed up in that amazing designer dress, all aglow courtesy of fancy makeup. My long hair was on display—beautifully styled into artful waves, flowing down over my shoulders. In the after shot, I was a bedraggled waif. Kinda cute looking I must admit, but so much thinner and not one ounce of glamour to be found.

'What am I to do Mum? They know I'm here and will be wanting to take more photos,' I wailed, despair clearly expressed in my voice and visible on my face.

'Does it matter?'

Mum, ever the pragmatist, failed to understand my concern.

'Of course, it does. I'm lucky that is quite a flattering photo. But next time it could be a disaster, or they could talk to someone down here who would tell a pack of lies about me. If I want to get back into acting, my image is so important. I know that may not happen but even so, the idea of people out there trawling through my life is just so disgusting. All I want to do is to go and hide. This is all so awful,' I wailed, tears now spilling down my face as I contemplated the misery that had become my life.

Yes, I know what you are thinking and totally agree: always the drama queen.

'If you really feel like you need to hide, then the solution is obvious,' Mum said with authority.

'Is it?'

'Go stay with your sister. She's not that far away, but far enough. If the press is looking for you here, they won't think to look in the next town. And if you stay away a week or two, they'll think you were just here for a holiday and leave us be. The article says nothing about the B&B, which makes me think that whoever let on that you were here, isn't a local. Maybe they just got lucky. I'm sure Amy would be fine with you staying. She's at work most of the day. Give her a ring. But ring her soon as it's almost time for her to head to school.'

Amy, answering the phone just as she was about to head out for the day, was immediately receptive to the idea of an unexpected guest.

'Of course. You must come and stay. There's heaps of room for you here, and it'll be fun having you stay. I should've thought of this earlier and asked you around. We can do sister stuff and bond. Maybe you can come with me to the huff and puff classes. They're starting shortly.'

'Huff and puff?'

'Yeah. Pre-natal stuff. Not my scene, but we mums-to-be are encouraged to attend to find out what we are in for. I'm in favour of total ignorance about the whole labour thing, but I gather that is frowned upon. I was dreading going by myself. Most likely, I will be the only one there without a partner. Maybe if we go together, everyone will think we are a couple?'

I hung up after agreeing with Amy that I would be waiting for her at her place by the time she arrived home that afternoon, and after being told the location of the door key—under the pot by the back door—no surprise that. Isn't that where a back door key is always located? You can tell we live in a safe community down here on the coast.

I dressed and headed out to find Mum and to receive my chores for the day. You guessed it! The usual chores, and heaps of them. The rest of the morning was kept fully occupied cleaning up newly vacated rooms and readying them for the next wave of guests. Nippa, as always, kept me company. By mid-afternoon, I was finished and had packed to go. Mum and I agreed that I would be on call to help her as required. Mum assured me that she could manage if there was not much to do and that she would call or text me first thing each morning if she needed me to lend a hand. We both thought so long as I arrived early and avoided the beach, I could escape detection.

'Unless those pesky journalists come here to stay, of course,' she said. 'And if they do, I'll charge them double or maybe even triple!'

Amy lived about ten minutes' drive up the coast towards Sydney, in what was once a quaint fishing village. Like many other places along the coast, in recent years it was becoming a victim of its own cuteness and popularity. Suburban development surrounded it and what were once paddocks for cattle had been converted into an ever-widening expanse of brick veneer and families. People have to live somewhere, I suppose, but as I approached this village and drove through the newly developed outskirts, I pined for how it once looked when I was a child. Must be getting old, I guess.

Amy lived a short walk from the main street in an old weatherboard cottage that once belonged to a fisherman or a farming family. It was not enormous—only the four original rooms protected by a front verandah and at the rear a largish extension that included an eat-in kitchen/family room and a bathroom. Nothing fancy, but as it was Amy's first house, purchased once she had a secure teaching job, it was her pride and joy. It was Amy and Dad who organised the extension, dealt with the builders and the challenges brought about by delays and bad weather. Talking to them about it, you'd think they had constructed something grand like Buckingham Palace or some other palace. But it was Amy's home and quite rightly something she should feel proud of.

Feeling a bit like a spy in some espionage movie, I had kept one eye on the rear-view mirror as I left the B&B and drove to Amy's place. It was just another day, and the traffic was as usual—the school bus, the tourist buses, the occasional lorry, and the milk tanker doing its rounds. No sign of any paparazzi chasing me. Not that I would know what they look like anyway. As I drove along, it did occur to me that perhaps I might be over dramatizing this experience. It could be a sign of the boredom that was infecting me rather than my own inflated sense of self-worth. Or it could be both?

Whatever the reason for my overreaction, I was pleased to reach Amy's home, park the car behind the house out of sight, find the back door key, and let myself and Nippa in. With the house only having two bedrooms, it was clear which one was the guest room. It was the room that looked like it was in the process of being repurposed as a nursery. Opening the bedroom door, I could smell the new paint that coated the walls. Now a cheery yellow, the walls were a sight to behold—not quite egg yolk yellow, but not far off it. I just hoped the baby would be able to cope with it and not get the nightmares I was expecting to suffer myself. Checked blue and white curtains adorned the windows. A blue/white and yellow frieze adorned the wall at picture rail height with detail of little birds flying in formation. All very charming in an English country house sort of way I suppose. It was clear to me that Amy was fully embracing maternity. At least I had time to prepare myself for her arrival so I could think of something positive to say about the nursery decoration.

I deposited my bag and Nippa's bedding by the double bed that was still allowed to reside in this nursery room and headed out for the kitchen. With a cup of tea in hand, I settled myself at the kitchen table and waited for my sister, while trawling through the pile of fashion magazines that were stacked on a nearby occasional table.

It wasn't long until the sound of a vehicle moving down the side driveway heralded Amy's return. Ever the guard dog, Nippa sprang into action and in full bark, positioned herself by the back door.

'Well, that's a lovely greeting to receive when I return to my own home.' Amy's complaints were softened with a smile. 'Down, Nippa. You vicious hound you. No need to lick me to death. Welcome to your new home, and welcome little sister. My, you just attract controversy.'

Dumping her handbag and school folders on the kitchen counter, Amy enveloped me in a heartfelt cuddle, then stood back to contemplate me. I did the same. Amy, with her long hair pulled back into a ponytail, was still dressed in her work clothes—sensible navy, cotton trousers and a multi-coloured floral smock-like top. The top was so baggy it was impossible to tell if the baby bump was yet showing.

'Give me a moment to get changed out of these things. I feel so grotty. Working all day with children just attracts mess. Then we can sit down and catch up. I suppose you've already found your bedroom. It's not that hard to find in this dollhouse!'

With that she headed down the corridor. I leaned back in the chair, took a sip from my mug, and contemplated the backyard view through the windows. A large expanse bearing signs of many decades of neglect. Although someone—Dad maybe?— had been busy recently, paving a small area outside the back door and erecting a pergola. Beyond that, was an expanse of dead lawn, bedraggled untended fruit trees and a half-hearted attempt at a vegetable garden.

When Amy returned, now changed into black leggings and a fitted top, it was clear, even to my untrained eyes, that she was a different Amy to the one I saw at Christmas. She was a vision of curves. Moulded bosom bulging out from her top and below that a sweep of tummy, not yet the bulge of full term, but a considerable development from the concave stomach that our Amy usually sported.

'Look at you! My, haven't you grown! Definitely pregnant now. Has anyone noticed?'

'No. Not yet. I've discovered that if you keep wearing the same clothes day in day out, no one even notices the changing me. It's like no one ever looks too closely so long as I just appear to be the same.'

Amy paused and smiled, 'Although I did tell the principal today.'

'And?'

'Oh, it all went fine. We've had a few teachers off last year on maternity leave and I think Diana, the principal, you know, thought I was just being a bit of a copycat and following in their footsteps. She hardly asked me any questions. It seemed like all she was concerned about was when I planned to go on leave and for how long. Didn't even ask how I was feeling. Not that I would have told her.'

'And how do you feel?'

'Tired. So tired. The up chucking stopped a while back, but there are still some foods and smells I cannot abide. It's good you're here, you know. Not that I'll be much company. In bed by 8.30 most nights, but just having someone else around in the evenings to talk to will be fun. How are you by the way? Seen any press snooping around today?'

'I'm okay. I'm finding it all a bit off that anyone would spy on me or even that they would think my life was of interest to anyone else. Anyway, Simon and Tom tell me that if I lay low for a little while, the media's interest will move on to harass some other poor unfortunate victim. Thank you for letting me stay by the way.'

'It's my pleasure. You know we should have done this ages ago. I've been an appalling big sister. So neglectful leaving you to your own devices. Though I suppose you had Simon keeping an eye on you. Not that I'm saying he's a responsible adult! Come on, let me show you around my kingdom and then we can sort out dinner. I warn you. I am not a great cook. I've already sorted out tonight's dinner, but don't get too excited. It's pretty basic.'

'Basic is fine with me. However, as the new house guest, it will be my pleasure to look after the pregnant one. Just tell me what you like to eat these days, and I will make sure I cater to your every craving!'

The guided tour didn't take very long. We started on the front verandah, where Amy, with visible pride, pointed out the few period details that still remained on this worker's cottage. Details that had something to do with the way the verandah was constructed, the trim on the original front door, and the curved shape of the glass pane above the door. I contented myself with making admiring noises, which seemed to be sufficient for Amy. The two front rooms were neat and tidy, just like my sister. One room was furnished with a small lounge and two tub chairs grouped around a tiled Victorian era fireplace. Again, my tour guide drew my attention to the original tiles—some sort of art deco lily design that was considered significant. I admired these and the pine mantelpiece. The wooden boards lining the ceiling, and the walls painted a warm cream colour, made the room lighter and larger than I expected. Underfoot, the same polished floorboards that lined the hall shone with a warm honey glow. All in all, it was a welcoming room, and

I could see myself relaxing in here with a book and a glass of wine.

The other front room was Amy's bedroom. It was a vision of pale blue walls with clouds of white netting swathing a four-poster bed. Restful prints of seascapes lined the walls.

'This is beautiful. You've done a great job, Amy. And I've already checked out the nursery. You certainly have got the nesting bug big time.'

'I got a bit excited when I bought this place. My first home and all that. Dad has been a great help. You know how he loves a project. You've probably already noticed that he has been busy in the garden. He often pops over when I am at work, and it is a surprise when I get home to see what he has been up to. I couldn't do it without him. I tell him that and he goes all bashful. You know how he is!'

Like all siblings, we laughed at the foibles of our parents and shared that moment of closeness—two sisters united in a tolerant understanding of our father's eccentricities. Moving to the kitchen, I settled Amy at the table and sought instructions as to what to make for her dinner.

'Tonight, it's easy. All you have to do is reheat the casserole I prepared earlier. It's in the fridge. See, in that orange casserole dish? Tomorrow though, you're in charge. Something simple please, and not too spicy or I'll get an upset tummy.'

The casserole, some chicken tomatoey Italian thing served with pasta, was delicious. I could see I would have to lift my game if I was to serve anything equally tasty when it came to my turn to cook tomorrow. As we ate, we chatted companionably about this and that. Amy's challenges with this year's class. All the children in her class that year were about eight years old.

'They're so young. Still babies really, although they consider themselves so much older now they've left the infants' school behind. I've never taught Year 3s before. Usually I get given older kids, so the last few weeks have been a bit of a shock—to me that is. And I suppose to them. But we're muddling along. I think they're much more settled this week and starting to learn. I'm a bit sorry I am going to disrupt their year when I go off on leave. With a bit of luck, we will have a hand over, so they can get to know the new teacher before I leave. I've been checking the dates and I'm fairly certain I will be gone before the end of term three. That is, assuming I keep feeling well enough to be on my feet all day.'

Amy's forehead wrinkled in thought and her expression became solemn.

'Leaving in term time is the one thing I feel bad about. Hopefully by then though the kids will be up to speed, sick of me, and looking forward to a bit of variety with a replacement teacher. Let's hope.'

A banging on the front door interrupted our conversation. I stood up.

'You stay there, Amy. I'll go see who it is. I can bring them down here to you, assuming that is that it isn't a Mormon or someone selling something. Keep the weight off your feet.'

'I'm not that big yet! But alright. You go.'

I headed down the corridor to the front door. There was no peep hole in the door, so I had to open the door fully to see who our visitor was. There was a man standing there. Clearly having come straight from work, he was dressed in stained shorts and a grotty T-shirt. He smelled ... how do I say it? ... fishy? His face, weather beaten and suntanned, had fine white lines around the eyes where the sun had not reached—evidence of a default expression of scrunched up features when facing the elements. His hair was sun bleached and ratty—not much different in length to mine now that I think of it. His arms were muscular and tanned like his face. This man was a bit taller than me and somehow vaguely familiar. We stood and contemplated each other. Like me, it was obvious he too was not certain about my identity. There was something about him that I had seen before. Then I remembered.

'Robbie? Robbie Timms, is that you?'

This stranger continued to contemplate me and then, like a

light being switched on inside his brain, his entire face illuminated with comprehension.

'Well, I never. It's Frankie. I would never have recognised you without that hair. What happened? Surely, you're too young to lose it all.'

Yep, that's Robbie. Not the smartest tool in the shed. But as I recall, his charm used to make up for his lack of intelligence. He must be the only person in the area that is unaware of my recent history. Now that could be a good sign. Not sure about his current choice of aftershave however, if that's what it was. The fishy aroma had intensified as we stood there in contemplation of each other. I remembered my manners.

'Come on in. You must be after Amy. She's out the back. We've just finished dinner. Have you eaten?'

With a shake of the tangled mess that is his hair, he indicated he hadn't, which was confirmed as he replied, 'No. Just straight off work. Wouldn't mind something if you have any leftovers though? Just popped in to say hi to Amy. Haven't seen her for a while, you see.'

Now this sounded interesting. I hadn't realised Amy and Robbie were friendly. Unless he was a mate of that loser Shane. Maybe that was it.

Amy's reaction as I entered the kitchen closely followed by Robbie made me even more curious. Clearly Amy was not expecting to see Robbie, nor was she even pleased to see him here in her house.

'Robbie! What are you doing here?'

'I came to say hello and see if you are okay. You haven't been answering my texts and I was worried.'

'Well, I'm fine. You've seen me so now you can go!'

Amy had never been one for beating around the bush. That was blunt, but then again, that is how Amy is. Seeing Robbie's crestfallen expression, I felt the need to intervene.

'Umm, sorry Amy. I already offered Robbie the rest of our leftovers. You see, he has just come from work and hasn't eaten.'

Amy sniffed. I'm not sure if that was in disgust at my offer, or because of the aromas that were emanating from his person, increasing in impact now Robbie was standing closely to both of us. The smell of fish was so overwhelming to me that I hated to think how it was impacting on the pregnant one. Not too well I suspected, judging from the greenish tinge now appearing on her face.

I took Robbie by the hand and led him to the back door.

'Come and sit outside on the new patio and I'll bring the dinner out there. I'll get you a beer and you can relax. We'll join you out there in a minute.'

Robbie allowed himself to be escorted outside by Amy, while I rushed to find a beer I had spied earlier in the back of the fridge. At the time, I had thought it was a bit strange to see beer in Amy's fridge given her current condition. Now I wondered who these beverages were intended for.

Robbie fell onto the reheated casserole like someone who had not eaten for days. Amy, sitting a good distance from Robbie—out of smelling range I suspect—considered him warily as he ate. For a while, nothing was said while Robbie devoted full concentration to his meal. Then, once the bowl was scraped clean and no casserole remained, he leaned back and smiled at us both.

'That was amazing. I hadn't realised how hungry I was. I didn't mean to barge in on you like this and to eat all your leftovers. I just wanted to say hello and see … well, to see, Amy, if you want to go out for dinner this weekend.'

I pushed my chair back. Maybe I shouldn't be a witness to this conversation as I could tell from the glacial expression on Amy's face that she was not inclined to accept Robbie's invitation. I didn't want to be here when she delivered the bad news. Taking the now empty bowl, and with a muttered excuse about cleaning up, I started to move away.

'No, don't leave Frankie. What I have to say won't take long. Robbie, I haven't answered your texts as I didn't want to. There's no future for us and I certainly don't want to go out this weekend or any other time for that matter. It's not going to work. We have nothing in common. Forget it.'

His stunned face showed Robbie was having trouble processing this information. His mouth moved in the motion of words, but no sound emerged. Then, with a deep breath he tried again.

'But we know each other … and well.' With a glance at me, he continued: 'I thought you liked me, you know, before Christmas.'

'I was drunk.' Amy's voice was crisp and distinct just like the schoolmarm she is. Standing up, she pushed her chair away. Taking Robbie by the arm, she pointed him in the direction of the driveway that led beside the house and back up to the street. Robbie, his stunned gaze still fixed on Amy's implacable face, allowed himself to be led away. Then, as if a thought registered, he stopped, turned, and considered Amy in all her glory. His gaze travelled from face to toes and then back again.

'It isn't only Frankie who looks different. It's you too, Amy. Is that why you cut off contact with me? Didn't you want to tell me you were having Shane's baby? You know I could handle that. It's you I like—baby or no baby.'

Amy's silence told me everything. This man, standing before her with a beseeching look in his eyes, was the father of her child. Yet, he didn't know, and for some reason Amy had no intention of telling him.

Or maybe not yet. For something in Robbie's tone, or in the words he had just said, gave Amy pause and with a visible softening in her voice, she spoke:

'Robbie. Not now. Not while Frankie is here. I'll give you a call and we can talk, but not this weekend. Maybe next week.'

I turned away and left them to continue the conversation. Once inside, I busied myself with stacking the dishwasher, tidying the kitchen and once more, filling the kettle and putting it back on to boil. I had a feeling my sister and I needed to talk. This could take more than one cup of tea, so I searched through the cupboards and located a cute, floral china tea pot that so matched the chintzy prettiness that was Amy's home. As she entered the kitchen, Amy spied me busy with my activities and smiled in appreciation of my cunning.

'You're right. We need to talk. There are biscuits in that biscuit barrel by the kettle. I think we need a sugar hit as well.'

With a pot of tea made and resting on the table in front of us, stewing for the requisite three minutes before I would pour the tea into our mugs, I commenced the interrogation.

'Okay, out with it. What's going on, and why won't you tell Robbie he's the father of your child?'

'Wow. You don't beat around the bush. Go straight to the jugular don't you. Yes, he's the baby's father. It's a long story, but I see no point in telling him.'

'Well then, tell me. Out with it.'

So, she did.

Apparently on the day Amy visited Shane unexpectedly and found him otherwise engaged, she then went to the local bar to calm down. Her life, as she said, was in ruins and she didn't know what to do. All that she had thought would happen—marriage to Shane, living in this town, teaching, and raising a family safe and secure in a close-knit community—well, all of that was now up in the air. Amy thought that this future was what she had wanted. But now she wasn't so sure. On that day, the images of what she had just seen played over and over in her mind and she just wanted to wipe them away. So, she ordered a gin and tonic, and then another. When Robbie arrived at the bar on his way home after work, but this time already freshly washed and in clean clothes, Amy greeted him like a long-lost friend, which he was. Robbie had been in the same year at school as Amy and they had known each other growing up. They had been part of the same gang of school mates and for a brief time in Year 8, had gone out together to the movies once or twice. Amy had always had a soft spot for Robbie who, while excelling in sport, had been a bit of dunce academically—something Robbie was happy to admit. Fortunately, he was also happy to work alongside his father on his fishing trawler, which explained the all-pervasive fishy aroma and the weathered visage. But that evening, he was clean and in good cheer, having had a very successful catch out at sea. And a further catch awaited him in the bar as Amy was keen to equal the score with Shane. If Shane could muck around with her best friend, well then, she could do the same with his. One thing led to another and before she knew it Amy was back home at her place in a clinch with Robbie, who couldn't believe his luck. Not that Amy knew that at the time, but Robbie had continued to fancy Amy since that time in Year 8. They were busy that night. Amy was drunk and although she had some recollection of the use of condoms, she seems to think that in the wee small hours there was a further sleepy interaction that may not have included the use of a condom. That was most likely the fatal moment when the unrestrained sperm were able to run free.

'But you didn't tell him. Why not?'

'Because there was no point in telling him. By the next day, once I had sobered up, I realised what an idiot I had been. Yeah, I agree Robbie can be a sweetie, but really, he is not for me. So not smart.'

'Is Shane any smarter?'

'Good point. Alright then. Intellect aside, I just couldn't see a future. You know, picking up someone in a bar is not the best way to start a relationship.'

'But he wasn't a total stranger. You've known him like … forever. But that doesn't explain why you haven't told him about the baby.'

'Cause I don't want to!' Amy's face reverted to the same closed expression she had displayed on Christmas Eve when she dropped her bombshell on all of us. She had clammed up and for now, this was going to be the end of the discussion. I knew my sister too well. After all, she was behaving exactly like me. Making my excuses, I took the now empty mugs to the sink, gave my sister a quick hug as I bid my farewells, and headed for bed with a sleepy Nippa stumbling along behind.

Chapter Eighteen

That night, Charlie came to me in my dreams. It was the Charlie I once knew and loved—hair surf besprinkled, showering droplets of sea water with every movement; sea-green eyes sparkling with happiness and gazing at me with a smile so full of contentment, his obvious joy seeping into my very being.

I was asleep. I know that. But the Charlie I saw felt so real. Even when I woke, my senses screamed with delight from having seen my Charlie again. It felt like he had visited me from wherever he existed now, just to share his love for me and remind me of the joy we both experienced for that short time when we had once been together.

I lay there in that half world that we all visit when we first wake, when our dreams still feel so real and are fully recalled for a moment before they slip away as full consciousness hits. As I remembered what I had just experienced, I felt so sure that it had been Charlie. Not a Charlie of my memories, but a Charlie who had returned with a purpose. To deliver me a message. A message that I was loved, to cheer up and get on with life. And to no longer grieve for him, as he was happy.

I couldn't rationalise what I had just experienced, and I'm sure the sceptics that live among us would say it was my sub-conscious being creative. Yet, my overall feeling was a profound feeling of gratitude. Gratitude that Charlie had once been in my life, and for the times we had once shared. Gratitude that this message of love and hope had been delivered to me for whatever purpose, and that now I had his permission to move on.

Out in the kitchen I could hear sounds of Amy moving around while talking to Nippa, who I could only assume had decided I was a lost cause and that there was a better chance of a breakfast titbit to be found from Amy.

Scrambling out of bed, I wrapped an old silk robe I had found on a hook behind the door around me and headed towards the kitchen.

My sister greeted me with a cheerful grin.

'Just in time. There's a pot of tea on the bench stewing. Help yourself. Found my old robe, did you? Doesn't look too bad on you. That colour green really makes your eyes pop. Come tell your dog to stop pestering me, will you?'

I made myself comfortable at the table and tried to distract Nippa by encouraging her to beg for dog treats. Her absolute focus on food is most impressive, and all of a sudden, she obediently ran through all her learnings from puppy school. She sat and, on command, lay down like a true professional. Amy was impressed.

'Not bad for a puppy. She's learnt really quickly. Must be the blue heeler in her. They're so intelligent,' Amy said.

'It could be from her other parent—possibly the neighbour's Corgi. They're meant to be smart.'

'Oh. Is that the other part of her genetic makeup? Unusual combination.' Amy gave a little sniff and then, diverted by a new thought, continued:

'What do you plan to do today? Apart from hide out from the press?'

'I don't really know. I'll contact Mum to see if she needs a hand. Maybe go for a swim?'

I looked out the window and considered the day. It was sunny with fluffy bunched clouds. Not too hot and not too cold. A perfect day for the beach.

'And organise your dinner too, of course. Is there anything else you want me to do? Get groceries, wash your clothes or clean?'

'No way,' Amy laughed. 'You're not my slave. Just relax and enjoy yourself.'

She put her mug down, pushed back the chair, and with bag swung over her shoulder, she headed for the door.

'Gotta go now, or I'll be late. See you this afternoon after work.' And with a wave she was gone, out through the door and away for the day.

First thing I did was ring my mother, who assured me she didn't need my assistance as she only had one room to prepare for guests who were expected later in the day.

'Are you sure?'

I felt like I was at a loss as to what to do. For once, I almost welcomed the idea of cleaning rooms and making beds as it would at least keep me busy. Mum, knowing me all too well, came up with a suggestion.

'You have a day to yourself. Treat yourself. You've been such a help lately and have had no time off. Why don't you go for a swim? It's a perfect day out there for you and Nippa to go to the beach. Just not a beach near us. And maybe take Nippa up to the farm for a play with their dog? Didn't Archie say you were welcome any time? Your dog needs to be socialised, don't forget.'

Now why hadn't I thought of that? All of a sudden, I really wanted to see Archie again, to get to know him better. It took my mother to show me what needed to be done.

'Not a bad idea, Mum. I might give him a ring. Now let me know if you need me tomorrow. All I need to do here is to make a nutritious dinner for your other daughter.'

After the call had ended, I sat at the table and contemplated the unexpected bonus of a day free of demands from others stretching out before me. I realised that it had been years since I have had free time. Really, the last time was when I was at school, when the summer holidays seemed to last forever. Even when I lived in Sydney, every day was busy, and since I had returned home as mother's little helper, I had been fully occupied. Now, if I wanted to, I could do absolutely nothing all day, apart from make sure that some sort of meal was ready by the evening.

A determined nudging by a small dog brought me to my senses.

'No, not absolutely nothing. You're so right, Nippa. You still need entertaining regardless of what I want to do.' I smiled down at my constant companion.

'Come on. No slacking around, you lazy mutt. Let's get moving. I'll ring Archie and see if he wants a visitor later today and you can do a bit more training with those cattle.'

Her ears pricked and she watched me intently as I reached for the phone. Sometimes I swear she could understand everything I said. With the number located and dialled, I waited for Archie to pick up. It rang and rang and, just as I was about to disconnect, he answered. He sounded a bit puffed.

'Sorry. Did I make you run for the phone? It's Frankie here by the way.'

'It's okay. I was just in another room and couldn't remember where I'd put the phone. But I'm here now. How are you, Frankie? When are you coming to visit again?'

'I'm fine. Well, sort of. A long story, but if Nippa and I could visit this afternoon then I can fill you in.'

'I've got a better idea. I've finished the chores till this afternoon. How about I meet you at the beach and we can have a dip, maybe fish and chips, and if you are still happy to hang about, you and Nippa could help me with the afternoon milking?'

Suddenly, I couldn't think of anything I would rather do than spend the day with this gorgeous man. Then I remembered the paparazzi. Surely it would be okay if he came up here to a nearby beach well away from my hometown. I explained my dilemma to Archie who was immediately intrigued.

'You mean we could be photographed, and I might be splashed over the mags as Frankie's hot new love interest? Sounds good to me.'

'Don't get too many tickets on yourself,' I laughed. 'With a bit of luck, there will be some new scandal and all this media interest in little old me will lapse.'

'Never!' he said, ever the gentleman.

We met down at the main beach. It was a rather protected beach, good for children and those seeking a gentle swim. We both waded into the welcoming water followed by my dog, who this time was determined not to be left behind. No going out too deep today as my dog made it clear her responsibility was to bring us back to the shore to safety. She swam around us like a circling shark, occasionally scratching me or Archie as she tried to scrabble into our arms.

'Ouch, Nippa, don't do that,' I said as I pushed her squirming body away.

'I give up. Back to the shore for me. The dog wins.'

'Anyway,' said Archie. 'I'm starving. Must be time for lunch. We farmers have been up since sparrow's fart, and we need regular feeding. Come on, you two. I know the place for the best fish and chips in town, just across the road there. Then we can sit on those benches and admire the view.'

He grabbed me by the hand, and we ran out of the surf chased by an energetically barking dog.

I don't know what it is, but somehow freshly cooked fish and chips taste so much better when eaten at the beach, when one's fingers and lips are freshly salted with sea water, and one is hungry from swimming. We ate quickly, or as quickly as hot steaming food permitted. Nippa sat by my feet and watched each chip and piece of fish as my fingers propelled them into my mouth.

'Take pity on your poor dog,' says Archie.

Clearly a soft touch that man.

'You can see she is starving. Still growing too. A bit of fish or a chip or two won't hurt her and will give her the energy to round up the cows.'

'More like chase and scatter them!' I replied.

But I weakened and shared some of our lunch with the ravenous dog.

After we had eaten our fill, I leaned back on the bench and updated Archie on my latest run in with the press. He thought it was funny. I did not!

'You didn't see the photo. I look like some starving waif. With a photo like that it is so easy for them to spin some tale of doom and gloom when in fact the opposite is true.'

No sooner than the words came out of my mouth than I pulled myself up. Was that really correct? Was I really enjoying myself? With wide eyes, I stared at Archie who gazed back at me, now grinning widely.

'Well?'

'Well, what?'

'I take it all is well then? Not doom and gloom after all.'

I nodded.

'You know what. Now I think of it, coming back here was the right thing to do. I can't believe how easy it has been to slip back into life here. I'm not saying I like the chores I have to do to help Mum, but it has been fun spending time with my family and Nippa—and getting to know you too, of course.'

Mindful of my manners, I felt I needed to acknowledge the increased contact with Archie as a positive in this—my new life.

'I'm glad you feel that way as I had something to run past you.'

'Mmm?'

Archie looked slightly ill at ease, as if he was about to broach a sensitive subject. I searched my mind for what could be bothering him. Had I done something or said something that could cause offence? Not that I could think of. We had really only just started to get reacquainted. I gave him a wide-eyed, encouraging look as if to urge him on.

'Go on. Spit it out. What is it?'

'Well. I was just wondering if you would like a bit of extra work. You know, helping me in the afternoons. You might have noticed it, but Dad is not doing so well. He's getting on and I suppose having worked hard all his life, his body is just wearing out. He still likes to help in the mornings. I think that's his best time of day, but by afternoon he has had it a bit. Jo, our neighbour, tries to help out when he can, but he has his own farm to run, and I feel reluctant to ask too much of him. I saw how much you and Nippa seemed to enjoy your visit the other day, and I wondered if it would be possible to help me in the afternoons ... say Monday to Friday.'

As he progressed through his request, Archie's expression became more and more plaintive, almost as if he were half expecting me to refuse. I'm not sure how I felt about this request so remained silent as I considered my options. Archie, clearly anxious, interpreted my silence as an indication of reluctance.

'I'll pay you, of course,' he rushed on. 'An hourly rate. Whatever is the going rate. And all the fresh milk you might want.'

I smiled, and he smiled back, his feeling of relief visible.

'Done! You had me with the offer of free milk. But can you afford it? You know how much Nippa drinks!'

With a murmured exclamation, Archie jumped up.

'We have to rush. It's time to get to the farm. The girls will be lined up at the gate wondering where we are. Somehow, I lost track of the time. Too much to talk about, I guess.'

We stood and walked shoulder to shoulder back to the carpark, and then parted company at our respective cars. As I followed Archie's car up the highway back towards the Saddler farm, I contemplated the ease with which I had fallen into this newfound friendship. He was so like his brother to look at—same colour eyes, mannerisms and facial expressions, yet taller and more muscular, I suppose as a result of all those years of manual work. Even though there was still so much I had yet to learn about this man, I felt at ease with him, as if I could trust him. Maybe that was because he was Charlie's brother and as I recall, much loved by Charlie. Or maybe it was just as simple as the fact that Nippa liked him. But whatever, I was happy to have the opportunity to spend more time with Archie and get to know him better.

We soon arrived at the farm and as Archie had predicted, the cows were waiting, and with a bit of mooing from some, indicating their dissatisfaction with the current arrangements. Archie's father was hovering nearby. I observed their interaction as I pulled up and parked my car. I could tell that Charles Saddler was not impressed about something and was making his displeasure known to his only son. As Charles gesticulated and yelled at his son, Archie stood by patiently and said nothing. I sat still in the car, uncertain as to what to do. Should I get out? Or stay in the car until the storm blew over? Or just leave? Archie looked across and waved at me to get out. I pulled a face. His father turned to see what his son was waving at, saw me and frowned. The tirade continued, now with a finger pointing in my direction. I leaned back into the car seat. What did I do to provoke this reaction?

I must have sat like a frozen dummy for only a minute, although it felt like much longer. I felt helpless and unable to do anything but watch as Archie somehow calmed his father down, turned him around and pushed him in the direction of the farmhouse.

I sat in the car and watched Archie as he approached me.

'I'm sorry, Frankie. I have no idea what got into him then. It's like he just lost it for a moment. Anyway, he's calmed down now. I said you and I are now in charge of the afternoon milking, although I will need his help on the weekend. He's been a difficult man for as long as I can remember, but some days I swear he is getting much worse.'

Archie ran his hands through his wiry hair as if in despair and grimaced as if he didn't know how to go on. Feeling reluctant to add to his distress, I decided to not make an issue of what I had just witnessed. In any event, the cows were signalling their need for attention by escalating their vocalisation and needed to be dealt with.

'No matter,' I said. 'We have work to do. Come on, let's set up and get on with it. Don't worry about your dad. We all have challenges with our parents.'

Okay, so that was a lie. As far as my parents are concerned, I couldn't ask for better, but occasionally it didn't hurt to exaggerate in order to share the pain.

We busied ourselves with the afternoon's milking. I worked alongside Archie as I tracked with him through the increasingly familiar rituals. It wasn't until we were out supervising the calves feeding that I felt the need to check up on him.

'Are you alright? Seeing your dad like that can be a bit distressing.'

'Yeah, I'm fine. Thanks for asking though. Sometimes it would be a help to have a sibling with whom I could share the load. It's times like this I really miss Charlie. I feel sorry for Mum though. She cops the worst. She always has, but somehow, she keeps being positive. I don't know how. Anyway, I hope you can still manage to help out. That is, if you can cope with us Saddlers.'

I smiled and assured Archie he wouldn't be able to keep me away. And I meant it. So much to entice me to this farm—these adorable calves and this rather interesting man. Provided I could keep as much as possible out of the way of the bad-tempered father, I assured myself I would be fine. After all, what could possibly go wrong? I had my incredibly brave guard dog by my side—the guard dog who was at that moment hiding between my legs, cowering in fear, psyched out by a mob of hungry calves.

Chapter Nineteen

My life settled into a regular rhythm. Each morning, I checked with Mum if I was required at the B&B. Some days she needed me to do my usual—make the beds and clean. But other days I got a reprieve from domesticity as the holiday season was finally drawing to a close. Now we were in early autumn, and the visitors to our region were either older tourists or young families who tended to stay for longer. These visitors were not tied to the school holidays and had time to enjoy the stable autumn weather and late warm currents that make swimming at the beach so much more enjoyable.

My arrangements with Archie continued. Monday to Friday I was up at the farm from about two o'clock each afternoon. This was enough time to help with the set up for milking—to prepare the feed and ensure the equipment was all where it was meant to be. Nippa and I still were tasked with bringing the cows into the dairy yard. I tried to kid myself that Nippa was making great progress, but really, she had a long way to go. We had good days when she obediently trotted at my heel and obeyed any commands that I gave. Then we had bad days when I am sure she was operating according to the orders given by some inner demon. She would bolt to the dam upon our arrival and refuse to come out, or she would scatter the cows just as they were heading in the direction of the dairy. Scattering the cows was done just for the fun of it. However, I had great faith in these cattle. A small pup was no match for them. One afternoon, both Archie and I were reduced to tears of laughter as we watched the matriarch of the herd line up Nippa and charge. That seemed to instil some respect in the dog—at least for a day or so.

Did I enjoy helping Archie? Yes, I think so. There was so much about the experience that was fun: being outdoors, learning a new skill, being surrounded by animals, and—let's be honest—spending time with Archie. Being with Archie had turned out to be much more fun than I had expected. Like his brother, he had a touch of larrikin in him. He could jest and pun with the best of them—when time permitted, that is. Most days we were focussed on getting through our tasks in time. Sometimes, when our day's chores were finished early, and I didn't have to rush home to prepare early dinner for Amy, I would linger. Archie would boil the kettle he kept up at the dairy, and we would drink instant coffee sweetened with condensed milk while sitting on an old bench outside. These were the times I enjoyed most. We talked about everything: current affairs, local gossip, what we have been reading, and ourselves. There was still so much I didn't know about this gentle giant. For instance, I was coming to learn that he could be a thoughtful and articulate person with a mind that was often focussed on matters unconnected with his daily life. He told me he studied Agricultural Science at university and really enjoyed his life living away.

'Why come back then?' I asked.

'There wasn't much choice really. Mum and Dad needed help with running the farm. Once Charlie was gone, it was either I came back, or we sold the farm. And I didn't want that to happen. After all, this farm has been in Dad's family for generations, and it would be hard to let it go. The timing was right. I had just finished my degree and so I returned all fired up with bright ideas as to how to bring the farm into the 21st century and beyond.'

'And have you?'

With a snort and a shake of his head, Archie made it clear that he had not been successful.

He explained: 'It's not that easy trying to convince my father to change. I can't really blame him. After all, he has been milking cows all his life and selling the milk to the co-op. He sees no reason to try any other way. *If it's not broken, why fix it?* is his usual response when I try to talk things through with him. He owns the farm, inherited it from his father, but I really need him to agree to try something different. Even when I show him how our returns are falling each year, and our expenses keep increasing, I just can't change his mind. His solution: *Get a bigger herd.* As if we could manage that! But I won't give up! I'll keep on trying and maybe in time I'll wear him down. I know change is inevitable if we are to survive on this property. I just have to convince him of that. It's only him I need to persuade. Mum understands.'

'What would you do if you could?'

I was genuinely curious by now. I had just thought all dairy farms were the same.

'We can never compete on a large scale. Our farm is too small, as is the set up in our dairy shed, and we don't have the funds or the people to expand. What I have in mind is to go into the premium market. You know, like a sort of boutique dairy—selling a premium product from superior cows. I already know our girls are pretty special and produce top quality milk, but with a bit of marketing and maybe some fresh blood into the herd, we could really shine. There are a few other dairy farmers in the district who are talking of banding together, forming a cooperative of our own and developing a local brand of premium milk. We will need to establish a small processing plant on one of our properties, but it's doable with a bit of planning. Then we could market this product at a higher price to those independent grocers around the region and at the nearby farmer's markets. Maybe one day branch into cheese. But that's a long way off. I just have to keep working on Dad.'

I smiled at Archie encouragingly and wished him luck. It sounded like a good idea to me. But what would I know? I was just an apprentice dairy farmer—and some days I wasn't even sure I was going to make the grade. Like on those wet days when the laneway and the dairy yard were an everlasting quagmire of mud and cow manure. When, even in my gumboots, my feet failed to grip in the slushy ground, and I slipped and slithered as I fetched the cows. I was working by myself on those days, as the not-so-obedient Nippa resolutely refused to leave the comfort of the car.

But when the rain slowed, and the sun ventured forth from behind the clouds and shone on glistening grass and steaming black and white rumps, I had no problem delighting in the beauty that surrounded me. I could even see the humour when I slipped and fell in the mud as I tried to exit the dairy yard. Well … just. It didn't help that Archie appeared to find my situation hilarious as I grudgingly accepted the offer of his hand to pull me upright.

'The look on your face as you went arse over,' he laughed, while flicking some mud (or I think it was mud) from my cheek. 'You were adorable,' he smiled.

That softened the blow somewhat. So, slightly mollified, I permitted myself to be led back into the security of the dairy.

Most days milking was pretty much done, cleaning complete and calves fed by 6 o'clock. Unless we were particularly efficient, there generally was no time for socialising as I would be in a rush to get onto my next job: looking after my sister.

Being the youngest in the family, I've never really had anyone to care for until Nippa came along and inflicted me with her demands. However, her care had been pretty straightforward and rarely begrudged by me. But a pregnant sister? That was something quite different. Being mindful of my responsibility to provide adequate nutrition for my growing niece, I was diligent in my preparation of delicious and nutritious meals. As always, I consulted my mum, who was a mine of information about best recipes. Then I had to take into account my sister's preferences, which were changing on a weekly basis. There were a few occasions where I had not kept up and served a meal that was not to Amy's liking. The first time I did this I had to laugh as the look on Amy's face was priceless. Clearly, she was appalled by my evening offering, but was not sure how to tell me in case I would be offended. As if! Her reluctance to eat the food I prepared just meant there was more for me! All those hours of manual labour not only left me exhausted by the end of the day, but also ravenous.

Amy was also feeling exhausted most evenings, but we still found time to get together for a bit of a chat. It was fun, especially as Amy treated me more like an equal rather than the annoying little sister I used to be.

'You know, Frankie ...,' she said thoughtfully one evening as we relaxed after dinner was tidied away, '... as far as I'm concerned, having you coming to stay has been the best thing. When I think about it, in all those years I still lived at home, we had never spent much time together, just the two of us. When I left home, you were still a little brat. Hah! Don't scowl. You know I'm right. You were always snooping around my room when I wasn't looking and getting into my stuff. Trying on my clothes and stealing my makeup! But now, it's so different. Like I've got a new best friend and someone who is here waiting for me at the end of the day.'

'Well, you could get a dog for that, you know. A dog who would be waiting for your return after work. Mind you, it's kinda fun hearing your news each afternoon. Do you realise you behave in exactly the same way every day?'

'What do you mean?'

'Well, you race your car up the driveway, scream to a halt, slam the car door, and you are yelling out to me before you even reach the door. You know, saying things like: You'll never guess who did/said what today? Always a new adventure. Sometimes I think I'm back on the set of that soapie with a new drama being enacted each day.'

'Yeah, I know what you mean. It's never boring. Temperament and tantrums, and hundreds of children. Their behaviour is totally unpredictable. Let alone that of the teachers. It can get a bit angsty, but I think I'm going to miss it when I go on leave. A baby, no matter how demanding, can't compete with a misbehaving classroom of young tyrants!'

With the passing of each week, I would observe the changes in my sister. The gentle swell in her stomach was becoming more pronounced, as was the amazing chest she was developing. We were both lost in admiration for her bosom.

'It's so unfair,' Amy would wail, while standing sideways admiring her chest in the bathroom mirror. 'Why can't I have this set the rest of the time? Why only when I am pregnant when no one would want to crack onto me anyway?'

'Well not exactly no one. What about Robbie? He seemed interested and he knows you're pregnant. It didn't seem to put him off.'

'Leave it, Frankie.'

Amy's look was stern. That schoolmarm look again.

'Don't go there. I really don't want to talk about him.'

So, I stayed quiet, but somehow Amy then decided she needed to continue the discussion. It was almost as if she was continuing a conversation with herself but speaking it out loud. I sat very still and just listened. This was all so interesting!

'He's rung me several times, you know. Says he just wants to chat. Asks me how I am and what I've been doing. In many ways it is easy to talk to him on the phone when I don't have to look at him and he doesn't see the new me.'

And you don't have to smell him, I thought. But did not say a word.

'He's asked me out to the movies on the weekend. I said I'd think about it, but I don't think I can go. It's just … I feel so ashamed of what I did that night. Getting so drunk and just being so easy to be picked up. I can't help thinking about that night. How determined I was to get back at Shane and how reckless I was. In a way it was lucky for me that Robbie was at the bar that night. If he hadn't made the first move, who would I have ended up with? I could have gone with anyone. No, I should never have slept with him. What was I thinking? How can he want to see me again after that?'

As she spoke, it was obvious Amy was working herself into a state. Her hands twisted against each other, and her face was flushing bright red—with embarrassment or anger, I'm not sure.

I reached across the table and placed one hand on hers to try and comfort her.

'Hey. It's alright. You're only human. We all make mistakes. I certainly can't criticise you. Look at me and what I did in Sydney. You were hurting and so, you were a bit reckless. But it's done and dusted now. You can't go back. Fixating on the past won't change what happened. And really, I don't think Robbie disapproves. If he did, he wouldn't still be in contact and trying to see more of you. It seems to me the only person judging you is yourself. And maybe, just maybe, it's now time to be a bit kinder to yourself.'

Amy smiled at me. Her hand reached out from under my hand and clasped mine with a comforting squeeze. 'You know, little sister, you've become incredibly wise for one so young. Maybe no longer a brat! Perhaps I need to just let go and forget the past.'

She gave her bump a rub and added, giving a slight smile:

'After all, I have a future to look forward to.'

Chapter Twenty

Thoughts of my life in Sydney had fast receded. My every waking moment was focussed on the tasks at hand—helping Mum, being apprentice dairy hand, chef to the pregnant one, or taking advantage of a perfect wave down at the beach.

There had been no further mention of me in the media as far as I was aware, and there was certainly no sign of any paparazzi hanging around. Although Mum assured me it was safe to return home, I declined, telling her I was happy to stay with Amy and give her a hand. My parents seemed to consider this an acceptable excuse and didn't argue any further.

Occasionally, I would miss my Sydney wardrobe. Not that I needed it for day-to-day activities. After all, who needs a little black dress when scrubbing out a bathroom or feeding the slobbering calves? But on the odd occasion Amy and I went out for dinner, or to see the latest movie, I found myself wistfully thinking about those gorgeous clothes still hanging on the racks in Simon's spare room. Or at least, I thought that's where they still were.

Then, one morning Tom rang. It was early. I had just waved Amy off and was about to text Mum to see if I was needed that day at the B&B when the phone rang. I answered it without looking, saying a cheery:

'Hello Mum.'

A deep, instantly recognisable voice put me straight. 'No, Frankie, darling. It's not your mum. Just little old me. Your favourite agent. Have you time to talk?'

'For you, Tom. Of course. All the time in the world. What's up and how are you?'

'Fine, fine. All good here. Way too busy but can't complain. Now I thought I should ring you as the police have just been in contact. We need to have a chat.'

Hearing that, my stomach plummeted, and I quickly sat down onto the kitchen stool.

Tom continued: 'Don't panic, Frankie, but the cops tell me they'll be summonsing you to appear at the coronial inquiry next month. The coroner has apparently decided a hearing is necessary after all. You know, to hear evidence on the circumstances of Gino's death. You were there—obviously. So, you need to give evidence.'

'Evidence?' I squeaked. 'Evidence. About what?'

'What happened on the night.'

'On the night? Tell them everything?'

I could feel the panic start to rise.

'You'll be answering questions of course from the counsel assisting the coroner. They'll talk you through the events of the evening, so the coroner can get a good picture of what took place.'

Oh no. That is so not a picture a coroner or anyone else needs to have.

I squeaked on. 'Surely they have enough information. I gave a statement to the police when I was still in hospital. Remember? Won't that be enough? Can't I just refuse to attend?'

'No, Frankie. You are what they consider a material witness. Of course, your statement will be tendered and become part of the evidence, but there may be other questions they want to ask. Not definitely, but there may be. After all, to be blunt, among other things, the coroner has to rule out the question of whether you dragged Gino to his death. We all know the rail snapped, but there has to be evidence to prove this and rule out other possibilities.'

He paused, as if struck by another thought. 'Frankie, you sound a bit odd. You're not ill, are you?'

'No. Just terrified,' I replied.

'Look, I can't say it won't be distressing for you but I'm afraid it is unavoidable. You must attend. I've already thought this might be how you would feel. So, I had a chat with Simon, and we've arranged for a solicitor friend of ours to be there at the inquest—to represent you that is. He'll be there to protect your interests and if he sees the questioning going along in any direction that might be ending up in blaming you for the incident, he'll go into battle on your behalf. Are you okay with that?'

Am I okay? Not sure. This whole affair was so outside my life experience, but I supposed having someone there with me on the day who was familiar with legal process had to be an advantage. I nodded, and then realised I was on the phone, not Skype. As you could guess, I was rattled.

'I suppose that will be fine,' I said slowly, dragging out each word, my method of delivery clearly giving lie to the words I was saying. I was so not fine, but I now understood that my attendance at the inquest was inevitable.

'When do I have to be in Sydney? I'm assuming I must see the solicitor some time before?'

'That's right. I'll ring the police to confirm the date and let you know. Maybe you should arrange to get up here a week before. That'll give you time to get organised and also give you the opportunity to see all your friends. It's time you got reacquainted with the city and with us.'

After the call ended, I took a moment to sit and focus on calming myself. I had a vague recollection that shortly after the incident I had been warned there was a chance the coroner might convene a hearing, but I had blanked that out. Giving the statement to the police officer had been painful enough. At the time I just wanted to run away and forget what had happened. Certainly, I did run away—back to my parents, just like the small child I still was inside.

But forget? No, that wasn't possible. Sometimes at night I still dreamt of that moment when I hit the water, the skirt of my dress billowing around me, soaking up the water and dragging me down. I would wake, choking and thrashing about just as I must have done as I sank down into the harbour's depths. No, I had not forgotten. But maybe it was time to accept what had happened. I could not change the outcome, but somehow, I must find the courage to understand that my time in Sydney, the good and the bad, all had contributed to make me the person I now had become. Perhaps it was time to accept that I, like everyone else, could also make mistakes. Perhaps, like my sister, I also needed to be kinder to myself.

But this was easier said than done. For the rest of the day, I brooded on my conversation with Tom. I mulled it over while ferociously scrubbing out bathrooms at the B&B and as I raced Nippa along the beach. I was still preoccupied with these persistent thoughts when I arrived at the farm and headed for the dairy, head down staring intently at the ground.

Archie, standing in wait by the dairy gate, greeted me. 'Looking for treasure, are you? There's nothing here on this farm but cow pats. And they're no use to anyone around here. They're everywhere.'

I looked up and stared into his face so warmly welcoming. It was so tempting to share, but what would he say? What would he think of me then? For some reason, Archie's good opinion was now important to me.

'Spit it out.' This time he spoke in a gentler, more persuasive, voice. Archie opened the gate and ushered Nippa and me in. Well, only me really. Nippa was more preoccupied in jumping up on Archie than moving quietly through the gate.

'You savage beast you. Think you can attack me, huh? Down. No jumping you. Come on, let's help your mistress get the cows in and she can tell me what's bothering her. Friends remember, Frankie. I've shared my worries with you. Now it's your turn.'

As we walked down the laneway to the closed gate behind which the girls were queueing, I explained what had happened this morning. Archie listened and didn't interrupt. He just let me dump my concerns on him.

'It's not like I didn't know this could happen. Tom and Simon both warned me there could be a risk the coroner wouldn't find cause of death based on the witness statements alone and would want to hear further evidence in case there was some safety issue to be considered. But the thought of talking about that night is terrifying and makes me feel ill. There's also the prospect of running the gauntlet of the press at the inquest. Now that will be just plain terrifying!'

'You won't be alone,' Archie reminded me. 'Simon and Tom will have your back and there's this solicitor who'll also be there to protect you. You've dealt with the media before and don't forget, they still love you—the innocent victim in all of this.'

'How do you know that?'

'I may live the isolated life of a simple farmer, but I'm not completely out of touch,' he said with a smile. 'You were the rising young actress, loved by all. The mystery about how you just disappeared seems to fascinate people. So young, so glamorous, and so badly treated by the management of that show. If they could see you now—up to your ankles in cow shit—they'd feel even sorrier for you!'

'Bastard,' I said, elbowing him in his side. 'You knew about what happened all along? But you never said anything. Why?'

'Old news, I guess, and really—haven't we all moved on? The Frankie I see every day is the one I'm interested in knowing.'

What did he mean by that, I wonder? Could it be my friend here fancied me? But just as this question was taking shape in my mind and before I could ask him, Archie rushed on, almost as if he was feeling embarrassed that he had said too much.

'You know, this inquest could be a good thing for you.'

I snorted in disbelief.

'Yeah, really. You see, this could be a way of everyone getting closure. Not just you, but his family too and the cast. So many people were affected by what happened on that terrible night, and no doubt so many questions are still left unanswered. If the coroner can set things right, then that might bring some comfort and let people move on with their life. You just have to be brave, Frankie. I know you can. Look how you managed after Charlie died. '

We reached the gate and the milling cattle. With the conversation over, we focussed on the job at hand. Yet, I still found time to smile across at Archie and mouth my thanks. He contented himself with a thumbs up as we both moved behind the cattle to encourage them forward. Nippa, I noticed, was nowhere in sight. My not-so-brave cattle dog was fast maturing into a wimp.

Chapter Twenty-One

Unlike the last time, this time when I caught the bus to Sydney, I knew to where I was headed. The scenery we trekked through was familiar and the trip seemed to be so much shorter. Like last time, Simon met me at Central Station. It was a more subdued meeting, but still welcoming. We cuddled, searched for my luggage, and headed off to locate his car, which was some blocks away. Simon grumbled as we walked along a crowded street.

'This city. I swear it gets more crowded with each week. The trouble I had finding a car park tonight! No wonder I very rarely bring my car into town. It's just too much trouble. Ah, here we are.'

His car was located in a cramped and dingy laneway. With my luggage stowed in the back seat, we both piled in and headed off down busy roads to Balmain. This time, the lights of the city were familiar to me and no longer a novelty, although it had been some time since I was last here. As if reading my mind, Simon intruded into my thoughts:

'It's been a while since you were last here. How long do you reckon?'

'More than six months, I think. You brought me home just before Christmas, remember?'

'That's right. Seems longer ago than that, but I guess that is because I've been so busy. The office is booming. So much work. But we've all missed you. Ruth and I at home, and the gang at work also. They want to catch up if you think you can manage it.'

'I've missed them too. There's no one quite like any of you

down home,' I said, thinking of the much simpler life I had been living. Like I had been existing in a different world.'

Ruth must have been listening out for our return for no sooner had Simon parked the car in a vacant space immediately in front of the house (a miracle according to Simon), than the front door opened. A beam of light shone forth, and a figure rushed out the door and down the front path with arms open wide.

'Frankie, darling Frankie. You're home at last. We've both missed you so. Without you there's been no one here to referee our spats or make Simon tidy up.'

I was immediately wrapped in loving arms and squeezed tight. Then Ruth loosened her arms and stepped back while still gently holding onto me. I could feel myself being examined by critical eyes and inwardly cringed. I was so not looking too *Sydney* at the moment.

Ruth's words confirmed this.

'Let me look at you. My, you look so different to last time I saw you—at Christmas when you were so successfully channelling *cancer chic* (you see? Ruth still has that PR flair for words!) Still favouring the waif look, I see. But really, who is doing your hair these days? It's a bit ... well, I don't know how to say it ...'

'Scruffy?'

'Yes, that might describe it. But you look fit. Sort of muscly and with an outdoors glow about you. Is there a good gym down your way?'

'Sort of, I guess. The dairy farm gym I suppose you could call it. That and the daily bathroom cleaning workout have been doing wonders for my fitness. Maybe I should start a blog and share my gems of wisdom.'

'Hah,' said Simon as he followed us in and plonked my bags down just inside my bedroom door. 'As your PR adviser, I suggest you hold off on that idea until you rework your image. No one is going to take advice from someone who looks like they were dragged in by the cat!'

'A bit of respect, laddie,' said Ruth as she hit his arm in mock anger. Even I could sense the electricity that sparked between these two and regarded them with interest. Has something been going on here in my absence? Was my beloved brother somehow involved with gorgeous, gentle and kind Ruth? Fantastic if that was the case. I couldn't ask for a better person to keep my brother in check. I made a mental note to keep a close eye on these two while I was staying with them—starting with monitoring who sleeps where.

We headed into the kitchen where Simon ferreted in the fridge and located a chilled bottle of Australian sparkling.

'I've been saving this to share with you, Frankie. It's one of Australia's finest and made by a client of the firm. We can always get more at a discount if you like it. Ruth, any chance of locating some glasses in this dive of a kitchen?'

He popped the cork to cheers from us and then poured the sparkling wine into three glasses. Silliness prevailed as we each took turns in proposing toasts. We drank and toasted each other over and over again, in between bouts of giggles from all of us.

Simon leaned back in his chair, wiped his lips with the back of his hand and gazed at me thoughtfully. 'Hairdo aside, it seems to me, Frankie, that you look amazingly well for someone who has spent more than six months in quarantine in that hick town. Whatever you have been doing must be agreeing with you. Do share,' he said with his trademark wicked grin.

'Hick town! Not at all. It's been great to be home and yeah, it's surprising even to me that I have settled back so easily. It has helped being busy of course—with Mum and helping Archie.'

'Archie?' chimed both Ruth and Simon.

Oh dear, I forgot. They know nothing about Archie. I know how Simon's mind worked and I suspect Ruth was just as bad. So, I continued as if there was nothing to be suspicious of and that my working arrangements were all very boring and matter of fact. Which they were, although I was starting to suspect that I might not mind if there was something else going on. You see it was such fun spending time with Archie. Could it be the fun you have with a friend? Or could it be something more?

Resolutely I pushed that thought to one side and focussed on the questioning faces in front of me.

'You remember Archie, Simon?'

Simon shook his head.

'Nope. Can't say I do.'

'Archie Saddler. Charlie's brother.'

'Oh, that Archie,' Simon said knowingly with wide open eyes and then shook his head.

'Nope.'

'He was at school about the same time as our Amy. Maybe in her year? I haven't bothered to ask her. Anyway, we have got to know each other, largely because of that dog you all gave me for Christmas. Well, she came from their farm. Archie needed some help with the afternoon milking, and I was looking for something else to do so I now lend a hand during the week. Beats cleaning showers and making beds, and I get paid too. It's pretty full on. Lots to do and I think I've got potential as an animal handler. I found I actually like the cattle, especially the calves.'

'And Mum tells me you're living with Amy. Aren't the parents good enough for you?'

I shook my head.

'No, not at all. It all happened when the press was hovering a while back. Mum suggested I move over to Amy's place. I can't believe I didn't think of it myself. It's been fun. Mind you, she's pretty bossy, but so far, I've passed muster. Lucky for me, she's focussed on the baby and her job. I'm not sure if I'll stay once the baby's born, but I guess if Amy needs me then I will.'

Simon and Ruth exchanged glances and some silent communication passed between them. I took such mastery of silent messaging as confirmation that they were definitely much closer.

'So, you don't think you would like to return to Sydney permanently and maybe find some more acting work? I'm sure Tom could hustle you up some work if you wished.' said Ruth.

I shook my head.

'I don't think so. I wouldn't rule it out, but it's like my life has moved on. Anyway, if the inquest is a complete disaster, then an acting career will be a non-event.'

Not long afterwards, I was shunted off to my room with orders from Simon and Ruth to rest and try to sleep in. I tried to linger so I could discreetly discover the current sleeping arrangements of my housemates. But they were ahead of me and disappeared into separate bedrooms. I could only assume that it must be the early days of any possible romance.

I settled into my familiar bed and smelled the distinctive smells of this old, often shut up home. That smell of old timber overlaid by remnant smoke odours embedded in walls from wood fires long ago was still detectable, and underneath it all there was a lingering musty odour of age and lack of ventilation. With a sigh, I rolled over and invited sleep to come. And it did.

The next day was Sunday. We had arranged to meet the old work gang for lunch at a café in a rustic restored factory in downtown Alexandria. It was obviously on trend, judging by the masses of people in hipster attire already there or queuing for a table. We took our places in the queue and miracle of miracles, a table was soon ready and prepared for us.

The time spent queuing had not been wasted. I had been swamped with affection and questions from my old workmates. Lena, Jasmine and Mark took turns peppering me with inquiries about life down the South Coast.

'Is living there the same as how life is portrayed on the TV soapies?' Jasmine asked, a city girl through and through.

'No way,' I explained. 'Much more boring,' I said. 'But with better surf and no crowds. Also different to the city in that everyone knows who you are and what you have been doing. That takes a bit of getting used to!'

Now settled at the table and our orders taken, I applied myself to catching up on their news. No point my doing all the talking as I had nothing exciting to report. I suspected my stories regarding the intricacies of dairy farming would so not do it for this gang.

Lena assured me that I was much missed in the office. Not only for my sunny personality—at this Simon choked on his drink—but also for my help managing the workload. She assured me that work had been incredibly busy with so many new, exciting and demanding clients. At this, the others all took turns to interrupt and talk over each other as in their enthusiasm they detailed the various catastrophes, or near catastrophes, they had dealt with as part of the day-to-day challenges of being in PR. I listened and found myself missing life in the world of public relations, where every day brought a new adventure and most evenings presented some exciting social opportunity—a launch, a first night, or just cocktails with clients. Nothing like that in my hometown.

Over shared platters of middle eastern delights, the chatter and laughter continued. It was so easy to forget why I had returned to Sydney and just let myself relax into the camaraderie of good friends, fine wine and fantastic food. It wasn't until sometime later, as we sipped our coffees, that reality returned. Mark brought me back to Earth when he asked what I had planned for the following week. Simon and I exchanged glances.

'Well, it's the coronial inquiry later in the week and I understand I have to spend some time with my solicitor before that,' I said.

Mark looked embarrassed, as if he has been caught out referring to a topic that was unmentionable in polite company. You know, like I had the pox or bad breath or something like that.

'Oops, sorry,' he muttered and looked anywhere but at me. I felt sorry for him. Sure, I didn't want to talk about it, but it looked like it would be impossible to now avoid the conversation.

'It's alright, everyone. I know it's a bit like the elephant in the room, but there's no point in ignoring why I'm here. Of course, I should be here to spend time with you all, and it's an added bonus that I can today. But next week I have to face up to what has to be done and give evidence if that's what the coroner wants. I keep hoping they will change their mind and not call me. But if it happens, so be it. I'm pretty terrified though.'

To a reassuring chorus of encouragement from my support team, I smiled and assured them I would cope—somehow.

Chapter Twenty-Two

Simon had arranged for me to meet the solicitor early the following week. He must have more empathy than I thought as somehow, sensing my apprehension, he assured me that he would accompany me to the first meeting.

'Not that you really need me there. You can manage on your own, but I suppose a bit of moral support might come in handy,' he said, much to my unspoken relief.

'Thanks. I'm sure it will be fine, but you never know ...' my voice trailed off as I miserably contemplated my brother. 'It's just that I have never been to an inquest before. I've no idea what will happen and the thought of giving evidence ... well, quite frankly it terrifies me. How will I know what to say? And I suppose the press will be there. It's just going to be awful. I can sense it.'

By now I was trying so hard not to cry. But I was failing. Tears welled and fell. My nose started to run with snotty drops as I choked with rasping sobs. That's right—my crying has never been a thing of beauty. I am not the sort of sobbing woman that people rush to comfort. They're more likely to turn away in disgust. Simon, to his credit, stayed by my side, passed me a box of tissues, and gave only a minor wince when I blew my nose with a loud honk. He looked thoughtful and observed me as I calmed myself.

'Frankie. Trust me. I know you can do this. Think about some of the emotional scenes in which you were involved on that soapie. Weren't some of those a bit fraught ... a bit stressful?'

'I suppose so. And?'

'What I mean is … weren't you worried that you couldn't manage it, yet somehow you did? I seem to recall you working yourself into a right state some nights when you were learning your lines.'

'Yeah, I remember many nights like that. So?'

'You pulled it off. You did it and performed convincingly. Would it help if you approached your giving evidence as a bit like an acting scene? You've already given a statement to the police. You'll still remember what it says, and chances are the questions will, by and large, be about the contents of that statement. So, remember your lines, be respectful and polite, and act. And tell the truth of course. You owe that much to Gino after all. There must be a reason why the railing snapped and maybe we'll find out why and prevent it from ever happening again.'

Sometimes Simon spoke a lot of sense. Not that I would ever tell him that. There's only so much flattery a sibling should give. I pondered what he had said and could feel myself becoming much more comfortable about what I was about to face. Sure, I was still feeling nervous, but I knew what happened on that night. After all, I was the one physically closest to Gino when the railing gave way. I was familiar with my statement and as my solicitor assured me, he would also be in court with me, and I needed to remember that his role was to protect me. A bit like having my own Rottweiler beside me, he told me.

The solicitor, an old university friend of Simon's, was called Ernest—a name well chosen by his parents as it was so in keeping with his manner. He was serious, methodical and seemingly trustworthy. Physically, he had the appearance of a bodyguard— maybe even a bit Rottweiler like. He had black hair, brown eyes, and those well-developed muscles of a dedicated gym goer. I liked him on first sight. This was a man I could trust to have my back.

I met with him on two occasions that week. Once with Simon. This first time was a *get to know you meeting*. At this meeting, Ernest outlined the procedure at the inquest and what I should expect. He told me that I should assume I would be called to give evidence early on during the coronial hearing, as I was one of the witnesses who could describe the events of that night. The more detailed expert witnesses he would expect to come afterwards. They would be called to give evidence about what could have caused the collapse of the railing.

At our second meeting, this time without Simon's presence, Ernest and I reviewed the statement I gave to the police. Ernest took me through it line by line to confirm that the details were correct. He then asked whether I had left anything out or whether there was anything I had remembered since giving that statement.

'You know any little aspect, no matter how small, that could explain why the incident happened?'

'Not really.'

I wrinkled my forehead in thought.

'You see, I had drunk a fair bit that night and it is all a bit of a blur. It's like I said, I was just by myself in the corner, wishing I could go home, when Gino appeared, sweet talked me and for once my defences were down. Normally, I would tell him to go jump, but in the nicest possible way as he wasn't a complete sleaze. Maybe, because I was a bit tired or feeling slightly down, his charm seemed to work and … yeah … I remember laughing and then kissing and it becoming a bit passionate. Do I have to give all the details?'

'Only if you are asked and only what you can recall. The counsel assisting will most likely be interested in the moment in time when the railing collapsed. What can you remember? Was it a snap? Or was there a warning crack before you tipped over?'

'It's so hard to say. Like I said, it is all a bit fuzzy, and I really was focussing on the kissing and the rest. I wasn't paying attention to the surroundings. When I play it back in my mind, one minute I am clasping Gino, the next I am falling. And, you know, even if there had been the sound of a snap or the like, the music was really loud and I'm not sure I would have heard it.'

'There's one other thing,' Ernest drew a deep breath. 'It's possible they might try to say you pulled him into the water—

deliberately. You need to be prepared for this. You may or may not be asked such a question.'

'Are you kidding? Why would I want to? I had no issues with Gino. Sure, he was a bit of a lad, trying it on with all the females. But he did it in such a charming way he had lots of interest and never had to force himself on anyone. And anyway, did you ever see the size of him? There's no way little old me would have the strength to pull him over. No way!'

Ernest nodded his head, as if satisfied with my response.

'Yes, that should do. Just answer the questions politely and concisely and make sure your responses are consistent with your statement. Oh, and remember, I'll be there to object to any line of questioning that looks a bit dodgy. It shouldn't come to that as the cause of death looks fairly straightforward. I suspect there will be some interest by the boat owner or their insurer, who might be trying to get a finding of a defective handrail, so they can go after the manufacturer.'

I left Ernest's office feeling somewhat comforted. Over a cup of coffee in a nearby trendy café, I tried my hardest to recall the night but with no further success. My memories were what I told the police at the time—alcohol induced fuzzy.

I finished my coffee and headed for my favourite department store, mindful of Ernest's directive to wear something to the inquest that was sombre, stylish, but not too sophisticated. I was to look respectable with a nod to the latest fashions, but not too designer. He told me I should style my look to appear like a well-dressed, ordinary person and not someone who was mega rich.

With an outfit selected and purchased, I made a quick visit to a nearby hairdresser for a tidy up. My hair, still very short, shaggy and sun streaked, didn't lend itself to much by way of extreme styling. Yet afterwards I was rather happy with my artfully feathered, gamine hairdo—a bit Audrey Hepburn, I thought. Now, all I needed to do was find some fake pearls and I would be the proper lady.

The night before the inquest, I was a mass of nerves. Ruth and Simon took me to a local trendy eatery for dinner and did their best to cheer me up.

'You'll be fine, Frankie. It was an accident. Nothing you nor Gino could have predicted,' said Ruth, patting me on my trembling hand.

'Yeah,' agreed Simon. 'Sometimes shit happens. There's nothing you can do or say that will change what happened. Things go wrong every day. This is just another one of them. We can't bring Gino back, but maybe we can make sure it never happens again.'

I nodded and tried to focus on the menu before me. Somehow, I was not at all hungry, but did my best to eat something to please my companions.

My parents and my sister were both in contact that evening. Mum and Dad rang and bombarded me with love and affection and assurances that my dog was pining away without me. I found it hard to believe the latter as I was sure young Nippa was being over indulged and spoilt by her pseudo grandparents.

Amy texted wishing me good luck and then immediately rang to share what to her was more exciting news than any court appearance.

'You have to come back straight away as soon as you are finished with that inquest. Things are much more exciting down here. The sprog is turning into a real dynamo. You know those fish flutters I was feeling in my tummy? Well, they've turned into real thumps. By the time you get home you should be able to feel it from the outside. Such fun! Now it is starting to feel like I am really pregnant and there is an actual baby in there.'

'Don't worry. I'll be back home as soon as I can.'

After ending the call, I stared thoughtfully at my phone. What I had just said, I meant. This city no longer filled me with excitement. Despite Tom's ongoing promises of an acting career still ahead of me, I felt no urge to return to those days. Maybe I didn't have it in me to be an actor. After all, the part in *On the Rocks* had never actually tested me. What I was doing in that soapie wasn't really acting and was more like an extension of my life as a surfie chick. In many respects, to succeed in that role, all I needed to do was be myself.

But it was more than that. Since I returned home, there had been an amazing change in my life, and in me. Incrementally, my focus had moved away from the big city and away from myself. Maybe my time away had helped me work through the grief of losing Charlie, and once more opened me up to creating a life in a small coastal town. Or maybe I was finally growing up and becoming an adult. Yet, whatever the reason, I had been changing. With each day, I had become more closely connected to the abundant natural environment, and more accepting of the necessary cleaning and tidying tasks—although sometimes, I really resented the bathroom cleaning. Why is it that guests always dump towels on the floor and splash water (or worse) everywhere? With every day, I had been given the opportunity to delight in contact with the sea and with the surrounding countryside.

Some of this was not a change, more a refresher. From when I was a small child, I was always the beach girl, but now, as a result of my work on the Saddler farm, I was starting to wonder if there wasn't also a bit of farm girl in me. Tramping through grassy paddocks and the connectedness with the elements felt so real and was starting to ignite some primal feeling inside of me. Even when I walked so carefully avoiding cow pats or was trying not to get stuck in the mud, there was always some subliminal part of me that was registering the bird song or sensing the wind on my cheek. It was all so authentic, and nature had me at her mercy—too hot, too cold, too wet, animals too demanding, too uncooperative, or too friendly. But nothing was fake or pretend. I did a job and I saw the outcome.

I had no doubts. I would return home as soon as I could. The answer was clear. There was no other life for me. Why then had it taken me so long to realise this?

Chapter Twenty-Three

I'm not going to drag you through the coronial inquiry proceedings blow by blow. Let me just say it was as awful as I had expected. Representatives from the press were there in droves. Flanked by Ernest and Simon, I ran the gauntlet of the media pack when we arrived that morning. In accordance with Simon's directions, I put my head down and walked into the courthouse ignoring the scores of questions being hurled at me. Actually, it was easy to ignore their questioning. With all the noise from their cacophony of shouting, it was almost impossible to distinguish between the individual voices.

That morning I had been a mass of nerves. If I had eaten any breakfast, I would not have kept it down. I felt awful. But at least I could console myself that I would present well on that night's TV news or in the printed press. My outfit was perfect. Well, in my opinion it was—a black strappy dress with matching bolero jacket. Not too short and not cut too low, and with a double strand of fake pearls that looked convincingly real. I also wore matching pearl earrings. I thought it set just the right note. Ernest also seemed to approve, judging by the quick once over he gave me when we collected him on the way.

The coroner's court was not in the central business district as I had expected. It was located a short distance away in Glebe. The building was a triumph of all things sixties and built in a Soviet bloc style—grey, functional, and not a thing of beauty. Located on such a busy road, it was a relief to run the gauntlet of the press and get inside away from the noise.

Proceedings commenced promptly at ten. I sat up the back of the room beside Simon and Ernest along with quite a few other people. In the crowd, I could identify some other members of the cast, all dressed in sombre colours. There were also some suited men—the other witnesses perhaps? Gino's widow arrived just before ten and sat in the front row. Her image of grieving widow was somewhat contradicted by the way in which she hung off the arm of her new man. Some top shot footballer or so I had read about in the latest gossip magazine the day before when I was at the hairdresser.

The coroner, a woman of severe appearance, commenced the proceedings by reminding us why we were there and what her role in the proceedings would be. She explained that the legislation gave her the responsibility to make a number of findings: the identity of the deceased (pretty obvious in this case); the date, place and cause of death (again, a no-brainer); and finally, the manner of death. She also noted that as the coroner she had an additional power if she thought it appropriate—to make any recommendations. These would be recommendations that, if implemented, would improve public health and safety in the future. Quite a responsibility really. Already the coroner had my sympathy.

Several people were called to give evidence as to what happened on the night. They included the producer of *On the Rocks*, Dana da Silva, who had made the arrangements to hire the cruiser for the party, the skipper, and the crew member who had been in the vicinity when the incident happened. Then I was called and with trembling legs, I walked to the witness stand and was sworn in.

My evidence was straightforward. I was shown my statement, asked if it was correct and made by me, or something technical like that. I said it was and the statement was then tendered. I was then asked a few questions by the counsel assisting. These were questions largely about what I could recall about what happened. As I had said in the statement, I didn't remember much, and I reminded my questioner of this. There were some questions about what exactly I could remember when the railing gave way behind us. I was able to explain it all happened so quickly that the main thing I remembered was hitting the water and the chill of the harbour as I sank. From one line of questioning, it was apparent there was some thought it might be possible that I had pulled Gino over with me. Not possible I firmly responded. He was so much bigger and stronger than me. At that point, I was feeling rather cross. How dare they try to imply it was my fault. It was Gino who was the instigator of our contact. Not that I said that.

I was asked if I recalled hearing a noise—a crack or some sort of sound as the railing gave way. Again, I was able to explain that the music was so loud it was impossible to hear anything else. Conversation was next to impossible unless one shouted and I would expect any sound, like a crack of something breaking, would be drowned out. Probably not the best choice of words in the circumstances and maybe that is why the barrister doing the questioning let the matter drop.

There were a few questions about what I could recall when I hit the water—was I aware of where Gino was, for instance. As I spoke, I thought back to what I could remember of those few moments when I hit the water, and how the water's coolness shocked me into a momentary state of awareness before I lost consciousness. My dress, with its full skirt, had billowed out as I fell. When I hit the water, I suppose it then acted like some sort of anchor dragging me under. I explained that, even if I had had time to look for Gino, I was too panicked to do anything as I felt myself being sucked under by the sodden weight of my clothes. And, I added, it was dark around me. I could hear splashing and assumed it was Gino. I remembered calling out and then sinking, my calls being choked as I inhaled water.

There were no other questions after that, and I was excused. Surprisingly, I was thanked by the coroner for my assistance. My distress at reliving the events of that evening must have been all too obvious.

Ernest and Simon escorted me from the court, and we headed to a nearby coffee shop. The press had given up on their stakeout. Presumably, they had all the photos they needed, and we were able to walk along the footpath unimpeded.

We found a vacant booth at the back of the coffee shop. With our orders taken, we relaxed, and I was encouraged to debrief.

'Well done you,' said Ernest. 'You didn't need me there at all. You managed perfectly on your own.'

'I told you she would be fine,' smiled Simon. 'Just no one believed me. But I know my sister. She's tough. Mind you, I think you were let off lightly. Not many questions at all, and none about what you and Gino were actually up to when it all went arse up—literally!'

I tried to repress a shudder and failed.

'It was hard enough giving evidence. I'm not sure how I would have managed if they had gone into the details.'

'Burst into tears. Works every time,' advised Ernest.

'I almost did. When he was asking me to describe what happened after we had landed in the water, I could feel myself choking up. You know, remembering the sound of all that splashing makes me wonder if I had been able to get to Gino, could I have saved him? If it wasn't for that dress …' my voice trailed off as I contemplated how different the night would have been if say, I had worn trousers and not some flowing gown.

'Maybe, maybe not,' said my brother, ever the pragmatic one. 'It's amazing you didn't drown as well. Especially with that amount of alcohol in your system. Speaking of which, I suppose the evidence about the autopsy will record the amount of cocaine in Gino's system. That, on top of the alcohol he no doubt consumed, would have slowed him down. Tom tells me Gino wasn't much of a swimmer at the best of times. A bit ironic for someone who had a starring role in a seaside soapie. But there you go.'

After that we chatted desultorily about this and that: Ernest's *get fit* programme and how he would much rather do nothing.

Simon waxed lyrical about the latest must-visit restaurant and must-see bands etc. Me? Well, I just sat there, trying to drink my coffee with still trembling hands and not really listening at all to the conversation that flowed around me. Simon glanced across with one eyebrow raised.

'Penny for them?'

'I can't believe it's over. Ever since that awful night, the thought has been lurking at the back of my mind that there would have to be an inquest and I would be called to give evidence. The thought was always hovering there in the background like some sort of boogie man, even though I did my best to try to ignore it. Now it's done and dusted. I'm not sure if I should be feeling elated that it's all behind me. Well, I don't. I think I feel numb. Is that it? Is it really over?'

I looked across at Ernest. Surely, he will know the answer to this.

'It's over for you, that's for sure. The rest of the proceedings will be taken up with technical evidence about what caused the rail to break away. That is, if it is clear what happened. There may be no explanation. But if there is, then it could be a public safety issue and the coroner might wish to make an observation or a recommendation in her decision.'

We left soon after that. Ernest headed off to the bus stop to catch a bus to work. He gave me a quick hug and after urging me to contact him at any time if I had any questions, he ran to wave down an approaching bus.

Simon and I headed down a side street to find the car. He put his arm around me and for once I found comfort in my brother's reassuring closeness.

'Are you okay? Do you want to come back to the office and see the gang? I'm sure I can find something for to do if you like.'

I shook my head.

'Best I go back to your place. I think I need to be by myself this afternoon. Just to clear my head and give some thought to what I should do now. It's like everything has ended and I don't know what to do next. Like I can't go back to how it was. Does that make sense?'

'I suppose so,' responded my brother, never the deep thinker.

He left me out the front of his cute Balmain cottage, parked his car, and with a casual wave, he wandered down the road to the ferry terminal. I let myself inside the house and stood still, not able to decide which room to go into. If such a simple decision was beyond me, how could I possibly decide what to do with the rest of my life?

But I was not to know that the decision would soon be made for me.

Chapter Twenty-Four

When Amy rang me the next day, I knew immediately that something was wrong. The tone of her voice gave it away. Not her usual high energy and in command tone, but a quieter, more subdued Amy spoke.

'What's wrong?' I asked. No point in beating around the bush.

Then I heard sobs. Quiet sobs. Not the dramatic ones that I'm known for.

'Tell me. What's wrong?' I repeated.

'I didn't know who else to talk to. Sorry to hassle you like this when you have problems of your own.'

'I have no problems anymore. They're all behind me,' I said.

With a feeling of relief, I realised that this was entirely true and not just something I was saying to appease my sister.

'So, tell me.'

Amy explained that she had been to the health clinic that morning. She had woken up feeling anxious about the baby as it had been almost twelve hours since she had felt any movement. Amy told herself that it was because she had been so busy at work and maybe the baby was just resting. But when there was still no movement by the morning, Amy was starting to feel seriously concerned.

'It's not like I've had a baby before, but it just seems strange that the baby has suddenly gone quiet. So, I rang in sick and made an appointment to see the GP. Anyway, the doctor tried to find a heartbeat with their ultrasound but said she couldn't find anything for certain. The doctor said there was a slight chance she could hear a heartbeat, but she wasn't sure if it was my own. She told me to get to the hospital, where they will do some further tests and I'm on my way now. Someone is taking my class, so I don't have to worry about them—not that I am at the moment. It's a bit of a drive, as you know, but I'm hoping you can meet me there?'

'Absolutely,' I said.

There was no doubt in my mind. I had to be there as soon as possible to help my sister.

'I'll take Simon's car. Have you rung Mum?'

'I don't want to worry her until I know for certain something's wrong.'

Her voice transformed into a wail. 'Oh, Frankie. I've just got a bad feeling about this. Everything was going so well. I was over all that up chucking and was feeling fine. Had started to accept I was going to be a mum, and was even beginning to enjoy being pregnant and now … I'm just praying it's all okay. But somehow, I think it isn't. Please get here as soon as you can.'

'On my way as soon as I call Simon. Text me with the details of where you are, and I'll be there as soon as I can. Hang in there.'

After I hung up, I rang Simon who immediately offered me the use of his car. I'd planned to take it anyway.

'It's not like I need it. I hardly ever use it anyway. Take it and hang onto it. If I need it back, I'll contact you. The keys are on the hook in the kitchen.'

'I know,' I said, jangling the keys in my hand.

'Let me know how you and Amy get on. If there's anything I can do to help, please call. Glad you can help, Frankie.'

The car went like a dream, and I contemplated whether I could somehow forget to return it. I can't see why Simon really needed it in the city and it sure beat driving Mum's little puddle jumper.

The drive took forever. Not that there was a lot of traffic to contend with, but because my thoughts were racing, everything seemed to be taking longer, even when it actually wasn't. My mind was in overdrive, contemplating a myriad of dire possibilities and wishing for a positive outcome. I did my best to bargain with the gods or whoever it is up there that controls our fate. Generally, I'm not much of a fan of deities, but in this instance, I was sure Amy needed all the help that could be found.

True to her word, Amy texted me with the details of the hospital and ward where she was waiting. It had been a few hours since I had left Sydney, and when I finally tracked her down, I found an Amy so much different to the one I farewelled the other week. Sitting forlorn and alone in a chair outside an empty hospital room, her appearance was somehow diminished. Smaller and less colourful than the Amy I last saw. She looked up at the sound of my approach. Reddened eyes in a blotched face regarded me. No sign of hope in that face. I could only assume that the news was bad.

Still dressed in her everyday clothes, the type of clothes she wore to work—bright shirt and sensible trousers—she looked like any other young mother-to-be waiting for a check-up and passing time by rubbing her swelling belly. Yet, the sorrowful look on her face made it clear that this was not just any routine check-up. I drew close and sat on the chair next to Amy, clasped her in my arms and rubbed her back.

'Hey. I'm here,' I said, stating the bleeding obvious, but by that stage I really didn't know what to say. Yet, somehow my words, or just my presence, seemed to be enough. Amy looked at me and through her tears she spoke.

'It's not good news I'm afraid. The nurse did an ultrasound but couldn't find a heartbeat. She's sent for the obstetrician. He will do some other test, can't remember its name though. She was trying to be reassuring, but I could see from the expression on her face that she had no doubt my baby has died. I have to wait while they track him down. There's nothing I can do but wait. It's the waiting I can't stand.'

'Oh, Amy. I'm so sorry. I wish I had been here with you and not up in Sydney. To deal with this on your own is just so awful.'

'You're here now.' Amy managed a watery smile and then continued: 'Last night I sensed something wasn't quite right. But I convinced myself it was just that me and bub were tired, so I went to bed early. It was strange. I slept so soundly. No baby kicking me awake, I suppose When I woke this morning, I felt different—heavy—like the baby was a blob with no kicks and rolls of life like she had been. I did what the books said. I had a glass of really cold water to shock the bub into moving, but nothing happened. Then I thought a sugar hit might work. I had a Mars bar for breakfast—can you believe it? Tasted so good, but again, nothing! Just my worst nightmare. Deep down I already knew motherhood was never going to happen to me.'

Her voice ascended into a wail and then converted into racking sobs. They were dry sobs, but it was clear from Amy's reddened eyes and puffy face that she had spent much of this morning crying, yet her distress had not eased.

'Amy, I'm so sorry,' I said, my back rubbing intensifying. After all, I was at a loss as to what else I was expected to do. It's not like I could change the situation.

We both looked up at the sound of determined steps coming along the linoleum corridor. A gentleman with greying hair and an important manner approached, flanked on each side by two nurses. We were in their sights as they bore down on us. The obstetrician I assumed. He stopped in front of us, cleared his throat, then looking directly at Amy, he spoke.

'You must be Ms McAdam?'

Amy nodded her head.

'Yes, but you can call me Amy.'

'Very well, Amy,' he said as if conferring upon her a great honour. 'Before we hook you up to a CTG monitor, I'd like to do a further ultrasound. We have a more sophisticated machine here than the one that was used earlier. I understand the earlier ultrasound may have been inconclusive so it's best to be sure. Come this way please,' he added, gesturing towards a room not that far from us.

The doctor glanced at me and continued, 'And bring your friend with you if you want.'

'My sister. She's my sister, Frankie, and yes, I do want her with us.'

'Very well. This way please. Sister, would you please prepare the patient and call me once all is ready?'

He turned to the other nurse. 'Matron, was there anyone else you wanted me to see?'

Matron shunted the doctor off in the other direction while Amy and I were escorted into another room and then into a room off that. It was set up with a bed and some equipment beside it. Amy was directed to disrobe and lie on the bed, leaving her bra and pants on. I went to leave, but my sister grabbed my arm.

'No, don't go. Really, don't. I need you here as I'm dreading this. I have a very bad feeling.'

Her bad feeling proved to be correct. The obstetrician was meticulous in his administration of the ultrasound device. Over and over, he ran the handpiece sensor over Amy's belly. The implement ran smoothly across her skin now glistening with the lubricating gel. With each pass, he pressed the device firmly on her skin as both he and the nurse peered intently at the screen. An outline of a body, the baby's body, was discernible on the screen. Yet both his face and the nurse's face were intense as they looked for signs of life in that body, now lying strangely still.

After some time, and it seemed like hours, yet I suspect it wasn't, the doctor looked away from the screen and sadly contemplated Amy. In a gentle voice that I had not expected him to possess, he spoke:

'I'm so sorry, Amy, but I am unable to find a heartbeat for your baby. I've looked from all angles and unfortunately there is no doubt. There is no heartbeat nor any foetal movement. For whatever reason, and we may never know why, it looks like your baby has died. I know this is a lot to take in, but Amy we need to deliver your baby as soon as possible.'

'Deliver? You mean cut my baby out?'

'No, Amy. I would be encouraging you to give birth to your baby naturally, rather than have a caesarean section. It is important for your own body that the birth is as natural as possible, and that we don't do a surgical intervention. You may not appreciate it now but believe me, I've been through this with many other mothers and in my experience the loss and grief are somehow more manageable if you can find the strength to labour and bring this little one into the world. I don't know why that is but trust me it seems to be. If your loved ones can be with you to greet your baby, so much the better.'

His face softened and in a gesture that amazed me, the doctor continued:

'We will be with you—the hospital staff and myself. This is not something you should go through on your own. We will all be there to greet your baby. I suggest as you get dressed, please take your time to think about what you want to do and then come out and see me. I'll be waiting to hear what you decide.'

After the doctor and nurse left the room, I helped Amy off the bed and stood by helplessly as she reached for her clothes. I tried not to stare at that rounded belly—thirty weeks of life, or life no longer. Gently curved, her belly was a thing of beauty and should have been something to celebrate. Amy caught my glance and smiled weakly.

'It is what it is, I guess. What the doctor said just now comes as no surprise, but I had hoped against hope it wasn't to be the case. You know, just now when I hopped off the bed, I could feel that things really had changed. My baby is no longer. I could feel her body clunk and roll forward as I moved—a solid lump and no longer a squirming, living thing. He's right, I suppose. I now must see this to the end and if that means delivering my baby, so be it. But will you please stay with me? I'm not very brave, you see.'

'As if I'd leave you. And what about Mum and Dad? Do you want them here as well?'

A nod was all the answer I needed.

After some discussion with the doctor, it was agreed that Amy should stay overnight and be induced first thing in the morning.

There was a trundle bed that could be set up in her room, so I might also sleep over.

While Amy was being settled, I rang Mum and Dad and updated them on what was happening. I explained that they would both be needed there in the morning, to which they both immediately agreed.

'But what about the baby's father? Shouldn't he also be here?'

'I don't know, Dad. I'll try to discuss that with Amy. Not sure about my chances.'

As I expected, Amy was adamant that she didn't want Robbie Timms anywhere near her.

'No way, Frankie. Why do you think I would want him anywhere near me when I'm about to give birth—whether it is to a living or a dead baby? It's so none of his business. Anyway, have you forgotten? He thinks it is Shane's baby.'

I mulled this over. Somehow, something didn't quite seem right and proper about Amy's approach, but I couldn't put my finger on why I felt uneasy. I tried to explain.

'Okay. I get it that you don't want Robbie to see you in labour. But don't you think there is something else here? I'm not sure how to explain it, but doesn't he have a right to say goodbye to his child?'

'Why?'

'I'm not sure how I can explain it exactly. It's just a sense that it isn't quite right to keep him away even if I am having trouble articulating it. Maybe your baby is entitled to be farewelled by both parents. Perhaps that's what I mean. Think about it. This may be the only baby Robbie may ever have ...'

I was interrupted by a snort of laughter from Amy. The first one I had heard today and, in these circumstances, a welcome one at that.

'Don't you believe it. He's a well-known ladies' man. Always off with someone. He's bound to have more children.'

Well, that made me see Robbie in an entirely new light. Who would have thought it? As much as I would like to learn a bit more about this man's hidden talents that make him irresistible to women, I reminded myself to focus on the matter at hand.

'Never mind that,' I said. 'Think about it. Really think about it and forget your feelings for this man. Think about what you ought to do. What is the right thing to do? Me—I have a gut feeling that he is entitled to say goodbye to his baby. In any event, if he finds out the truth after you have buried this baby, do you think he would forgive you, or would this be something you might regret? Believe me, living with regrets is so not a good idea. Trust me, I know.'

Amy's glare in my direction was all the answer I needed. I held up my hands in mock surrender.

'Alright. Alright. I get it. I'll back off but promise me you'll think about what I just said.'

I took a deep breath and focussed on something else equally important—to me that is—the case of my rumbling tummy.

'I don't know about you, but I so do not want to brave the hospital food. How about I do a pizza run? You text me the details of whichever room they finally allocate to us, and I'll bring us back some food. I assume you are allowed to eat. Otherwise, you'll just have to watch me enjoy my dinner.'

A pillow hurled in my direction was all the answer I needed. Amy would be ok—for now.

Chapter Twenty-Five

I suppose any mother will tell you it's not called labour for nothing. This was the first time I had been witness to childbirth and I now understood that the term *labour* was no understatement.

Maybe it might be different if all that hard work culminated in the birth of a living baby. Maybe then the joyous feelings would sublimate the pain and exhaustion so that what had preceded the birth became a fuzzy memory.

In Amy's case, the emotion that surrounded us throughout the following day was of sorrow and grief. The physical pain of giving birth was also wrapped up in the heartache associated with an untimely death.

The day started early with another nurse arriving to prepare Amy. She explained to Amy that she was a midwife and had just started her shift.

'I'll be with you all day,' she said to Amy, giving her a reassuring smile. 'If I'm not in the room with you and you need me, just press this red button here and I'll be right in.'

She took a deep breath and continued: 'We'll be in this together. This is not the first still birth I have helped to deliver. I'm so sorry you and your baby have to go through this, but I'll be here with you to help in any way I can. And I'll be here with you afterwards, as will my colleagues. You and your baby are most important to us. You'll have time to be with your baby to say goodbye. That is so important.'

By now, we were all in tears, midwife included. The box of tissues was handed around. Noses honked and then the nurse focussed on the task at hand. I was dismissed from the room while some sort of suppository or pessary was administered—possibly the same as what she had last night—something to do with softening the cervix to prepare for birth. I so did not want to know anything more about that!

Sometime later, Amy was attached to a drip, which was then turned on and we waited … and waited. I understood that whatever was meant to happen could take a little while to start. We sat and talked about nothing in particular. Mum and Dad were expected shortly once they had fed and watered that morning's guests.

The contractions, when they started, seemed mild at first but quickly ramped up, more quickly as a result of the administration of the drip than if Amy had commenced labour naturally. Or so the midwife explained to us. I did my best to help my sister. I made my hand available to be squeezed and allowed her to lean on me as she walked around the room, as far as she could while still tethered to the drip. Just as I was starting to tire, Mum and Dad appeared and took over the support role. Amy greeted their arrival with an anguished cry. I guess it is only natural for any of us when we are in distress to want our mother and father to be with us. Almost as if we believe they can still make things better like they did when we were children.

I retreated to the corner and allowed my parents to comfort their daughter and give her courage.

'Come on, my girl,' Dad urged as his hand was now being squashed by Amy in response to a contraction.

'You're doing great. Not long to go,' he stated positively, yet with an anguished look at the midwife.

'Why don't I check and see how things are progressing?' said the midwife. 'It won't take long, and we'll then know where we stand. The cafeteria is still open. So, while I keep an eye on Amy, I think you could all do with a coffee.'

We actually had a tea, and after we drank that and ate a chocolate biscuit—or two—we felt somewhat stronger. No wonder nurses are always suggesting people have cups of tea. We sat around a hospital issue table, quietly sipping, and lost in our own thoughts.

As we filed back into the delivery room, we heard the midwife saying:

'No. Not long now. Let's get you in a comfortable position. You have done so very well. Why don't we get your parents to stand on each side of the bed? When I tell you to push, Amy, you can start, and we will be there to help. Your body will tell us when the time is right. I suspect it shouldn't be too much longer.'

Amy's wail in response was not encouraging. 'It hurts so. Dad, I want it to stop. Make it stop. I want drugs.'

'It's not possible, Amy,' the midwife spoke calmly yet firmly. 'You're too close. The drugs won't have any time to take effect. By the time we get them into you, and they start to work, it will all be over. Trust me.'

In Amy's robust response, she made full use of various colloquial expressions I was not aware she knew and made it very clear she had no trust in anyone present in the room.

'There. I knew it. She's in transition,' the midwife sighed in satisfaction. 'I'll just slip on some fresh gloves. Do you now feel the need to push?'

'Of course I bloody do!' came the response.

The midwife, with one hand on Amy's belly, focussed on what was happening inside.

'There,' she said. 'Another one is coming. When it grips you, just push—right down into your bottom. Do your hardest. Here goes. Let the contraction wash over you and push like you never have before.'

As Amy grunted and swore, the midwife peered into Amy's nether regions and murmured encouragement.

'Good girl. I can see your baby's crown. Your baby is on its way. Next contraction, give it your best. Squeeze your dad's hand, share the pain, and push. Bear down. Now!'

From my perch on the windowsill, I watched in stunned horror.

The noise was primeval. This was nothing like those glamorous birth scenes you see in the movies. You know, where the mum-to-be barely raises a sweat. Amy looked more like that character from *The Exorcist*—eyes popping, face slick with sweat and speckled with the remnants of an earlier vomiting episode. The bedding, crumpled around her, was stained with blood and faeces. The words that spewed from her mouth would be akin to something from the same movie, yet neither Mum, Dad nor the midwife appeared to be fazed. Presumably, this was par for the course for childbirth. I decided then and there that pregnancy was not for me.

Things sped up. The gap between the contractions was almost non-existent as Amy, in accordance with the midwife's instructions, bore down and grunted with the effort of pushing this child into the world. The doctor, who had surreptitiously snuck into the room, was on hand to manoeuvre the baby into the world when with one enormous yell from Amy, the head was revealed. With gentle hands, the doctor eased the child out of Amy's body and into her arms.

I watched with stunned horror as my niece—for now I could see the infant truly was a girl—was gently wiped and placed, still naked, onto Amy's chest. Amy's arms reached out to clasp her close to her heart while Mum and Dad drew close to coo in amazement.

I watched the doctor and midwife confer. Clearly, their work was not yet completed for I could see the cord that still linked my niece to Amy. The doctor asked if anyone would like to cut the cord or if they happy for him to do so. Amy nodded in my direction.

'Let Frankie do it.'

'Me?'

Amy nodded. 'Please?' Her pleading, with a voice now hoarse from all that grunting and screaming, nearly brought me undone. Of course, I would do as she asked. With trembling hands, I cut the cord and took my first glance at this new baby, gazing at her through eyes now blurred with tears.

She lay so quiet and still in her mother's arms. Despite a slight bluey/purple tinge to her lips, this baby looked exactly like I would expect a newborn to look. She was rather small, in a dainty way and not like a drowned rat. I suppose her petite size was to be expected as she was only 30 weeks in age, or thereabouts. Her eyes were closed and to all intents and purposes, you would think she was asleep. She looked so peaceful, totally unscathed by the trauma of birth. I reached out and gently stoked her cheek, which was still warm with the residual heat from her time in Amy's body. This warmth was deceptive and for a moment fooled me into thinking we might have it all wrong and that at any second she might stretch and come to life. Yet, the discolouration of her lips brought me to Earth. I was just deluding myself. She was well and truly dead.

We were all crying now. Mum, Dad, Amy, and me. To see this perfect little child and know there was no future for her, seemed beyond our comprehension. The room was awash with grief.

The doctor brought us back to the present by reminding us that the placenta still had to be delivered. He injected Amy with some sort of needle that was meant to speed up the process. The midwife gently eased the baby out of Amy's clutching arms with a murmured comment about *cleaning up the little one* and *wrapping her in something warm*. As if that would make a difference.

A short while later, my niece was returned to a much more comfortable Amy, placenta now having been safely delivered after another agonising few moments.

Our baby, swaddled in a soft, white blanket and with a tiny white beanie on her head, looked almost doll like. With her eyes still shut and her face wiped clean, she returned to her mother's arms. Amy traced her daughter's face with one tentative finger.

'You know, I had no idea what she would look like. She had always been just this blob in my stomach. But now …,' her voice broke, '… now she is her own person. I can see that she is an individual. She is not me and not her father, but a mixture of us both. Look, she has my nose.'

'And possibly your chin,' Mum observed.

'But certainly not your hair,' Dad said.

'No. That's just like her Dad's,' said Amy.

'And speaking of her dad,' Dad added. 'Shouldn't he be here to say goodbye?'

Amy sighed deeply and I watched her start to roll her eyes.

'No, Dad. Don't go there. He doesn't need to be here. Please leave it alone. It's my decision and mine alone whether I choose to involve her father. And I choose not to.'

But my parents were not so easily dissuaded. I saw them exchange glances and communicate some hidden message. Then Dad, in response to Mum's nod, went into battle.

'Amy, my dear, you know we love you and as our first born you have always been special.'

'Don't I know that?' I muttered under my breath. But Dad heard and turned to me with a smile.

'Yes, you're also special. My last born. Always my baby. Both of you, listen to me. Your mum and I have tried so hard to not interfere with you children as you lead your lives, believing that it is important that you learn from your mistakes, and I suppose also to let you fully claim ownership of your successes. But this time, Amy dear, I feel we have to say something. This child is not yours alone. She also has a father, who we both believe has a right to say goodbye.'

As Amy went to speak, Dad held up his hand.

'No, Amy. Please let me finish. In times not that long ago, this child would have been whisked from your body, taken away and disposed of before you even had a chance to say your farewells, let alone see her. Imagine how you would feel if you had no idea what your baby looked like and were not permitted to hold her like you are doing now. Imagine if you did not know who she resembled and were given no time to share her with us, her loving family. How awful it would be if you were expected to go on with your life as if she had never existed. Of course, what you are dealing with now is certainly a tragedy, but can you see how much worse it would be if you were denied the opportunity to say goodbye.'

'But he doesn't know he's the father. So, it can't be the same for him as for me,' Amy protested.

'He will find out sooner or later. This is a small community. You know how secrets have a habit of getting out. I'm not a betting man, but I would say it's a dead cert that people will know— especially as we already understand Shane is telling everyone that will listen that he is not the father. Amy, think about it. Can you live with yourself denying this child's father the chance to say goodbye? It's not like you need to have a relationship with him or even see him again come to that, but somehow your mum and I feel this might be healing for you. The right thing to do and all that. Please think about it? That's all I can ask. Trust me, sometimes as your father, I do get it right.'

Dad and Amy stared deep into each other eyes as if they were exchanging further hidden communion. Amy looked down and contemplated the small bundle in her arms. Then she looked up and at me. Clearly a decision had been made.

'Alright then. I will do it. Frankie, would you please ring Robbie and tell him what's happened? Say if he wants to see his daughter he needs to get here tonight. I'm not sure how long I will be allowed to keep her with me.'

'Robbie? You mean Robbie Timms?' Mum and Dad exclaimed in unison.

'Yeah.' Amy was immediately defensive. 'Is that such a surprise?'

'No, dear,' Mum said in a soothing voice. 'He was in your year at school after all. That explains from where the baby got such a gorgeous amount of hair and maybe her long arms and fingers. Well, I never. I didn't realise you liked him.'

'I don't. It was a one off and look where it landed me.'

The tears returned. Time for me to leave. With a scrape of the chair, I stood up and headed for the door, muttering something about ringing Robbie now.

'Take my phone,' Amy called. 'You'll find his number in my contacts.'

Robbie answered on the second ring with a surprised hello. Clearly, he knew this was Amy's number. It made me wonder if their contact had been more extensive than my sister had led me to believe.

'No, Robbie. It's Frankie. I've just borrowed Amy's phone. Have you a moment to talk?'

In a puzzled voice, he assured me he had, having just finished work for the day. Then I commenced the difficult task of bringing Robbie up to date. At least he knew Amy was pregnant, so I didn't have to give him that shock. Once I explained what had happened and how Amy had gone into labour, he was all care and concern and asking what he could do to help. Now came the tricky bit. I took a deep breath.

'You see, Robbie. The baby died some time yesterday. We're not sure why and the medical people say we may never know, but you see Amy's little girl was born today and ...,' I drew a deep breath and rushed in. Might as well get it over with. '... Amy is wondering if you would like to come into the hospital this evening and say goodbye to the baby.'

'Me? Of course. If she wants me to, I'll be there. But why would she want me to say goodbye?'

Like I've said before, Robbie Timms is not the smartest tool in the shed. You'd think he might have connected their bonk with Amy's pregnancy, but there you are. He clearly hadn't. It was now up to me to spell out the bleeding obvious to him.

'The reason Amy is asking if you would like to say farewell to the baby is because she is your daughter. Amy thought you might like to see her before the funeral.'

That's a total lie, I know, but I don't think Robbie needed to know that it is the last thing Amy would have wished.

There was silence at the other end of the phone as Robbie processed this unexpected information. I hope he wouldn't take too long as Amy's phone battery was almost flat.

'My baby? A daughter?'

It's almost as if he is musing out loud to himself, so I said nothing and waited for him to say more. I just wished he would hurry up. Then, with a decision made, he spoke: 'I'll be there straight away. Well, as soon as I've had a shower and got changed.'

Thank goodness for that!

'I'll tell her to expect you.'

After giving him the ward and room details, I ended the call. Returning to the hospital room, I handed Amy back her phone, gave her a kiss and cuddle, and told her I would return in the morning. By now, I was feeling totally overwhelmed. If I was feeling like this, then I had no idea how Amy felt, but I hoped Mum, Dad and Robbie could help her. As I could not. I needed time away—on my own, by the beach, and with my dog.

Chapter Twenty-Six

There is no other way of saying it. The funeral was awful. It was meant to be a private funeral for family members only and that was exactly how the notice in the local paper described it. But as we live in a small community, it came as no surprise that our wishes were ignored.

Maybe it was for the best that our grief was shared with those with whom we share our everyday lives, although I'm not sure Amy initially felt that way.

The day of the funeral Amy and I arrived at the church early. The coffin was already in place on a trestle before the altar, the lid now firmly in place and covered in a mass of yellow and white blooms. The size of the coffin—so tiny—its size emphasising the tragedy of the situation. A life ended before it had begun. Arm in arm, Amy and I stood still and contemplated the scene before us.

'You know,' said Amy, 'I'm glad I had these last two days to be with her, my daughter. I can finally accept she is gone. All that is left is the shell of what my daughter once was. The baby that wriggled and kicked inside me is no longer. Whatever spirit that moved her has moved on and I must accept that her body must now be let rot.' Seeing my expression of distaste, she continued: 'Hey don't come over all squeamish on me, Frankie. That's the natural order of things. Maybe one day there will be another. I certainly hope so. Robbie and I have been talking about how we must let our daughter go.'

'Robbie?'

My incredulous reaction must have been apparent in my tone.

'Yes, Robbie. You'd be amazed at how sensitive he has been. I certainly have been.' She looked up. 'Ah, here he is now.'

'Over here, Robbie,' said Amy as she waved to Robbie.

Robbie, dressed in a sombre navy-blue suit with wet slicked hair combed back, was totally unrecognisable from the everyday Robbie in his fisherman attire of grotty T-shirt, shorts and work boots. Reaching us, he wrapped his arm around Amy and drew her close. I watched Amy in amazement as she leaned into him and together they contemplated the tiny coffin that held their daughter's remains. Something certainly had changed between the two. They whispered to each other, and both gently placed some items on top of the coffin: a rattle from Amy, and a bathtub toy—a multicoloured fish—from Robbie. I silently backed away, being conscious that these three people, this little family, needed to spend some final moments together.

The funeral commenced with a brief address by the minister, who spoke of his sorrow in christening Amy and Robbie's daughter in the hours after her birth. 'Fleur' she was named—a name he assured us had been selected by Robbie and Amy for their daughter to commemorate the blossoming of her into their lives. Sitting beside Amy, I was conscious of how Robbie squeezed Amy's hand tightly when the minister said this.

After the minister finished speaking, both Amy and Robbie stood and moved to stand beside their daughter's coffin, splendid in its blanket of daffodils and jonquils and trailing greenery.

Amy consulted a crumpled sheet of paper in her hand and, in a trembling voice, she started to read:

Under my heart you landed and made your nest. With each day of morning sickness, you grew and wrapped yourself around me. But I did not mind. For every day you claimed a bigger part of me. My heart was yours to command. I was your slave, your serf, your devoted nurturer. My heart was no longer my own.

Under my heart now lies an empty space. Desolate and no longer full of hope and joy for the future. I see no future, only the knowledge that somehow part of my heart left my body with you. Farewell my little flower, our beautiful Fleur. Farewell until the day we meet again.

With trembling hands, she passed the sheet of paper to Robbie who, in fits and starts, read the following words:

Our daughter, Fleur, left us before her time at only 30 weeks of age. All the things we took for granted have been taken from us—the chance to teach her about life, love and this community. We will never be able to teach her to swim, surf or share her with you. All we can do is be thankful she didn't suffer and that she can now rest here with her family, and that one day we will be reunited with our beloved daughter.

He looked up at the now crowded little church at the congregation of friends and family and added:

'Thanks everyone for being here today to share in our sorrow. I speak for Amy and her family when I say that we appreciate your concern. I know it won't make the pain go away, but sharing our grief with all of you will, I hope, lessen the load. Thank you.'

We stood and sung a song. Amy had agonised over the choice of hymns that would be appropriate and in the end she and Robbie had agreed on something that wasn't too sorrowful—one they both liked. To the not quite tuneful singing of *All Things Bright and Beautiful*, the tiny coffin was carried out by Robbie and my father. We all fell in behind and followed them to the graveyard out behind the church.

There's not much more I feel I can say. The burial of such an infant was one of those life events I never ever want to repeat. A life cut short before it even had a chance to start. As I stood by my parents and Simon, and watched the desolate parents commit their daughter to the earth, I sensed someone approaching me and felt an arm reach around and draw me in. I knew who it was before I even turned. I knew from the earthy smell of him and the strength in that arm drawing me close. A whisper in my ear:

'Are you okay, Frankie?'

I turned and shook my head, trying to give him a watery smile.

'No. Not really. I just want this to be over, so I can run away. Is that too bad of me?'

'Nope.' His voice dropped to an even fainter whisper so no one else could overhear. 'Dog, beach and swim. Sound like a plan?'

'Works for me!'

Chapter Twenty-Seven

Aweekend. A chance for a lie in and to take it easy all day as no dairy duties awaited and for once, no house maid obligations to fulfil. At my usual waking hour, I stirred and, realising I could linger in bed for a much, much longer time, I rolled over and snuggle under the doona, relaxing back into glorious slumber.

But it was not to be. The shrill ringing of my phone intruded as it rang over and over. Why did I not turn my phone off? On and on it rang until, with eyes still shut, I reached towards my bedside table and knocked the phone flying.

'Bugger.'

Yet still it rang. At least it was not broken.

'Alright, alright. No need to get your knickers in a knot. I'm coming.'

Awake now, I sat up, then leaned over, tummy pressed to the mattress as I rummaged around to find that useless phone.

Finally, with phone retrieved, I repositioned myself and answered the call. Already I could see the caller was identified as my brother. No need to be polite then.

'Simon. What are you doing? You woke me up. It's Sunday. Shouldn't you also be asleep?'

'Sleep? Who needs sleep when there are Sunday papers to read?'

'Sunday papers? What do you mean, and why tell me?' I asked, a feeling of dread settling in the pit of my stomach.

Somehow, I suspected this call was not to be about the sharing of good news.

'Little sister. You just can't keep out of trouble, can you?'

And then he explained. The Sydney Sunday paper, which is always full of gossip, trivia and well … let's just call it, light reading, has this time excelled itself. An expose spread over three pages and entitled, *Special Investigative Report – How a soapie got wrecked On the Rocks.* You guessed it—the report dished the dirt on my old soapie and the cast in amazing and accurate detail. An unnamed informant shared with the journalist the inside scoop. Isn't it funny how such sources are always unnamed?

And what a scoop it was. Tales of the freely available drugs, the addiction by certain actors to that white powder—didn't everyone know that already?—the sexual romps among the cast and crew—again, surely no surprise. Hadn't Gino's antics been shared enough already? The falling out between director and producer—well, that was news to me, and the fake romance between Luke and me.

'Of course, it was fake! It was acting,' I said.

'I don't think that is exactly what the journalist had in mind when it was said to be fake. What is said in this article is that the speculated romance was fake because Luke already had a partner—of the male gender—and that you colluded with keeping this from the public who, according to this article, *had a right to know.*'

'As if they did. Poor Luke. How is he coping? He must be devastated that his secret is out.'

'Ah, so you knew, did you? Well then, if that part of the story is accurate, maybe the rest is as well.'

'Come on. Of course, I knew. Both he and Harry are my friends, and I respect their privacy. It really is no one else's business. If Luke knows about this article, he will be devastated. He'll be thinking his career will have gone up in smoke.'

'Not necessarily,' said Simon, who was wise to such matters. 'With a decent bit of media management, he can make the most amazing story out of this—if he wants to, that is. Ten years ago, he would have had to kiss his career goodbye, but in these more enlightened times, creating a whole new career may still be possible.

But he needs to come clean, confess and all that. To be honest though, I suspect that this is the end of his time on that soapie.'

'Most likely and that outcome is probably something he can live with. Luke hasn't been happy there for some time. In fact, he's been complaining ever since I left. Luke told me he felt like he'd been sidelined in the plot, and I seem to recall he had already been talking to Tom about his options.'

I realised I needed to find Luke and offer him whatever assistance he felt he needed. I'm pretty sure there won't be much support coming from his other cast members if my memories of them were correct. They would just throw him to the wolves. With that in mind, I ended the call to Simon.

'Simon, I've gotta go. I must ring Luke and see how he is. If I need you to do anything I'll ring back. And thanks for letting me know. I can't believe it! I actually thanked you for waking me up on a Sunday morning. I must be losing it!'

'Nah. It's the least I could do,' came the complacent response. 'Always happy to share the latest gossip. Talk soon little one.' And with that, he hung up.

With trembling fingers, I scrolled through my contact list until I located Luke's mobile number. He had an unlisted phone number, so I hoped he would be answering any calls on the basis they would be from friends. But no, it went through to his voice mail. I left a message asking him to call me, hung up and waited.

Almost immediately, he rang back.

'Sorry I didn't take your call just now. I've been screening my calls.'

'Luke, that's perfectly fine. I totally understand. Simon just rang me and told me the news about the article in today's paper. I've yet to read it, but I gather they've outed you among other things. How did the journo know? You don't need this!'

'Too right I don't. Not only is the press hounding me, but so are Ivo and Dana. Those two want to meet me to have a serious discussion about my future. You'd think I was a murderer or something and not in a committed relationship with my partner. But I guess all they care about are their ratings and the fantasy world they have constructed. As if I care,' he said in a slightly defiant yet trembling voice.

'Oh Luke. What a bummer. Are you okay? Is there anything I can do for you?'

'Well, actually. Now you mention it, you probably can. If you don't mind, that is.'

'Anything. Of course.'

And that is how I agreed to provide a refuge for Luke down here, down the coast. I agreed to this without even consulting the parents because I knew they wouldn't mind. Of course they didn't and as Dad reminded me, we were now experienced in hiding people away from the press.

Luke didn't arrive until late afternoon. By then he had met with Ivo and Dana and agreed on a way for him to exit the production. A slight tweak of the storyline, which involved him reuniting with me. But I'm getting ahead of myself.

He had also had a long conversation with Tom, his agent, and with my brother. Whatever had been discussed, had filled him with optimism. The Luke that arrived at our place was not the same Luke that I had been speaking to earlier that day. I could see as soon as he got out of the car that he was relaxed and smiling—and alone.

'Where's Harry?'

'He's staying at his sister's place until things die down. You know how private he is. The last thing he wants is to be grilled by the media. He says he's fine though. Just can't understand why anyone would care about our private life.'

'A wise man he is. Come on,' I said, taking a carry bag which clinked in a way that boded well. 'Come and meet Mum and Dad, and then we'll get you settled. I think Mum has put you in the spare room inside. You'll be away from the guests unless you want to mingle with them?'

Once inside and with introductions out the way, I settled Luke on the lounge and immediately started to grill him. That is until Mum called a halt to proceedings.

'Frankie, child, give the poor man a break. Poor Luke, he has only just arrived and must be exhausted after the day he has had.'

Turning to Luke, she continued: 'Please forgive my thoughtless daughter, Luke. Sometimes I despair.'

'It's okay, Mrs McAdam. I'm used to her, and I suppose she's entitled to find out what is really happening. I suppose you might like to know too?' he said, giving my mum a cheeky grin. It was a wise move as it softened her reaction to being called Mrs McAdam—so ageing!

Not surprisingly, Luke hit it off with both my parents. After all, I like him so why wouldn't they? Our evening went smoothly— early dinner, as it was clear Luke was exhausted, and then we farewelled him to an early night with a promise to have a proper chat in the morning. That evening, as I prepared for bed, I wondered what Luke had meant when he said something about the soapie story line contemplating a reunion with me. Surely not?

I tried not to speculate but somehow, I think I failed. That night, my dreams were populated with a range of scenarios that all saw me back being part of the cast and involved in a succession of adventures, each more outrageous than the last. In one such dream, even Gino made an appearance as he once again tried it on with me. All that lingered as I woke was a feeling of outrage that even the dead could be expected to return to that soapie. Still, at least it was now daylight, and I would have the opportunity to find out what Luke had meant with that cryptic comment last night. I would be kind and not grill him until after breakfast was completed. I could be very considerate in that way!

I got up early—I really wanted to know, you see. And waited. And waited. Sleeping beauty was having a lie in. Mum sternly told me to not be so impatient and to have some regard for the *poor young man* who had been through a most trying experience and just needed to rest. She's a born nurturer that one.

Clearly, my impatience was getting on Mum's nerves. She shunted Nippa and me out and told us not to return for a good half hour.

'Go and run the fidgets off—both of you,' she ordered.

When Mum had that look in her eye, there was no point fighting back. I knew from experience that if I did, I would just lose. So, I put my running shoes on, and with my buddy leading the way, we headed off to the beach and ran and ran.

But still, my thoughts kept up with me.

Chapter Twenty-Eight

Luke was awake and up and about by the time I returned home. Not only that but he had also found time to produce yesterday's paper and was discussing it with both Mum and Dad.

I walked in through the back door and was confronted by the sight of three people standing by the table, heads together, peering intently at the newspaper spread out before them.

Mum was the first to speak. 'My goodness. If only half of these reported goings on were true, it would appear the real drama occurred every day on the set and not on the TV,' she exclaimed.

Judging by her intrigued expression, I wondered if she was interested and not appalled by the alleged activities.

Dad however was made of sterner stuff. 'Well, for my part, I'm glad our Frankie is no longer part of that set. What debauched goings on,' he muttered in disgust.

Glancing at Luke, he continued: 'Luke, it seems to me you would be best to scarper as quick as you can from that lot. There has got to be a better life for you somewhere else. Surely not all workplaces are a mess of drugs and sex.'

Luke, ever the gentleman, prevaricated: 'Vince, I think this report might be somewhat exaggerated. Or it may be that I wasn't in the know—on the outer so to speak. It all seemed rather tame to me. Sure, we all knew about Gino and his behaviour, but he seemed to get away with it every time. He could charm his way out of any situation. But the drugs ... well, I didn't know.'

By now, I was inside and standing next to Luke. His distress was obvious in the way he held himself so tightly, and by the way he was worrying his bottom lip—a rather endearing habit of his. You see, I knew Luke very well. He couldn't hide anything from me. I put my arm around him and leaned into him.

'Luke. All this stuff isn't what's worrying you, is it?'

'No. It's that,' he said as he pointed to an image at the bottom of the page labelled: *Luke and his partner Harry* ****

'Well, at least they didn't give Harry's surname. Respecting his privacy, I suppose. And you must agree, it is a lovely photo of you both,' I said as a pathetic attempt to ease his distress.

Mum and Dad both made concurring sounds while Luke pulled an anguished face and did further damage to his lower lip.

'What am I to do? I can't lie. Harry is my partner, but if I acknowledge the truth of this article, there goes my career,' he said, despair evident in every syllable uttered.

'Does it have to be so absolute?' asked Dad.

'Yes!' both Luke and I responded in unison.

'Well, if it does, does it really matter?' asked Mum before elaborating. 'After all, and as I often told my children when they were little—not that they listened to me, of course—the most important thing is to be true to yourself. Seems to me you've been living a lie—a glamorous lie, and a lie it would appear you have been living in collusion with our Frankie. Maybe, Frankie dear, it is time you and Luke set the record straight. After all, there must be others out there in the same boat as you, Luke, who will be expecting you to be honest with yourself and them. Sort of being a good role model to others. Think about it.' She smiled kindly at Luke as if to take some of the sting out of her parental guidance.

Linking my arm through Luke's, I dragged on him with all my might. 'I've an idea. Things are never as bad on a full stomach. Let's leave Dad to cook us a decent fry up, and we'll go and wait outside for our breakfast. Then you and me, and that smelly dog of mine, will go for a long work and nut out some sort of plan. And I seem to recall you said Ivo made some sort of suggestion to you. Time to share that with me as well. Come on. You never know, this might be just the opportunity you have been looking for.'

'What opportunity are you talking about, Frankie?' asked a mystified Luke. 'Breakfast, a walk, or what?'

'Your future silly!'

Dad excelled himself and cooked a breakfast to die for: perfectly poached eggs, crispy bacon, fried mushrooms topped with some soft Persian fetta, and heaps of sourdough toast. Two cups of coffee later, we were both ready to waddle off on our walk with Nippa racing off in front of us.

'Come with me,' I said. 'I know the perfect spot to sit and make plans. This way.'

With Nippa leading the way, I led Luke to my favourite thinking spot—down the dirt track to the headland where we stopped by a flat rock. This rock was perfectly shaped for sitting and had a view straight out to sea, or if you preferred looking to the left, down onto the beach. The rock was big enough for both of us … just. The hound collapsed at our feet, her panting all out of proportion to the exercise she had just endured.

I took my time, choosing my words carefully. After all, Luke was one of my dearest friends and I wanted to help, not hinder.

'It seems to me that both our lives have been turned upside down by that soapie. I've come out the other side and you are still in the churn and are yet to work out what to do. Yet I think there is no way back for you. After that newspaper article, things can never be the way they were. That image of Luke, the hetero actor, is no longer sustainable. The real you now has the opportunity to shine through. Does it matter if people get to know who you really are? Really?'

'Yes!' his voice trembled.

'I'm not sure it will. Be brave. You have a choice. Gino didn't— the damage inflicted on him from that soapie is permanent. But for you, I think it is different. It is now time to work out what it is you actually want to do. Maybe Tom and Simon can help you.'

'Or you?' Luke said hopefully. 'You know, I mentioned how Ivo said perhaps you could come back and entice me away? You know, something like you suddenly appearing in the community and luring me away to a new life?'

I seemed to recall him hinting as such last night—something about his character leaving on a quest to find me. But to be honest, I gave it no conscious thought, apart from a passing curiosity. My dreams though, that was another matter. And that could just be the result of an overactive imagination—or indigestion. After all, my contract had been terminated months ago. With a sinking feeling, I contemplated what was potentially on offer. A chance to return to Sydney to a role on that show and possibly a chance to redeem myself.

This could be all I had been pining for all those months ago immediately after Gino's death. I could become the soapie surfie queen again, maybe wave Luke/Drew off, and then perhaps go on to bigger and better things. Images of me, the star in my own show, hair long again and with hordes of admiring followers, blossomed in my imagination. Fame, adulation and success. What was there not to like? If such a future was so desirable, then why the sinking feeling in my stomach? Why the trembling and clammy hands. What was my body telling me that my imagination wasn't?

I took a deep breath and looked down at my feet and at the blue/black brindle dog lying there, quietly snoring and drooling on my running shoe. What would I do with her if I returned to Sydney? How could I leave her behind when she was so much a part of my life? Anyway, did I really want a life where I would be on the set pretending to be someone else for ten, twelve or fourteen hours a day? Was that the real Frankie?

The answer was clear if only I had the courage to commit.

I took a deep breath. 'Luke, I don't know what you should do. That is something you must determine. But I do know for me there is only one way forward. I cannot go back to that life I led in Sydney. Sure, there were good things that happened to me there—meeting you and Harry stands out as one of those highlights. But forcing myself to return to that show is just so wrong on so many counts. Too many sad memories for one. Most importantly though is that it no longer feels right for me. My life, and my future, is here.'

As I said these words, I knew deep within me that I was speaking the truth. I knew because the sick feeling settled, my hands stilled, and a feeling of absolute certainty overwhelmed me. For whatever reason, this coastal community was where I was meant to be.

Luke smiled at me. 'You are a brave one, Frankie. I just hope your determination is enough to inspire me. Yep, I think you might be right. I must be true to myself and move on. It's time. I owe it to Harry!'

'You sure do! Don't worry, we will all be there with you as your cheer squad. You know what I think? I'm wondering why you are still here with us and why you aren't at home with your man.'

Chapter Twenty-Nine

It was a day like any other. I followed the now familiar routine without conscious thought. Helping Mum with the cleaning in the morning, then enough time for a quick swim before I headed up to the farm in time to call the cows in for milking. Nippa and I wandered down the hill to the paddock gate where already half the herd were waiting patiently to be let in. Once I opened the gate, Nippa and I stood still and let them amble through. Just like humans I thought as I watched them push through. Invariably, there was someone in the herd who had to be there first, always in a rush to get the job done and move on to the next thing. Or maybe they were only greedy and wanted a first go at the food. They were just like my old classmates, you know the ones that consistently came top of the class and scored the best desks or could be relied upon to know the answers to those tricky questions? That was so not me. I would be the one, like those cows over there, who were in no rush at all and didn't mind being last. They had better things to do and were still standing in the dam happily munching on the weeds that grow by the edges, soaking up the warmth of the late afternoon sunshine.

Still, on that day, things went fine. The dam paddlers were eventually persuaded to leave their watery sojourn—probably helped along by Nippa, who launched herself into the water with much splashing and barking. Then there was the task of persuading Nippa to vacate the water and follow me. Eventually though, a thoroughly soaked dog and a slightly damp me brought up the rear, as the remaining cows meandered along the laneway that led to the dairy.

Archie and his father were already busy with the first contingent, and milking was well under way by the time Nippa and I arrived.

Archie, with raised eyebrows, perused my damp attire and the dog now busy shaking droplets in all directions.

'Been having fun, have we?'

'That rotten dog you gave me just wouldn't leave the dam. I blame it on the cows. They were having such a good time paddling around that Nippa had to join them! Not only did I get wet trying to get her out, but then she shook all over me. Lucky it's a warm day. Now what do you want me to do?'

Archie pushed his hat back and gave his head a thoughtful scratch.

'We're pretty good here. I've filled up the tank for the calves. How about you take that over to their feeder and set them up. Then while they're feeding, would you duck into the hay shed and grab a bale of hay for the calves? Just one bale will do.'

I made a mock salute and with a brisk *yes boss*, Nippa and I set off to do our chores. After several months on the job, I liked to think of myself as an experienced farm hand and I was now well accustomed to the ritual of feeding the calves. With the milk tank on the trailer and hooked up onto the quad bike, I drove to the calf shed and went through the process of connecting the tank to the *milk bar*. The calves, jostling and mooing in their excitement, made me laugh and Nippa bark. The chaos quickly settled into contented slurping.

The hay shed was a short distance away from the dairy. It was made of the usual construction common to most farms—a large, rusty, corrugated iron shed enclosed on three sides to protect the precious hay from the weather. Being late summer, the shed was almost at capacity, stacked with bales of freshly cut, fragrant hay. Big round plastic covered bales of what they call *silage* were stacked outside and would be given to the milking herd, if need be, during winter. But the smaller bales of pasture hay, Archie told me, were given to the calves to bring them on and accustom them to eating such stuff. Mind you, given their appetites, I think they would eat anything!

I parked the bike and wandered inside. The hay shed, like many farm sheds, was home to many mice, and Nippa, with a quick woof, was off on the chase.

I found a bale that was reasonably accessible and started the process of lifting it and carrying it to the bike. Not as easy as it sounds. The bale was heavy with good grass—and prickly. As I put the bale down to get my breath, I saw Archie's dad approaching, shovel in hand, with a look of grim determination on his face.

'Charles? Is everything all right? Is there something you need to do? Can I help you?'

'Yes, yes,' he mumbled as he approached and pushed past me.

I shrugged and bent down to pick up the bale of hay. Then, I felt tremendous pain as what I later learnt was the result of the shovel being brought down hard on the back of my head. Not that I knew this at the time however, as the blow was so hard it knocked me out. That is what might have saved me for Charles only hit me once, apparently being satisfied that he had done the job.

From then on, my recollection remains scattered. I recall trying to regain consciousness and fighting the dense smog that seemed to inhabit my head and my lungs. My lungs? My brain registered the smell of smoke, but it was beyond my ability to rouse myself and move. I was vaguely aware of barking followed by a frantic yelling. And then, the feeling of being lifted and moved away from the smoke. Words floated around me still punctuated by the frantic sound of barking.

'Frankie, are you okay? Answer me. What happened? You're bleeding. I've called the ambulance and the fire brigade, but I need to get you away from this. Maybe Dad can help.'

Dad? No way. Even in my concussed state, I knew that was a bad idea. A spasm of fear and adrenaline coursed through me and with that my eyes flew wide open.

'No. Not Charles,' I croaked. It hurt to speak. The smoke had done something to my voice.

'He hit me. With the shovel, I think. I don't know why. And fire brigade? What's happened?'

I struggled to sit up. Bad idea, as the world swam around me, and little stars danced a samba across my vision. I lay back down again and squinted up at Archie, a dark shadow against the too bright daylight.

'What?' Shock was apparent in Archie's voice as he stared down at me in disbelief. He shook his head and continued to speak, almost as if he was trying to understand what had happened. 'I'm sorry. I don't get it. I was wondering why it had taken you so long and was wandering up this way to see if you needed a hand. Then, I heard Nippa carrying on, barking like crazy at a different pitch to her normal sound, so I came to investigate. I found the hay smouldering and you sprawled out right next to it. If Dad did this to you, it just doesn't make any sense. Why would he do this, and where is he now?' He looked around. 'He's nowhere in sight so I need to find where he has got to. But first things first. I must put this fire out and get you looked at to see if you are okay. So, I'll prop you up there in the shade for the time being and see if the firefighting hose will reach. Back soon.'

He settled me against a wooden fence post under the shade of an old oak tree and disappeared. The world still shimmered, and stars rotated every time I moved my head. Not that I wanted to move my head as it ached so. I felt myself wanting to black out again and tried to fight the feeling.

Must stay awake, I told myself.

Nippa appeared and settled herself next to me. Even the little jolt I experienced as she nestled into me, sent ripples of pain through my body. My mind emptied and I could feel myself sinking into a semi-conscious state. There was no energy for curiosity or speculation as to what happened, or why.

Nippa's growling intruded into the pain and the black haze that had engulfed me. *She's growling. Why?* I struggled to open my eyes. Not a good idea as the brightness of the daylight pierced my skull with shards of pain. In response, my eyes immediately squeezed shut. The growling continued at a louder and deeper pitch. Nippa was clearly not happy. I heard footsteps approach. Hesitantly, I opened my eyes just a crack. Yes, there was the shape of someone approaching. Not the familiar outline of Archie. Anyway, Nippa would never growl at Archie. Even in my befuddled state, I sensed I was in danger. My innards tensed. I squirmed and tried in a hoarse whisper to call out for help.

'No need calling for help, Missy. There's no one here but you, me, and that infernal dog. I sent young Archie back to the house to wait for the fire brigade. I told him it was an accident and he believed me. My son cannot save you now. It's time you got what you deserved.'

Again, I squawked. Not that my rasping sound could be heard any distance away, but it was all I was capable of doing. My hand reached for Nippa as if for comfort. The last thing I needed was for her to bolt. I could feel the tension in her body as she kept up those well-known doggy sounds of warning. Maybe it was instinct, but somehow, I knew I had to keep him talking in the forlorn hope that help might soon arrive.

'Why?' I rasped. 'Why were you trying to hurt me?'

I sensed him drawing close. But not too close.

'You had to be punished. I knew who you were from the very first time I met you. You were Charlie's friend. I knew that, but I didn't let on. I didn't want you to be suspicious. I took my time waiting for the perfect opportunity when I could strike and give you the punishment you deserve.'

'Punishment? For what?'

'You killed my boy. If it wasn't for his hanging around with you, being tempted by your silly ways, he would have been safe and stayed up here on the farm where he belonged. You killed him, so you must die. It is only right that you die. An eye for an eye, like the Bible says. That way justice will be done, and Charlie can rest in peace.'

'But, but ...' my brain fogged with the pain of trying to make sense of what Charles had just said. How can I explain that it wasn't my fault? And in any event, would he listen to me?

'But I wasn't even there.'

That's the best my pathetic stunned brain could come up with.

'It's all your fault. Encouraging him with your silly little ways. Making him so besotted that he could talk of nothing but *Frankie this* and *Frankie that* until I felt like screaming. When Charlie died, they told me I had to let him go and get on with my life, but I knew I couldn't. I knew I had to take my revenge. For a time, I was stuck as to how to do it. You had moved away. But then things changed. Your father came out here to buy a pup and I knew it was only a matter of time until you would come into our life once again. It wasn't until after you visited the farm with that silly pup that I saw the good Lord had delivered you to me so that justice could prevail. I knew I had to move quickly for I could see, right under my eyes, that history was repeating itself. My Archie falling under your spell, just like what happened to our other son. Wasn't one Saddler enough? Did you have to ensnare both?'

'Archie? He likes me?'

'Oh, don't come on all sweet and innocent to me. I know your wicked ways, you Jezebel, you. But this time you won't get your way. I will make sure of that. Your time is up.'

His hands, grimy and surprisingly strong, reached for my throat. His intent was clear. I tried to squirm away but was unable to. Every movement sent my head spinning and I felt my body threaten to black out. My stomach churned with fear, and without any conscious thought, I vomited its contents all over Charles just as Nippa sank her teeth into his ankle. I'm not sure whether my actions or the actions of my pup caused Charles to step back, but somehow, we got a reprieve—sufficient reprieve to allow time for the cavalry, in the shape of Archie, to arrive.

'Dad! Dad, what are you doing? Leave Frankie alone. Can't you see she's hurt?'

Charles staggered back, making futile gestures to remove my vomit from his face, and glared at his son.

'Just you leave me be, lad. I have business to do here. This piece of wickedness killed my Charlie, and her time is up. It's a matter of justice. She has to pay for her sins.'

'Dad.' Archie's voice was almost pleading. 'Dad, come on. Give it a break. You're not well. You need to rest.'

Archie reached out to take his father's arm, as if to lead him away. His father shook him off and lunged at me.

'This time I won't fail. I thought I had got you when I hit you with that shovel. My Charlie is calling me. Can't you hear him? He says I must do it now, then he will rest in peace. Don't fight. You know this is what you deserve.'

He kicked out at Nippa, who once again had launched an attacking manoeuvre, laying into his other ankle.

'Will no one else get rid of this infernal dog or do I have to kill her as well?'

I pushed myself back as hard as I could against the tree. This time Archie was no longer as gentle as before and, with a manoeuvre I had seen him perform with unruly calves, he tackled his father facedown onto the ground. Then, grabbing him by the shirt collar, he hoisted him to standing position and, having twisted one of his father's arms behind his back, Archie frog-marched his father away from me and towards the house.

I could hear Archie's voice fade away as he spoke in quiet yet determined tones: 'No, Dad. I won't let you do this. Listen hard. This is not on. You cannot behave like that. Clearly there's something wrong with you and you're not well. Mum has called the ambulance and the police, and I expect they will take you to the hospital first thing. How can I get you to understand? Frankie had nothing to do with Charlie's death. She wasn't even there on the day. If Charlie had shown any sense and stayed with Frankie that day, the tragedy would not have happened. His death was all his own fault. Do you hear me, Dad? All Charlie's fault. He was driving too fast. Showing off probably and crashed the car. It's surprising the other families who lost their children through Charlie's bad behaviour haven't tried to lynch us. But they haven't. They have grieved with us.'

As Archie lead his father away, I squinted at their retreating figures. I heard the sobbing and the anguished *no, no, no* that Charles uttered, over and over again.

Me? I couldn't comprehend what had just occurred. My dog, my hero, relaxed into me once more, the job of protecting her mistress now done.

The last thing I can recall before I surrendered to the darkness was muttering brief praise to my dog—my saviour.

Chapter Thirty

Consciousness crept in stealthily. Gradually, I became aware of the muted sounds of bustle—the rattle of trolleys, the ebb and flow of conversation—the precise meaning of which failed to register. Then I became aware of a feeling of stabbing pain in my head, which called me to wake up. I stretched and opened my eyes just a crack. The strangeness of my surroundings jerked me to reality.

Where am I? What happened?

My memories were muddled. I struggled to recall why I would be in this strange place, which I was rapidly coming to identify as some sort of health facility. A hospital perhaps? I looked down and saw I was wearing some regulation issue attire stamped with a logo. A nurse came bustling in. Yep, definitely a hospital. Most likely the same hospital I visited recently with Amy.

'You're awake then? Good. You've been out for a while. How are you feeling?'

'Muddled,' I replied, feeling the back of my head from where the pain was still emanating in a throbbing beat.

'And no wonder too. You took a fair blow to the head. Best to leave it alone now. There has been a bit of blood and you don't want to start the bleeding again, do you? Now, are you up to seeing your parents and some young man? They've been waiting outside for hours.'

I tried to nod and winced as the pain spiked. The nurse immediately noticed.

'Very well then. Five minutes only, so they can see you are awake and okay. I'll let the doctor know, as he will want to examine you now that you are conscious. Don't get up as you need to rest. Ring me if you need me. The button is here,' she said as she placed a cord with a red button next to me on the bed and left the room.

Mum, Dad and Archie appeared soon after. They entered the room with care, treading softly and walking hesitantly as if they were expecting the worst. When they saw that I was awake, they all broke into smiles, and I was sure I could hear a sigh of relief from one of them. Maybe the sound came from Dad for he was the first to speak.

'Thank goodness you are awake, Frankie. We've been so worried. The doctor said the x-rays showed no sign of brain damage or fracture and that you just had bad concussion. But when you seemed so out to it, I was worried it could be something worse. Like your skull was fractured or something.'

He reached the bed and swooped in for a kiss. The jostling of the mattress as his body made contact, sent ripples of pain through my head and I tried not to wince and give a grateful smile. A weak one at that.

'Hi guys. Yeah, I'm awake, but I have a killer of a headache. That must be the concussion, I suppose.'

Mum moved closer and tucked the blanket firmly around me. Ever the mother.

'Yes, dear. They said you have to remain here under observation for a day, maybe two. You had us worried.'

'What happened?'

'A bit of a story,' said Dad.

'Maybe Archie can fill you in.'

Archie took my hand and looked carefully at me; his face etched with concern.

'I feel like it's all my fault. I should've noticed something was wrong with Dad. Well, I suppose I did. Just put it down to old age and early signs of dementia and that he generally was becoming a bit odd. But I didn't realise he was getting paranoid and dwelling on Charlie's death. Of course, he seemed rather unwelcoming when you first came to the farm, but I thought that was because he was never very good with strangers. I just didn't realise what was going on in his troubled brain and that he was fixated on you—and not in a good way.'

I stared blankly back at Archie. As I had no memory of what had happened and no background on which to pin it, not one word of what he was saying made any sense.

'You really don't remember, do you?'

I shook my head and then winced. *Really must stop doing that.*

'Maybe that will make it easier for you to accept and understand. You see, for some strange reason, Dad got it into his head that you were to blame for Charlie's death. I don't know why he could possibly believe that, and he certainly didn't share his suspicions with Mum or me. If he had, we would have set him straight—or tried to.'

'Me? I wasn't even there when it happened.'

'Yeah, I know. It makes no sense. The hospital last night said Dad's paranoia might have something to do with his dementia, or there might be something else going on. They're going to do tests. But whatever the result, Mum and I both agree that it is not safe to have him home. Dad could have killed you. It's only luck that saved you—and Nippa too, of course! I blame myself. I should have paid more attention to how Dad was deteriorating, and I certainly shouldn't have put you in danger,' said Archie, staring at me earnestly.

I felt like I was expected to respond, but really didn't know what to say. There was still no memory of the incident, and without any independent recollection of what Archie had just recounted, it made it all seem too bizarre to be true. Luckily, Dad saved the day. Patting Archie on the arm, he spoke:

'Archie, mate. Don't blame yourself. You weren't to know how sick your father is. I mean none of us did. I noticed he was a bit unfriendly whenever I saw him down the street and also when I came to collect the pup, but I just put it down to old age. At least now we have an explanation for his behaviour that makes sense and hopefully he can get treatment and be properly cared for. He must be terribly confused.'

Dad's words seemed to give Archie some comfort, and more comfort than I could manage in my current painful state. After a few more minutes, all three were ushered out by the officious nurse, who assured them they could return in the morning when the patient would be much more rested and feeling better. I certainly hoped it would be so.

No sooner had they left than I succumbed to sleep. It wasn't until first light of the following morning that my slumber was disturbed by the sound of people talking. It was a change of shift handover if I was to judge by the subject matter of the discussion. I heard a murmured discussion about the current status of the patient in bed 17 who had taken a nasty blow to the skull. They were talking about me! I listened intently. Apparently, I was expected to make a full recovery and would be encouraged to get out of bed today and move around. If all went well and my pain diminished, I would be discharged later that day.

I couldn't say the headache was fully gone. It still lurked in the background like a soft drumbeat, a warning not to do too much. Yet, after a quick shower, I felt so much better and was able to have a mouthful or two of a most disgusting breakfast. Once dressed in some of my own clothes that Mum brought into the hospital the day before, I even felt a bit more like normal, so long as I didn't try to touch the tender part of my skull. My memory of the events at the farm had still not returned and it was possible they never would.

The doctor came to see me after lunch and pronounced me fit to be discharged. I was still a bit wobbly and found that every jolt on the trip home in the car with Mum and Dad reminded me of my condition—a reminder that was all too obvious to Mum. Once home, I was parked on the lounge with my jubilant pup beside me.

The TV remote was handed to me as Mum bustled off to find me some refreshments.

'Now don't you move, you hear? You need to rest at least for another day or so. Doctor's orders, not mine!'

I lay back and allowed my dog to lie on the lounge and snuggle into me. Her enthusiasm made me wonder if I might have been missed. She licked me on the chin, and I contented myself with a sweeping pat along her back.

When Mum returned with a steaming mug of tea and a biscuit, she informed me that a visitor has just driven up the drive. The smirk on her face gave me a strong clue as to the identity of my visitor.

'Archie?'

'The same,' came a deep voice from the doorway, and Archie appeared bearing an enormous bunch of native flowers and a box of chocolates.

'I thought you might need a few treats,' he smiled, the tanned skin around his eyes crinkling with good humour.

With greetings exchanged, Archie then sprawled on the chair next to the lounge after telling me not to get up. Mum muttered something about getting Archie a drink and rushed out of the room. It was clear to me that Archie wanted to say something. He cleared his throat and looked down thoughtfully at his work-hardened hands. I waited.

'Umm ...' This was obviously harder than he expected. Archie, usually so articulate, was now seemingly lost for words.

'Umm ...' He tried again and then the floodgates opened. 'I wanted to see you today not just to see how you are, but also to apologise for the way my family has treated you. I feel like we have all let you down, especially me. I knew how much Charlie meant to you all those years ago. Yet, after the accident, I cut you out of our lives and I shouldn't have. You were grieving, and you should have had our support.'

'That's not completely right,' I demurred. 'You spoke to me at the funeral, remember?'

221

He nodded. 'Yes, I did. Just a few words in passing. That doesn't count. I should have done more and at the very least been in contact with you in the weeks following. You were only a kid after all. How could you manage to navigate life after the death of a loved one on your own? And then I'm so sorry I didn't pick up what was going on with Dad. I knew he wasn't too keen on you and put that down to him being a difficult old bugger. I should have known better. You know, if I had been a bit slower getting to you the other day, you would almost certainly have died. I keep thinking about how close it was that I came to losing you. It plays over and over in my mind. If something had happened to you, I know for sure that I would never forgive myself. And it is thanks to your buddy here that you were kept safe,' he said, rubbing Nippa's ears and receiving a gentle lick on the hand in return.

His words reminded me of a nagging thought—some sort of confused returning memory of something I thought his father might have said in the heat of the moment. Something I needed to investigate.

'You know, Archie, I'm still rather confused about what actually happened. I can't remember everything, although fragments of memory are starting to return. It's possible your dad might have mentioned something about how he objected to you getting too attached to me. Did I dream that or was he telling the truth? I know we are friends, but was he hinting at something more?'

Archie again looked down at his hands, giving them further scrutiny. He had a pained expression on his face. Maybe he had a splinter? I observed a wash of red rush across his face. Was the man blushing? His jaw muscle worked furiously, and he looked up to stare directly at me. The high colour was fading, but his eyes were awash with emotion and a hint of tears. Those eyes were so like those of his brother with their piercing blue/green gaze. They were eyes that could not lie and, like now, they showed every thought that this man was thinking.

I looked back and stared intently at him. He was so different from his brother and yet somehow so much the same. Archie was a man I could trust with my life. No, more than that. A man to whom I owed my life.

I nodded.

'So, it is true. Fancy that. Your father was aware of how you felt before I did. I must be getting slow with old age.'

I grinned. Suddenly, it all made sense. I marvelled at how I had totally underestimated the bond we two shared. What I had thought was friendship was more than that and it could, with time, form the foundation for a future together.

I reached out my hand and found it clasped between two calloused hands. He drew me up and into his arms and then, no surprise here, we kissed. After such a slow start, we seemed to move along with speed. Excitement built as our kisses deepened. Lost in the new sensations, in the touch and feel of each other, we failed to register the high-pitched barking of another being who also could feel the growing excitement and wanted to share in our happiness.

'Be quiet,' Archie commanded.

'Shut up,' I said. The not always obedient hound dropped to the ground and regarded us with puzzled eyes.

I turned to Archie.

'Now, where were we?'

Chapter Thirty-One

Dear reader, you may be anticipating a wedding by now and of course, I would hate to disappoint you. Yes, there was a wedding, but it wasn't the wedding you might be expecting. I wasn't quite ready for marriage at this stage. Not because I didn't love Archie. I loved him with all my being. As did my dog! But I was content to take things slowly. While there was no doubt in my mind that this was my man for keeps, after all that had happened in previous years, I didn't want to jinx it and so was happy to allow our relationship to evolve gradually. But my man thought otherwise. To my surprise, he stunned me one afternoon by getting down on his knees and proposing marriage and a life of drudgery as a dairy farmer's wife. It was a proposal made in the most romantic setting—not! Archie, kneeling carefully in the dairy yard just before the start of milking, surrounded by jostling and curious cows.

'Oh, give over you,' I said, pulling him to his feet before he was trampled by animals anxious to get to their food in accordance with the usual routine of the afternoon milking session.

'Is that a *yes?*'

'It's a *maybe.*' I softened my response with a smile and a kiss. 'You need to sweeten the deal. The offer of a life of drudgery needs a bit more work if you want to tempt me to accept. What else can you add to make your proposal irresistible?'

You can guess what happened next. He drew me in close and commenced with admirable thoroughness to kiss and cuddle me. But, as I explained once I had the opportunity to draw breath, all of this, while most appreciated, did not bring anything new to the deal. And then, seeing the hurt in his eyes I tried to explain:

'Bear with me, Archie. I've said *maybe*. I'm just not ready to move onto wedded life when I'm still adjusting to life on the farm with you. I love you and want to be with you, but can you please give me time? Does it matter if we never marry?'

I could see from his dejected expression that it did. You see, I had come to realise that my man was quite traditional in that way. Something in him longed to be part of a family, and to his mind that meant marriage. He really was a one-woman man and once he had made up his mind I was the one for him, he thought the next step was to seal it with a vow. Me? I was in no hurry. So much had already happened in a rush. Some days I felt like I lived in a whirlpool.

As soon as Elsie, Archie's mum, moved out and into town, Archie started to urge me to move in. Once Charles had settled into the dementia accommodation unit in town, Elsie made plans to move out. She found a small villa not that far from where Charlie was and moved in along with a selection of the furniture and goods from the farmhouse. I would have been happy for her to take the lot as there wasn't much to my liking.

I was a bit worried Elsie might feel I had moved her on and pushed her out of a home of many years. But that was not the case. Elsie went to great pains to assure me she was happy to leave, that she had never liked living in that old, draughty place—*so isolated and surrounded by horrible, smelly and scary cattle*. Once settled in her villa, Elsie was a new woman. We lunched with her most Sundays if she could spare the time, and her chatter was full of details of social activities and the occasional mention of her husband whom she still visited, even if he no longer recognised his wife.

As soon as Elsie had left the farm, Archie, Dad and I spent a furious few days repainting the interior, which I swear hadn't been painted for decades. We ripped up the floor coverings, recarpeted the bedrooms, and Dad found time to reseal the floorboards on the enclosed back verandah, lounge and kitchen. It came up a treat.

I convinced Archie that I would use some of my contract payout funds from that soapie to refurnish the house. He took a fair bit of convincing, but I insisted. If he wanted me to move in with him, I had to be comfortable, and that meant replacing his spine crumbling bed and finding some furniture to replace the stuff Elsie had taken. I had plans further down the track to convince my man to use some of my invested funds to further his dreams of upgrading the farm. But I knew that would take time, as my fiercely independent man didn't like being helped by others—just like me. You see, we did have a lot in common.

I said I felt like I lived in a whirlpool. That was so true. Not only was I becoming used to life as a partner—in work and in love (with all that entailed), but my sister then insisted I help with planning her wedding. Yes, that was the wedding I mentioned earlier. The death of their daughter had brought Robbie and Amy close and before I knew it, Amy was flaunting a rather attractive engagement ring selected by Robbie and given to her as part of a surprise proposal one date night. She was over the moon and posted a photo of hand and ring almost immediately.

With true Amy precision, the wedding was immaculately planned and went off without a hitch. The weather of course fell into line and delivered a perfect, late summer day. They were married in the afternoon in the small local church where we buried Fleur, their daughter.

As I waited in the church nave, my thoughts turned to the last time we gathered in this place, and emotions swirled in the pit of my stomach. I turned to watch my sister entering the building, her face reflecting the emotions I was feeling. Through watery eyes, she smiled at me, visibly steeling herself for entry into a place that held so many sad memories.

'Chin up, big sister. This will be fine. I'm sure that if little Fleur is here with us in spirit, she will be cheering her parents on.'

Again, a smile, but this time less watery. Then, with a shove, Amy propelled me through the door and into the church. With a whisper, she said:

'Love you, sis. Come on, let's go get them.'

Robbie's look when he saw his bride was a highlight of the day. It was like he couldn't believe what he saw. And I must say, I thought the same when I saw Robbie. They both made a very impressive couple, and as is often said, they both *scrubbed up well.*

Amy was a vision in ivory lace over a strapless satin lining. Her hair was elegantly upswept and hidden by a veil secured by a coronet of pearls and crystals. She carried an armful of roses of ivory, taupe and coffee shades from which trailed some sort of greenery—possibly ivy? Botanical knowledge has always been sadly lacking in my repertoire.

Amy had ensured that my bridesmaid's outfit was equally elegant. Again, it was a taupe/coffee shade with a strapless satin lining under a sheer silk chiffon overlay, which enhanced the ivory tones of Amy's gown. A coronet of flowers decorated my still very short curls. We looked a treat in the photos, let me tell you. And we were beautifully set off by the groom and my brother in their evening suits.

The wedding ceremony was full of heightened emotions. I think everyone was so happy for this couple after all they had been through. From time to time, I glanced back at the congregation during the ceremony and noticed surreptitious wiping of eyes with handkerchiefs—especially when Amy and Robbie read aloud their handwritten vows. It was all so heartwarming, possibly too much emotion as the relief was palpable when we exited the church. All that sentiment, while heartfelt, was also awfully draining. Everyone seemed to be eager to relax and get into party mode.

And we did. Amy and Robbie had hired the adjoining church hall, so it was only a matter of a few steps to the outdoor bar before the party began.

Like most country celebrations, the wedding reception was a relaxed do. To start with, we mingled outside near the bar, drinking beer or sparkling wine, chatting and catching up with friends while munching on finger food being distributed by circling waitresses. There was so much finger food I was beginning to wonder how we would fit in dinner. My oh so sensible sister had planned for all eventualities, and when we finally were seated in the hall resplendent with greenery and sparkling fairy lights, we were able to help ourselves to shared platters, so we need only eat what we wanted. I nibbled on a small helping of dip and vegetables, while my ever-hungry Archie ate as if it had been weeks since he last saw food.

The speeches were full of emotion and once again, I saw many handkerchiefs in play and heard an amount of not-so-subtle sniffing. Dad insisted on giving a short speech—about how proud he was of his eldest child and although overcome with emotion, he managed to hold it at bay for long enough to recount some outrageous tales about teenage Amy's antics.

Robbie spoke about the special bond he and Amy had as he smiled at his bride, and she beamed back. I saw her surreptitiously stroke her tummy, and I observed the glass of sparkling wine on the table before her remained untouched. Amy, noticing me staring, raised one eyebrow in query. In response, I mouthed *what?* Her answering nod told me all.

Twelve Months Later

The afternoon's milking was now complete. With the calves fed and the dairy washed clean, we both leaned against the railing fence. We watched the last of the cows taking their time as they ambled down the laneway, heading for the green of open pasture and the company of the rest of the herd.

I stood next to Archie, lost in contemplation of the beauty of this rural Eden as I soaked in the serenity of the scene before me. It was the same scene that presented itself to me every day, some might say with monotonous regularity. But I preferred to think of it as a simple message that life can be harmonious, marked off in predictable segments and anchored to meeting the needs of those gentle giants and their offspring.

My man, my Archie, with one foot resting on the bottom rail, contemplated his kingdom. No doubt somewhere in that brain was a consideration of the next chore on that long list of chores that happens to be the lot of the farmer. But in that moment, I like to think that he, like me, was appreciating the beauty of the lingering late afternoon sunlight lighting up the valley with a warm golden glow. That he too was listening to the contented low and moo from cows checking in on each other, and that he too was registering the growl and woof of dogs at play behind us.

He turned to me and with a smile, he asked:

'Well?'

'Well, what?'

'Is all well?'

'Better than that,' I smiled and, taking his hand, we turned away and headed across the yard for home. Archie pulled me closer and planted a kiss on the top of my head.

'If it's a boy, let's call him Charlie. Or even if it is a girl. I quite like the name for either gender.'

I rubbed my ballooning stomach.

'Fine with me. Charlie, Charlee, Charlize, or whatever.'

'*Whatever* it is!'

Author's note

For further information on donating hair to charity, please visit either www.locksoflove.org or sustainable salons.org.

Acknowledgements

A big thank you to Nick Haddow of Bruny Island Cheese and Beer Company who very kindly found time in his busy life to spend a day with me at his dairy farm down in the Huon Valley, Tasmania. Although I am the niece of a dairy farmer and have many happy memories of school holidays spent helping with the afternoon milking, my knowledge was rather out of date. I really enjoyed seeing how Nick and his team run their dairy farm, and I certainly enjoyed meeting the lovely cows in his dairy herd.

Thank you also to my test readers who enthusiastically read my draft story. Your feedback helped inform subsequent drafts and have much improved the plot. Of course, any mistakes are all my own.

I spent my childhood on the NSW south coast and wanted to bring to life the beauty of that area—coastline and escarpment. I hope I have tempted you to visit.

About the Author

Once a lawyer Dorothy now writes full time. She likes to write about the things that interest her – old houses, gardens, animals and occasionally about ghosts.

Dorothy lives in Tasmania in a romantic stone Georgian house with a long-suffering husband and a menagerie of animals.

Other stories by Dorothy may be found on Amazon Kindle.

www.ingramcontent.com/pod-product-compliance
Lightning Source LLC
Chambersburg PA
CBHW031318280626
47169CB00019B/2135